Takin' Chances
for the Holidays

Adrianne Byrd Donna Hill
Monica Jackson

Takin' Chances
for the Holidays

ARABESQUE®

TAKIN' CHANCES FOR THE HOLIDAYS

An Arabesque Novel

ISBN-13: 978-1-58314-749-8
ISBN-10:   1-58314-749-7

CONTENTS

FINDING THE RIGHT KEY

Adrianne Byrd

To The Adrianne Byrd Book Club,

You ladies are wonderful. Thanks for being there for me in my time of need.

We're more than a club, we're family.

Kimora

Every inch of my body aches—in a good way.

Elijah Thomas, as always, had tossed it up, flipped it and rubbed it down until I was practically speaking in tongues last night. The delightful scent of sex and candy tickles my nose and I slide on a smile before bothering to open my eyes. When I do, I'm surprised and elated by the pretty mess Elijah and I have created in our hotel suite.

I try to sit up, but then I'm quickly reminded of the silk scarves that bind my arms and legs to different bedposts.

Some days you really have to ask yourself if it's worth chewing through the straps to get out of bed.

"Ho! Ho! Ho!" Elijah emerges from a steam cloud billowing from the bathroom. "Merry Christmas." His tall, dark-chocolate body appears yummier while wrapped in a snow-white robe with the hotel's moniker printed over his heart. On his head sits a cheap red-and-white Santa Claus hat.

"Where did you get that?" I ask, laughing at his silly antics.

"Don't worry about it." Elijah's bushy eyebrows seesaw while his thick lips widen and he moves stealthily toward me. "Right now Santa needs to know if you've been naughty or nice this year." His eyes glint devilishly.

"What do you think?" I tease.

Elijah checks the camera on the tripod before he settles his weight on the edge of the bed and slides his large, callused hand up the inside of my right thigh before it disappears into the moist juncture between my legs. I should resist him, make him work for what he wants, but before I know anything, my breathing thins, my body melts and my eyes roll to the back of my head.

"Ah, that's my girl," Elijah praises.

His fine ass always could make me forget how to spell my name. In truth, he's the best Christmas present I could have hoped for—but I will never tell him that. For all his black magic in the bedroom, I know trying to hold on to Elijah is like trying to hold on to smoke. He has a habit of appearing and disappearing before the sun can catch him.

I'm surprised he's still here.

As I rock my hips in the same languid motion of his probing hand, my legs tremble and strain against the silk scarves. I doubt if I have enough energy to sustain another orgasm. If anything, it would probably wipe me out and put my ass to sleep.

"My baby is ready for me," he says, referring to the sounds my body makes as his strokes turn into plunges.

I'm ready—or at least I think I am.

The hotel robe flies across the room in a flurry, and Elijah crawls his sinfully chiseled six-foot-four body into bed and hovers over me. Briefly I feel the weight of his heavy, smooth organ against the lips of my shaved kitty, but I have no time to react before he slips on a condom and glides inside and fills me completely.

Watching Elijah work—his arm muscles straining to balance his weight, his washboard abs flexing while his hips pump and the delectable way he licks his lips as he gazes down at me—is such a mind orgasm. This is probably why I don't mind his taping our sexcapade—and the fact I get a copy.

I'm telling you, girls, my Christmas key party was the best idea I've ever had.

Coco

Why in the hell did I let that heffa talk me into going to that damn key party? In one night I've compromised my career in the district attorney's office. For what? A quick romp in the hay with my superior, Patrick Holloway?

My boss, for God's sake!

Squeezing my eyes tight, I pray when I reopen them I'll wake at home in my own bed—alone. No such luck. Patrick's snoring buzzes in my ear like a chain saw.

Dear God, why didn't you stop me?

I would cry, but it's been so long I'm not quite sure I remember how. It's not that I'm a hard-ass, like Kimora and Roberta claim. It's just that I've come from a long line of women who never indulged in such luxuries as feeling sorry for themselves.

Get up and dust yourself off.

I always smile when I hear my mother's voice. It's as if I have a tape recorder inside my head with all her sound advice. I don't need a video cam in heaven to know that she's up there shaking her head over my behavior.

I listen a few more minutes to Patrick's snoring symphony before I attempt to creep toward the edge of the bed. However, it's not the easiest thing in the world to escape a cocoon of satin sheets. You inch one way and then slide another.

"Where are you going?"

I freeze at the sound of Patrick's voice croaking out at me. Exhaling and then painting on a thin smile, I glance over my shoulder to meet his sky-blue gaze.

A white man. What in the hell was I thinking?

"Home," I admit. What's the point of sugarcoating it?

"So soon?"

His long muscled but pasty arms capture my small frame and drag me back against his body. I cringe, but my nipples harden at the feel of his rock-hard erection.

"Who said I was through with you?" he chuckles and then nibbles on my ear.

Hell no, my head screams, but my body melts against him. Something has to be seriously wrong with me. Patrick and I are like oil and vinegar—literally. My skin color has been my pride and pain for thirty-five years. I'm not just dark, I'm black. African-black. And in 2006 in America, it's practically a sin to be this regal and this…black.

"It's Christmas morning, and I want to play with my gift."

His hands dive beneath the covers, and to my horror, my legs open up to receive his gentle strokes. I'm shamed by the way I arch my back and thrust up my itty-bitty boobs. No, I don't have a handful, but I have sensitive coal-black nipples the size of marbles.

At one flick of Patrick's warm tongue, I'm nothing more than a moaning idiot aching for one last tumble before I take my butt home.

"You have no idea how long I've been wanting you. Wanting this," Patrick says.

His words strike me as curious, because up until last night we haven't been able to stand the sight of each other. We're both bossy, brass and refuse to give an inch toward each other. But I have no time to question him on this because in the next moment he slides into me with one *long* stroke.

Damn, he's pretty hung for a white boy.

My eyes drift to half-moons as I concentrate on my vaginal muscles. Squeeze and release, squeeze and release.

"Hot damn," Patrick moans. "Do you know what you're doing to me?"

I smile and push him over to take the top position. "I know *exactly* what I'm doing."

Ten minutes later, I have District Attorney Patrick Holloway spelling my name frontward and backward. I'll think about the repercussions of the damn key party tomorrow. Right now I have to teach this white boy a thing or two.

Birdie

The theme from *Shaft*—my cell phone's ringtone—drifts in and out of my head for quite a while before I realize it's not a part of my dream but someone calling. I frown, wondering who it could be at this time of morning.

Whoever it is is just going to have to try back later. This sleep is feeling too good for me to climb out of bed. When the music stops, I smile and snuggle closer to the pillow with snippets of last night's party flashing in my mind.

First of all, I had no business taking my big butt to Kimora's key party. When she'd told me the rules, it had just sounded like an excuse to have an orgy or something. That's just the kind of freak Kimora is. She's my girl and all, but she's still a borderline "hochie."

As it turns out, I have a little "hochie" in me, too.

It isn't long before my mind focuses on a pair of hazel eyes framed by long lashes. They were attached to a man with the most kissable lips I'd ever tasted.

There was drinking, dancing and even a little Mary Jane. Hell, it was like being in college again. Now, if I could only remember the name of that hazel-eyed gigolo that helped me get my groove back last night....

"Jason? James? Joel?"

"You rang?"

I bolt upright at the sound of the honey-coated baritone. However, my faux eyelashes are matted together, rendering me blind.

"Who is it? Who's there?" I back up so fast I overshoot the bed's edge, and the floor rushes up to smack my butt, and my head bangs against something sharp. "Ow."

Laughter rumbles above me, and I have to literally use my hands to pry my eyes open. Smiling down at me are those beautiful hazel eyes and a naked pecan-brown brother with pillow-soft lips.

"Hi," is all I can manage to squeak out.

"Hi, yourself." He winks back at me and stretches out a coffee mug. "I figured you might be needing this."

I know he's referring to the coffee, but my eyes drift to my mysterious man's package—if you know what I mean— and it seems like I still have some "hochie" residue.

Shaft plays again and two things bolt through my brain: One, today is Christmas; two, my kids are calling me.

"Damn." I scramble off the floor as fast as I can, all the while pretending the room isn't spinning beneath me. "Where in the hell is my cell phone?" I bend, I squat and then I belatedly realize I'm doing all of this and I'm still naked—all one hundred and ninety pounds of me.

Red-faced, I turn back toward my—what? Lover? Boy toy? One-night stand?

"Don't mind me." He smiles lazily. "I was just admiring the view."

I smile but then jerk the top sheet from off the bed and quickly wrap it around my body. Apparently I'm not the only one who has hit their head. The music stops just as I locate my phone buried beneath my favorite pair of jeans. I flip it open and read I've missed six calls from my babies.

"I, uh, have to return a call, er, uh—"

"Joel." He flashes a bleach-white smile. "Joel Hawkins. We met last night."

I nod stupidly, even manage a wobbly smile. "I remember now." From the corner of my eye I spot the room's adjoining bathroom. "I'll be right back."

Clutching the sheet, I dart toward the bathroom, but a surprised gasp jumps from my throat when the sheet is snatched from my fingers.

"Like I said, I was enjoying the view." He sets the coffee cup on the nightstand and eases back onto the bed.

When Joel winks again, I'm struck by how young he looks. "How old *are* you—twenty-five, twenty-six?"

"Twenty-three next Tuesday."

My heart sinks and I forbid my head to do the math. "I'll be right back." I turn again toward the bathroom and I don't dare breathe until I'm hidden safely behind the closed door.

"Twenty-three?" I whisper to my reflection above the

bathroom sink. What does that mean—that he was born the year Michael Jackson released *Thriller?*

I take a seat on the only chair available and quickly punch in my ex-husband's cell phone number. Drawing a deep breath, I brace myself for an onslaught of questions. And as soon as he picks up, Kenneth doesn't disappoint.

"Where in the hell are you?" he questions in a harsh, graveled whisper. "The boys have been trying to reach you all morning."

"I thought since you had them for Christmas, I would sleep in."

"You're not at home or you wouldn't be calling me back on your cell."

Einstein at work. "Put Terrence and Matthew on the phone."

"After you answer the question."

"I don't have to answer a damn thing," I snap. "Put the boys on the phone."

The line clogs with tension. Without seeing Kenneth, I already know his nostrils are flared and his teeth are grinding together. He wants to bark, but I know the children are close by and he has no choice but to stew in his anger.

Screw Kenneth.

He lost the right to question my whereabouts the minute his stuck his penis in my little sister—just like she lost the right to one of her front teeth. But I digress.

A few seconds later I hear Terrence—my eight-year-old baby—as his excited voice rushes onto the line. "Mama?"

"Hey, baby. Merry Christmas." On my small porcelain seat I lock my knees together and rest my head against the palm of my hand while Terrence hurries through the long list of toys his father had bought him. I have to bite my tongue about most of the items on the list. Kenneth *knows* how I feel about toy guns and certain video games, which is exactly why he'd bought them.

Divorce is a bitch.

Matthew is next, and his list has me cringing in my seat, as well. What the hell is a three-year-old going to do with a DVD player—other than break it?

A soft knock on the bathroom door reminds me where I am, and I realize that I've been in here probably thirty minutes. I quickly place my hand over the small receiver and call out, "Just a minute."

"Mommy, Daddy wants to talk to you," Matthew is saying when I return my attention to him.

"Tell him I'll have to call him back later," I say, needing a day off from arguing. Of course, Matthew doesn't listen, and the next thing I know Kenneth is back on the line.

"Birdie?"

I hang up. I'm so over his mess.

Standing from the throne, I glance over at the mirror again, and this time I'm horrified by what I see. My hair is pointing every which way but loose, my makeup is MIA, and my love handles are like yards on a football field.

He was enjoying *this* view?

There's another rap on the door. "Birdie, don't tell me you fell in?" Joel jokes with an infectious chuckle.

"A few more seconds." I laugh and rake my fingers through my hair weave. Thank God there's Listerine and

Dixie cups on the counter. After a quick gurgle and a splash of water to my face, I'm back in business.

"Go get him, girl." I wink at my reflection.

When I reopen the bathroom door, baby-face Joel is smiling and leaning against the door frame in his gorgeous birthday suit. The thing is, he's looking at me as if I'm the most beautiful woman in the world.

I can't tell you the last time someone looked at me like that—if anyone ever had. You know, I think I might keep him.

Seven days before Christmas…

Chapter 1

Kimora rushed through the doors of the American Liberty Bail Bonds office, her eyes wide as she searched for her cousin. She wasn't used to being up at this hour. Mornings were for the nine-to-fivers who slaved happily away in a five-by-seven cubicle—or something like that.

She'd never been to her cousin's little business and she was less than impressed with the cramped, noisy office sloppily decorated for Christmas.

"Where's Stephen?" she asked no one in particular.

"He hasn't made it in yet," a stout older Korean woman, manning the ringing phone lines, answered without so much as glancing in her direction.

Kimora walked toward her. "Do you know when he'll be back? This is an emergency. My friend is in jail."

The woman looked up. Her gaze dragged over Kimora's

short red skirt, exposed midriff and overflowing breasts. "You don't say?"

"Hey?" Kimora snapped. "What's your name? My cousin owns this place and I'll—"

"It's a little early for a catfight," Stephen said from behind her.

She pivoted with an instant smile and her arms stretched wide. "Stevie!"

Stephen's brows leaped when recognition settled in his eyes. "I'll be a monkey's uncle. Little Kimmy." He took her into his embrace, squeezed too hard and too long. "Well…you're not so little anymore, huh?"

Cousin or no, Stephen ravished Kimora's hourglass figure with his gaze and he even had the nerve to lick his lips.

"You could say that."

Another lick. "So what brings you here?"

"Says her friend's in jail," the Korean woman droned.

Kimora squashed her irritation. "Roberta Russell. Her last name used to be Washington. You probably remember her from high school."

"Birdie?"

"That's her." Kimora crossed her arms.

Genuine surprise colored Stephen's face. "Come on back to my office." He moved around her to lead the way. "Maura, hold my calls."

"Uh-huh."

Kimora watched the woman's judgmental eyes rake over her again and she couldn't help but flip the woman off before she followed Stephen. "Nice place you got here," she praised, hiding her sarcasm.

Stephen opened and held his office door. "It pays the bills."

She glanced up as she crossed the threshold and spotted the mistletoe.

Stephen's gaze followed hers, and then he smiled back down at her.

"It's not going to happen," she warned. There were still *some* things she wouldn't do.

"No, no." His face darkened with embarrassment. "Of course not. I would never—"

"Neither would I." She smiled and waltzed farther into the room.

"Please…take a seat," he offered.

Kimora hesitated. The place looked as if a tornado had ripped through it, and she questioned whether she should trust her weight in one of the chairs.

"Don't worry. It's sturdy," he said as if reading her mind. He took his place behind the desk. "So Birdie is in jail. What on earth did she do?"

"Punched out one of her sister's front teeth after she caught her in bed with her ex-husband."

Stephen whistled and leaned back in his chair. "You're kiddin' me."

"I wouldn't be here if I was." Kimora's smile tightened. "Can you help?"

Roberta sighed and leaned against the holding cell's iron bars. Her muddled and blurry thoughts were stuck on instant replay of last night's fight with her ex-husband—and her soon to be demised sister.

Though she'd clearly been the winner of the short fight, victory now left a bitter and foul taste in her mouth.

"I can't believe I fell for that man's bull again." She dropped her head and cradled it.

She and Kenneth had recently inked their divorce papers. The final straw that led to their breakup was because he had been sleeping with their next-door neighbor. She—and everyone in her cul-de-sac—found out about the affair when Mr. Winslet had chased Kenneth out of the Winslets' residence in his birthday suit. As fate would have it, she and the other stay-at-home moms had been re-turning home from PTA meetings that Kenneth had claimed to be too busy to attend.

There was nothing like public humiliation.

But there she'd been, just last week, falling for his lies about wanting to return home to be a better husband and father. He'd cried real tears while proclaiming he could never love another woman…and all the while he'd been banging her little sister, Jackie.

"When will I ever learn?"

"Roberta Russell!" a woman guard shouted. "Merry Christmas! You just made bail."

"Oh, thank God," Roberta murmured, standing. She needed to get home to her babies.

It took a few minutes to complete processing, but by the time she stepped out of the precinct she was ravenous for the taste of freedom.

"Birdie!" Kimora raced over and wrapped her arms around her. "I came as fast as I could."

Roberta peeled herself out of Kimora's arms and knuckled a tear away before it could be seen. "Thanks for havin' my back, girl. I owe you one."

Assistant District Attorney Courtney Brown read the text message from Kimora and shook her head in relief. The cryptic messages she'd received all morning from Kimora still didn't tell her why Birdie was in jail. *At least she's out now.*

One of the many reasons Courtney didn't race to her girl's aid was that she was due in court. Her whole team was just itching for the jury to find Wyclef Onwu guilty for the rape and murder of eleven-year-old Tina Else.

Originally she'd anticipated a slam-dunk case. However, Mr. Slime had hired another Mr. Slime, and from out of nowhere the State's case had fallen apart at the seams. Still, Courtney remained convinced they had the right man—he was just slippery, that's all.

Wendy Cox, Courtney's legal assistant, poked her head into the office. "The jury is still out."

Courtney gritted her teeth but gave Wendy a quick nod. Three days of deliberation was not a good sign.

District Attorney Patrick Holloway burst into Courtney's office without knocking. "Three days of deliberation is not a good sign."

Her eyes snapped up and irritation showed on her face. "I know." She hated how he always said the very thing that was on her mind.

"If we lose this one, the mayor will have my head."

"So you've told me." She crossed her arms. "Just as you've told me you'll drag me down with you if we lose." She stood from her chair and straightened out her jacket. "Threatening me every hour on the hour doesn't have me shaking in my shoes, so you can stop."

Red flames flared up Patrick's neck, and his own irritation polished his blue eyes to arctic daggers. "You're skating on thin ice with me."

"Ditto."

One punch. That's all she wanted—that's all she needed. Three years she had been working with this pompous son of a bitch, and for three years he'd been riding her last nerve.

Patrick shook his head as he turned back for the door. "I should have gotten rid of you years ago."

"I'm the best damn attorney you got, and you know it," she barked at his back.

He stopped and faced her again, but whatever he was going to say apparently crashed against the hard, grim line of his clamped teeth.

Courtney and Patrick were staring each other down in an intense stalemate when Wendy rushed back into the office without knocking to blurt the latest news. "They're in."

Courtney's heart plummeted to her stomach. She thrust up her chin and flashed Patrick a thin smile. "Let's go see what we're going to get for Christmas—a conviction or a new job."

Chapter 2

Twenty minutes later Roberta exchanged one jail cell for another when she pulled up to her double-mortgaged Colonial-revival home. On the outside it was picture-perfect: fresh paint, streak-free glass windows and grass cut to home-owners' association's regulation.

Inside her mother was lurking, undoubtedly ready to wag her finger and run down a list of what she should've, could've done. One thing for sure, it would be interesting to see if her mother would defend Jackie, as she always did. Actually, Birdie was curious to learn how Jackie had gone about explaining why she was in bed with Kenneth.

"Mommy's home!" Matthew, Kenneth's "mini me," jetted toward her with chocolate glop smeared across his face and hands.

Within seconds it was all over Roberta's clothes. "Does this mean you're no longer a bad guy, Mommy?" he asked, staring up at her wide-eyed.

The question broke her heart and choked off her air supply. She placed her purse on a nearby table and lowered herself to one knee. "Mommy was never a bad guy, honey." She pulled him closer, ignoring the chocolate.

Matthew frowned. "Then why did the police take you to jail?"

Birdie opened her mouth, but then her mother's sharp voice cut her off.

"Yes, Roberta. Why don't you tell your children why you were dragged away from home in *handcuffs?*"

Birdie's gaze snapped up to similar but harder, colder eyes. "Do you mind?"

Lauren Washington carefully folded her arms and flashed a thin, chiseled smile. "Not at all."

It was times like these when Birdie felt a kindred spirit to *Psycho*'s Norman Bates—all she needed was a good butcher knife.

Her older baby, Terrence, stood like a small shadow behind his grandmother.

"Honey, we'll talk about this later," Roberta said, affectionately rubbing Matthew's back and smiling. "Right now I need to talk privately to your grandmother. Can you and your brother go up to your room for a few minutes?"

Matthew looked as though he wanted to argue.

"Please?" she added, hoping to cut him off before he started.

Terrence stepped from around his grandmother's protective stance and lifted a hand. "C'mon, Matt. Let's go play race cars."

Matthew's small shoulders deflated as he turned toward his brother.

Roberta watched them as they exited the foyer and crept up the staircase. When they were finally out of sight, her gaze slashed toward her mother, but she remained silent until she heard the boys' bedroom door snap closed.

"Why do you insist on making me look bad in front of them?"

"Stop being so dramatic, Birdie," Lauren said, turning. "You don't need any help in that department." She strolled toward the kitchen. "Or are you saying that I had something to do with the cops showing up here last night and dragging you to jail?"

"Fine! I guess I should be the one to apologize for overreacting when I found my baby sister in bed with *my* ex-husband."

Lauren rounded on her, her eyes razor sharp. "You mean the husband that *you* drove away because you were ignoring him?"

"What?"

"C'mon, Birdie," Lauren said, exasperated. "How many times have I told you when you were growing up that blind, crippled or crazy, a man is a man—and he's going to behave like one? You and Kenneth had been having problems for a while. Do you honestly think that someone as handsome as Kenneth was going to abstain from sex that long? He has needs! And let's face it—" her eyes raked Roberta's full figure "—you've let yourself go."

* * *

The district attorney's office didn't lose its case—but it didn't win it, either. As the judge rapped his gavel to bring order to the court, Courtney's temples pulsed with a burgeoning migraine.

"A hung jury," Courtney whispered. She didn't see that coming. She sighed, massaged the worry lines from her forehead and glanced at the defendant's table. The slimeballs were congratulating each other.

Behind her, the victim's mother wailed and the father swore obscenities. Her stomach soured as she thought of meaningless words she could offer as comfort. *Hang in there. We'll get him next time.* She rolled her eyes as court adjourned.

Courtney stood and drew a deep breath before turning, but all that was behind her was two empty seats. Her eyes zoomed to the door in time to catch the Elses storm out.

Patrick elbowed her arm. "Hang in there, Ms. Brown. Technically it's not a loss. We'll get him next time."

Swallowing her irritation, she snatched up her briefcase. "We should have gotten him *this* time!" She stomped out of the courtroom. By the time she stood before a bank of reporters Courtney had her camera-ready smile in place. She reassured the citizens of Fulton County that the district attorney's office didn't view today as a defeat and vowed that justice would prevail in the end.

After catching her paltry speech on the six-o'clock news, Courtney powered off the television by remote and sulked her way to the kitchen for a bottle of wine. As she walked past the dining room, her eyes skimmed over the boxes of Christmas decorations she'd dragged down from the attic.

The way things were looking now, it would be Christmas Day before she bothered putting anything up. It was just as well. Christmas was just another day, as far as she was concerned. A paid day off.

Christmas was for families—and Courtney didn't have any family members left. She'd never known her father—her mother had taken his identity to the grave with her six short years ago. As far as Courtney knew, she had no brothers or sisters. Her mother's parents died when she was three, and the last of her mother's three sisters drowned in a boating accident just eight months ago.

So Courtney was alone.

She popped the cork to her favorite Pinot Grigio and then filled her wineglass to the rim. After one sip, her pity party was over. She had a ton of things to do. Turning and pulling open the freezer, she grabbed a Lean Cuisine and proceeded to nuke it.

Her mind raced with ideas of how to handle Onwu's second trial. Whom they should subpoena and whom they should steer the hell clear of. When the microwave beeped, she carefully took the plastic tray out and placed it onto a cool plate. Grabbing her "gourmet" dinner and her wine, Courtney headed to the living room, where her briefcase awaited.

The doorbell rang.

She groaned and wondered who was at the door. "Just a minute."

The visitor apparently grew impatient and punched the bell button until a musical solo jingled throughout the house.

"I said just a minute!" Courtney set her food and drink down on the coffee table and raced to the door.

The bell continued to ring.

"What the hell is your problem?" she asked, snatching open the door.

Birdie stood on the other side with a river of tears pouring down her round face. "I hate her!" she croaked.

Instantly Courtney's tough-attorney act melted away and she crossed the threshold to pull her best friend into her arms. "Oh, Birdie. What's wrong? What happened?"

Inwardly Courtney scolded herself for forgetting about Birdie's plight.

"My mother is an evil bitch!" Birdie croaked into her friend's shoulder. "She gave my sister the stamp of approval for sleeping with my ex-husband and then…she called me *fat!*"

"What?"

"I know. I mean, sure I've gained a few pounds but—"

"Not that! What do you mean Jackie is sleeping with Kenneth?"

Birdie's face scrunched up again before she released a mighty wail. "It's awful. My own sister!"

Courtney glanced around. "Come on in. There's no need to alert the media that your sister is a slut."

Birdie obeyed, nodding and sniffling. "I should have shot them instead of punching out her tooth."

"That's why you were arrested?" Courtney asked, closing the door behind them. She would have paid good money to see Jackie get her butt kicked. Lord knows this wasn't the first time Birdie's little sister had stolen something that didn't belong to her.

"Coco, I don't know what came over me." Birdie wiped her eyes. "One minute I was standing in the doorway, and the next I was Muhammad Ali on Joe Frazier."

"No!" Courtney's eyes rounded with astonishment but a smile curved her lips.

Birdie bobbed her head as she walked into the living room and dropped down into one of Courtney's posh armchairs. "Kimora came through in a pinch, though it's always scary to be indebted to her."

Coco snickered. "She'll probably make you go to that ridiculous orgy party."

"The key party. She's already hinted at it. But, girl, there's no way I'll ever go to something like that."

When Kimora strolled through the doors of Club Sexy, she was operating on two hours of sleep. However, being a professional party planner and club owner she took sleep deprivation as a way of life—and she loved it.

What other job would let her remain a perpetual teenager, pay her an insane amount of money and allow her to hobnob and sleep (though very little sleeping was involved) with the hottest celebrities?

Sable walked by with a tray of drinks. "Elijah was here looking for you," she informed Kimora.

Kimora, dressed head to toe in shimmering silver, froze in her tracks, while her heart raced faster than the music.

"Are you all right?" Sable asked, crossing back with her empty tray and counting her tips. "You look as if you've seen a ghost."

Kimora blinked out of her trance and followed Sable like a lost puppy. "Elijah was here? What did he say?"

Sable hurried her steps and glanced over her shoulder with a wicked grin. "I heard how he had you dick crazy, but damn, girl, is it dipped in gold?"

Kimora smiled slyly.

"Hot damn," Sable hooted. "Puff, puff, pass."

"I like you, but don't make me cut you," Kimora said, laughing, as they stopped at the bar. She had the feeling that she shared Elijah with too many women as it was.

"Two Heinekens," Sable ordered from the bartender and then turned toward her boss. "He said just to tell you that he stopped by."

Kimora forced herself not to show her disappointment, but she wasn't sure if she was successful.

"I did, however, take the liberty of inviting him to your singles' key party on Christmas Eve."

"And what did he say?" Hope flooded every pore of Kimora's body. It had been more than ten months since she'd seen Elijah, and her body hummed with anticipation.

Meanwhile, Sable shrugged as she placed her two beers onto her tray. "He just said he'd *think* about swinging by— and that was it."

Chapter 3

Every year, Birdie, Kimora and Courtney hooked up three days before Christmas for one last shopping spree. Finding great deals in the next-to-bare shelves and picking over bins was the great challenge for every shopaholic.

"You know Elijah's butt has to be married," Coco said, rolling her eyes and picking up a pair of stylish black pumps in the middle of her favorite shoe store. "He has to be. It's the only thing that explains his disappearing acts and the fact that you don't know where he lives or even have his phone number. He just pops up every once in a while, takes you for a tumble in bed and poofs into a cloud of smoke."

"Humph!" Birdie shook her head. Given her current situation, Kimora sleeping around with a married man caused her pinched expression to sour.

Kimora cut her eyes as she dramatically dusted off her shoulders. "I'm surrounded by player haters."

Coco set the pumps down, settled a hand on her hip and dropped her polished Ivy League voice to inject the right amount of street cred into her tone. "Ain't nobody hatin' on a man you ain't got." She wiggled her bare wedding finger for emphasis.

Kimora dusted her shoulders again, determined not to let anyone rain on her parade. "So are you hoes coming to my party or not?"

"Not!" Courtney and Birdie answered in unison.

"Why am I not surprised?" Kimora shook her head and strolled away from them to the next aisle of shoes.

Everyone knew by the slump of her shoulders and the firm set of her jaw that a pout was on the horizon. "You guys never come to my parties." She picked up a pair of boots, casually glanced at them and then set them back down. "It's not like you have anything else planned."

Birdie refused to be moved. "I'm a little too old for your freaky parties."

"Amen," Courtney croaked.

"We're all the same age," Kimora sassed.

"Our point exactly," her friends chimed.

"You're only as old as you feel." Kimora smiled. "And I don't feel a day over twenty-one."

Courtney shook her head. "I must be in the 'ancient' category."

"C'mon. It's not like you're doing anything anyway," Kimora complained. "Birdie, the boys leave tonight to spend the next week at Kenneth's place. What are you going to be doing? Drowning your sorrows in eggnog?"

Birdie lowered her eyes as her round face darkened with embarrassment. "I happen to like eggnog."

Kimora shifted her attention. "What about you, Coco?"

"What about me?"

"What do you have planned—shoving your nose in case files or actually putting up your Christmas tree for a lousy twenty-four hours?"

"No." Courtney refused to meet her eyes. "I plan to leave it up until New Year's Day."

"Sad." Kimora shook her head. "Both of you."

"Whatever." Birdie selected a pair of sensible mud-brown shoes. "Oh, these have just the arch support I need."

Kimora's hand jabbed into her hip. "Should we also pick you up some medical support hose while we're at it? Jeez, you guys act older than my grandmother. Who, by the way, would jump at the chance to come to this party if I invited her."

"That's a mental image I could've done without," Coco said.

"Face it," Kimora ranted. "You two need to get a life. Lord knows Kenneth isn't letting the dust settle under his feet."

Roberta's eyes snapped up and then turned ice-cold. "You want to be a bitch? I can get bitchy."

Kimora waved her forward. "Bring it on."

Birdie took a step towards Kimora and Coco placed a restraining hand on her shoulder. "You two stop it. Especially you, Birdie. The last thing you need is another assault charge. I swear you've turned into Mike Tyson this week."

"She started it."

Coco rolled her eyes at having to play mother to two

grown-ass women. "Kimora, stop pushing her buttons. We're supposed to be shopping, remember?"

"All I'm saying is you two need to loosen up. Have some fun. It's not going to kill you."

"Now that's debatable." Courtney turned away from the aisle. "We're finished here," she announced and headed for the door.

Neither Birdie nor Kimora moved. They eyed each other, assessing whether they should pick up the fight since they no longer had supervision.

"C'mon, Birdie. You know I didn't mean nothin' by it."

She did know that, but Kimora had a habit of speaking before thinking.

Kimora took her friend's silence as a peace offering and she walked around to Birdie's aisle and swung her arm around her shoulder. "I love you, girl. You know that." And to prove it, she planted a loud, sloppy kiss against Birdie's cheek.

Birdie cringed and tried to pull away. By the time she succeeded, she was laughing.

"Am I forgiven?" Kimora asked, laughing and leaning into her.

Hard as she tried, Birdie couldn't hold on to her anger.

"Forgive me or I'm going to kiss you again and grab your butt right here in front of all these fine folks." Kimora laughed and added, "Then the truth will really be out why you and Kenneth separated."

"Kimmy—"

"I'm going to count to two. One—"

"I forgive you."

Kimora kissed her anyway. At least her butt was spared.

"So what exactly is a key party?" Birdie asked.

"A singles' key party is just that," Kimora informed her girls, clustered around a cheap iron table in the middle of the mall's food court. "When the men arrive, they deposit their keys into a bowl. Everyone networks, plays games—"

"What sort of games?" Birdie asked above the rim of her giant grape drink.

Kimora's smile held a devilish glint. "*Fun* games."

"Sex games," Coco corrected, shaking her head. "You can count me out. I have a little more self-respect than that."

"Relax. You don't have to do nothing you don't want to do. It's not that kind of party, Coco."

"Uh-huh. What happens with the keys?"

Kimora's smile widened as she leaned forward for the juicy part. "Toward the end of the party, after everyone has finished networking, I bring the bowl of keys to the middle of the room. Each woman has to reach in and select a set of keys. Whoever's keys you draw, he's your...date for the rest of the evening."

Birdie and Coco looked at each other for a long moment and then burst out laughing.

Kimora rolled her eyes and waited out the tide of their laughter. "Yeah, yeah. Chuckle it up. At least I'm enjoying the holidays. I'm enjoying life, living in the moment."

It was Birdie's and Coco's turn to roll their eyes.

"But you should come, Birdie." Kimora tried to sound nonchalant. "Stephen will be there."

Birdie's mouth had just settled around her large corn dog, but she stopped from taking a bite.

Kimora's eyes dropped as she cleared her throat. "You know, he's always had a thing for you."

"I knew it." Coco chuckled into her drink.

Birdie's eyes narrowed as she ripped into her corn dog.

"And you know he really came through for you the other day," Kimora continued.

"So you told him I would sleep with him for bailing me out?"

"No!" Kimora protested a bit too hard and a bit too loudly. In the ensuing silence, her eyes darted from Birdie to Coco. "Well, not in so many words."

"I don't believe this." Birdie dropped her meal-on-a-stick back down onto her plate and leaned back in her chair. "Are you my friend or my pimp?"

"Are you sure you want to know the answer to that?" Coco whispered out the side of her mouth.

"I'm your friend," Kimora snapped, managing a flush of indignation. "All I told him was that you'd be there. I have no control over the set of keys you'll draw. What's wrong with giving the man a little hope?"

"You're kidding, right?" Coco asked.

"C'mon. Birdie had a real emergency and I played the only card I had."

"Well, you can just call him and tell him that I won't be there. I may be lonely, but I have a little more dignity and self-respect than to jump on the first man that crosses my path." With that, Birdie snatched up her tray from the table and stalked over to the trash bin to dump its contents.

Coco shook her head, but when she glanced up, she was stunned at Kimora's expression. "What are you smiling about?"

"Birdie." She chuckled softly. "She'll be there."

Coco glanced over her shoulder and watched her best friend before she sighed. "Maybe."

"So…" Kimora gave Coco her full attention. "What's going on with you and your hunky boss?"

Coco met her friend's gaze dead-on. "There's nothing going on. You know I can't stand the man."

"Uh-huh."

"I need to quit that place. I'm so sick of his micromanaging I don't know what to do. I mean it. I'm overworked, under-appreciated, underpaid," Coco continued, on her soapbox.

"Uh-huh."

"When I'm gone, then he'll know what a good thing I was." Coco glanced over at her friend. "What are you smiling about?"

Kimora shrugged. "Nothing. Nothing at all."

You're cordially invited to Kimora's Christmas Singles' Key Party

Rules: There are no rules.

Leave your inhibitions, your cell phones and cameras at home, because what happens at the key party...stays at the key party.

Patrick

It's Christmas Eve and I have a mind not to climb out of bed. What's the point? The prospect of dealing with my large, loud and meddlesome Irish family already has my temples thudding with an early-morning migraine. Where in the hell am I going to find the energy to plow through the next two days?

I push off the bed's blankets and ignore the massive army of goose bumps marching across my flesh. The alarm clock blares out from the nightstand, and out of reflex I slam my fist down on the off button and push myself out of bed.

Christmas hasn't always been like this. Once upon a time, I'd looked forward to the holidays. I'd anxiously participated in the unspoken but understood annual competition with the neighbors over who can squeeze the most Christmas lights on their house. No electric bill was too high. Death by building an elaborate nativity scene on the roof was deemed honorable and a worthy cause. But the real game was who had the best tree. Fake, spinning and prelit trees were automatically disqualified. A real tree was the only way to go.

Of course, everyone tried for the trifecta. But in truth, Lydia and I were the only ones to ever win that honor.

Lydia.

A river of guilt streams through my heart. Guilt. Not longing or pain—the emotions I should be feeling as a widower. What did it say about me when after six years I no longer missed my wife? In truth, each day it grew harder to remember the small details of Lydia's face or the exact musical notes of her laughter.

Does that mean I didn't love my wife—that she hadn't *truly* been my soul mate? And worse, what does it say about me when another woman's face fills my thoughts and dances in my dreams?

Laughing, I doubt Assistant District Attorney Courtney Brown has ever danced in her life. She is so strong, regal and serious. Her smiles are rare and her laughter nonexistent. Yet there's still something that entices, draws me like a magnet.

As quickly as the thought enters my mind, I dismiss it and turn on the bathroom shower. There is no point in fantasizing about Ms. Brown.

The woman hates me.

She also has a way of pushing *my* buttons. Every time I walk into her office with the full intention of being polite and charming, I end up walking out ready to smash something against the wall.

Women.

I step into the shower and dunk my head beneath the steaming flow of hot water and reach for my bottle of liquid Dial soap.

Ms. Brown resurfaces in my mind. Her wide onyx gaze triggers something raw and primal in me. I imagine waltzing up to her, in her tight gold pantsuit (my favorite color on her), and snatching open the jacket.

Even in my dreams Ms. Brown is no pushover. She slaps my face—*hard*, leaving a bright red handprint. Her reaction doesn't cool my passion but inflames it. Pushing her up against the desk, I rip open her blouse and devour her full lips. Her tongue draws circles on mine and arouses a deep guttural groan.

Entrenched in the daydream, I mindlessly lather my body. Somewhere along the way my large, rough hands have transformed into small, black, graceful ones with French-manicured nails.

In my mind, I free Courtney's dark breasts from her lacy black bra and fill my mouth with her even darker nipples.

When the queen sighs in ecstasy, I harden into smooth steel. With superhuman strength one is only blessed with in dreams, I yank off her pants and I'm pleased to see a lacy thong. Along the edges I catch sight of her black, downy nest of curls and I almost feel like a kid in a candy shop. Yet at the same time I want to hear her beg for it—to hear some solid confirmation that she wants it as bad as I do.

Then finally "Please" falls gracefully from her lips.

I push the small string between her legs aside and I quickly glide into her.

Vaguely, around the periphery of my mind, I'm aware of the shower turning cold. Just as I'm aware that it's my hand locked around my shaft and pumping wildly away like some prepubescent teenager.

Pushing reality out of my mind, I concentrate on my regal queen, whose head lolls back while her husky sighs play like sweet music in my ears. I'm lost in her feminine curves and soft, lush mounds. Tight. Wet. Perfect.

Suddenly it's difficult to catch my breath. My orgasm, originating from my toes, ruptures so fast and furious that I have to brace my weight against the shower's wall.

In my mind, I spill every drop of my passion into Ms. Brown's tight, hot body. But in truth, it and my courage swirl down the drain.

Joel

I've always had this thing for older women—and an even bigger thing for plus-size women. I don't know. There's just something to the adage "more cushion for the pushin'." Sticks and bones do nothing but bruise a brother, if you know what I mean. I need a little girth to stay warm in the winter.

Anyway, Christmas is looking out to be a real pisser. I've only been in Atlanta for a couple of months. I'm a rapper looking to hit it big in the A-T-L. My plan is to drop my little demo on Jermaine Dupri and then just blow up. But until that happens, I'm baggin' groceries at Publix.

It ain't so bad. Flexible hours, meeting new people and, starting at the first of the year, a brotha will even have health insurance. Medical *and* dental.

Anyway, because it's Christmas Eve, Publix closes early—and the place is a madhouse. It's cool, though. It keeps me busy. I don't even mind sporting the cheap red-and-white Christmas hat. 'Tis the season to be jolly.

"Paper or plastic?" I ask the next customer before glancing up. When I do, it's like—whoa! A sistah with the face of an angel, a creamy peanut-butter complexion and a thick-in-all-the-right-places body is standing before me.

"Plastic," she says, not bothering to glance in my direction. She frowns as she digs through her purse. "Where in the hell did I put my debit card?"

"Momma." A little boy with her beautiful eyes tugs her arm. "Can I get some candy?"

She gives a dramatic sigh, obviously trying to remain cool. "One piece," she announces.

"Me, too?" Another child pops up from the candy rack.

My gaze quickly searches her fingers for a ring, and my heart drops a few inches when I spot the gold band and sizable diamond twinkling back as if commanding me to back off. Hell, one thing I've learned about these well-to-do suburban women: their man ain't got nothin' to do with me. I'm all for hittin' and quittin' it. Then again, this sistah could get a brotha caught up.

"You each can have one piece," she tells the child, doing a great job of keeping the irritation out of her voice. "Here it is." She extracts her card from her purse and hands it to Shalonda, the cashier.

Shalonda, whose skinny ass has the hots for me, clears her throat, and I remember my job. I start cramming food into the bags, every now and then sneaking side glances at this angel's bodacious ta-tas. A brotha could feast for weeks off those things—for real!

The great thing about older women is that they always want to teach a young thug a few things. In my short lifetime, the school of *Find My G-Spot* has been the only place I like to get my learn on, if you know what I mean.

I'm packing groceries, smiling and daydreaming. I'm wondering what she looks like in the throes of passion, what she would feel like if I was buried between those thick thighs and how high she could scream when she came.

These are things I'm more than willing to find out—if given the chance.

I place all her bags back into the grocery cart and wait for her to show me to her car. She takes her receipt, promptly grabs her children's hands and begins to lead the way—still not sparing me a glance. However, I forgive her for it the moment she moves in front of me and blesses me with a glorious view of her tight pear-shaped bottom.

Lord have mercy.

Tears pool in my eyes. What I wouldn't give to touch, feel and kiss every inch of it. I am casually wiping the corners of my mouth to make sure I'm not salivating when the little man glances over his shoulder at me.

"What's up?" I say.

The boy eyes me suspiciously, but I hold my smile. Hey, I love kids, and a lot of times if you get along with a woman's kid, you're in like Flynn. I get no such chance today since my peanut-butter baby is obviously preoccupied.

"Momma, how come Daddy can't come to our house for Christmas?" the oldest child asks.

"Honey, we've already talked about this," she says, releasing his hand to work the automatic unlock button on her key chain. She pulls open the trunk of a nice white S-series Mercedes. I load the groceries while trying to keep my eye on the prize.

When she bends over to buckle the children in their car seats, my hard-on throbs out of this world. Finished loading the car, I close the trunk and wait. What am I waiting for? I'm not sure—a tip, a glance or a smile.

"Thanks," she says, still not bothering to look at me as she climbs into the driver's seat.

"No problem," I reply, but it's too late. She's already slammed the door and started the car. I step aside, mainly to make sure that I don't get run over—and it's a good thing, too. Baby girl doesn't even look in her rearview mirror before backing up.

Oh, well. A missed opportunity. Her loss.

Elijah

Whenever I'm in Atlanta, I center on one thing: Kimora's fine ass. I'm not BSing you. The girl is a freak—just the way I like it. There's nothing she won't do to please me in the bedroom. I'm here to tell you, that's a rare commodity indeed.

Black suburban women are uptight and domineering nowadays. They come to bed with a full list of things they will and won't do. A hand job is okay, but a blow job is out of the question. Vaginal sex is great, but if you suggest anal, it could get ugly.

If I say something to my girl, Kimora—I mean anything—the girl is down for whatever. That's perfect for a sex addict like me.

One thing to know about me I want—no, I *need*—sex like I need air. No BS. Kimora gives me space and allows me to take in all the air I need.

Yeah, yeah, I know what you brothers out there are thinking: I could just get myself a hood rat and be done with it. But you know and I know there's a world of difference between the two breeds. Kimora is that nice combination of classy on the outside and freaky on the inside.

Perfect.

With circumstances being beyond my control, I'm in Atlanta for the Christmas holiday and that means I plan to unwrap a special little somethin'-somethin' this Christmas. Right now I'm intrigued by this key party Kimora is throwing. I thought this kind of party went out with all things seventies.

Though, if I know my girl—and I do—this is going to be one hell of a party.

I open the door to my hotel suite wondering what I can do to kill time between now and the party. I want to do something—or someone. I want to play with something—or someone.

The pretty woman working the front desk had checked out my tall athletic frame with intriguing green eyes. She looks like someone who wants a good time. Unfortunately every playa in the world, including me, knows not to pull that infamous Kobe Bryant move.

I could pay through the nose and watch some porno, but that's only going to frustrate me, and I'm not all that into self-gratification, if you catch my drift. What I do like, however, is making my own movies. Something else Kimora and I have in common. They just don't make them like Kimora anymore.

So why don't I be a man and drop to one knee? Let's just say it's complicated. And my baby never pushes the issue.

Damn, I really do love that woman. But if I tell her that, it could cause a whole lot of drama I don't need.

With nothing to do, I walk over to the closet and pull out the digital camera, the tripod and the black suitcase—my Kimora fun box. I smile, already feeling that anxious anticipation for my baby. I snap open the case and remove silk scarves, handcuffs, riding crops…and one very special gold package that can only be opened on Christmas morning.

Kimora loves surprises, and I'm betting that this one is going to send her over the moon.

Chapter 4

Kimora loved getting ready for dates and parties. Preparation was just as much fun as the destination. A long soak in her favorite scented bubble bath with a cucumber mask and a glass of Pinot Grigio was just the beginning. Selecting the right body oil is as important as the right perfume. The objective: to be unforgettable in every way. Seduce a man with all five senses, and he'll be thinking about you when he's ninety-eight and using a bedpan.

Kimora loved being a woman, pampering her skin, playing with makeup and experimenting with her hair. Then there was selecting the right lingerie, the best outfit and, of course, the perfect shoes.

There was an art to being beautiful—one her mother taught her to appreciate at a young age. Sure, she could have married by now, but why, when being single was so much damn fun?

It was sort of funny. Even Birdie and Coco thought she secretly longed for marriage—the whole white picket fence, the two-point-five children and the family dog. Hell, Birdie had all of those things and she didn't look too happy.

From Kimora's viewpoint, the picket fence looked too much like a jail cell and the children like miniature wardens. But maybe she'd consider the dog.

Sure, Kimora knew her closest friends and even some of her lovers considered her a sex freak, but such labels never interested her. As far as she was concerned, they were created to make people comfortable. As Celie said in *The Color Purple*, "People don't like women being too loud or too free."

Kimora was comfortable in her sexuality—the rest of the world could go to hell. She smiled at her private musings and continued to take her time getting dressed.

Exactly three hours later a masterpiece had been created, and Kimora, as always, patted herself on the back and winked at her reflection. "Go knock them dead, girl."

Birdie had fixed an early dinner so she and the boys could have their own Christmas party. A little later their father would pick them up and they would spend Christmas with him and his family. It would be their first Christmas apart, and the thought had sent her crying to the bathroom more than once today.

Terrence seemed moodier than usual. One minute he was happy to open Christmas gifts on Christmas Eve and the next, resentful that she wouldn't be there to open gifts with them at their father's house in the morning.

After they'd returned from the grocery store, Matthew had finally stopped asking her the same questions and put on a brave and happy face.

It was most likely for her benefit…and she appreciated it.

With the dishes in the sink, the boys raced to the living room, where large and small brightly decorated Christmas gifts awaited them.

Seconds later the house was filled with happy squeals and exuberant laughter as her babies tore into their gifts. She grabbed her camera and proceeded to capture every moment on film. Soon their infectious laughter and wide smiles rubbed off on her and she forgot about her husband-stealing sister, her screw-anything-that-moves husband, her newly obtained criminal record and, lastly, her unsympathetic bitch of a mother.

No. *This* was what life was really about: her children—and, of course, trains, race cars and baseball gloves. The evening sped by in a blur and before she knew it, the doorbell rang.

"Daddy!" Matthew sprang to his feet like a jack-in-the-box and raced toward the door.

"Matthew, baby, wait," Birdie called after him. It was no use. He'd already opened the door, and Kenneth's deep baritone boomed into the house.

"There's my little man!"

Matthew burst into giggles.

Birdie rolled her eyes as she lumbered to her feet. Terrance remained planted before the tree and pretended to be intrigued with his gifts.

Birdie frowned. "Terrence, aren't you going to say hello to your father?"

He shrugged and continued to play.

"Ah, there's my other boy," Kenneth said, strolling into the living room with a wide grin. But when Terrence continued to ignore his father, Kenneth's gaze sliced to Birdie. "What's going on?"

She had a suspicion but didn't think it was the right time to voice it. "Terrence, baby, go say hello to your father," she instructed gently.

Terrence quietly placed his toy on the floor and shuffled over to his father like a condemned man walking toward the electric chair.

Kenneth folded his arms around his oldest son, but shot Birdie a hard, evil look.

"Okay, boys, grab what toys you want to take over to your father's and I'll go get your suitcases from upstairs." She turned and bolted out of the room. Pretending pleasantries with a man she wanted six feet under was not her strongest suit.

"We need to talk," Kenneth said, striding up the stairs behind her.

"Not tonight," she answered, not surprised by him following her.

"I want to apologize—"

"Not tonight." She rubbed at her pulsing temples as she entered the boys' room.

"I've been calling you all week," he huffed.

Birdie snatched up the small suitcases she'd packed

earlier, swiveled around and rammed one suitcase right into Kenneth's prized jewels.

"Oomph!" Kenneth doubled over.

Birdie's eyes widened dramatically. "Oh. I'm sorry."

Kenneth's eyes narrowed as he squeaked out, "Do you feel better?"

"Actually—" She thought about it "—I do."

Kenneth pulled himself straight. "I know what I did was wrong," he began, his voice still strained.

Birdie rolled her eyes and stepped past him.

Her husband gripped her arm and held her. "It was a mistake. I love you. I always have."

She met and held his gaze. "You sure do have a funny way of showing it."

"We belong together, Roberta. So let's stop playing games." He inched closer to her. "I know you miss me," he whispered.

Birdie hated the way his warm breath kissed her skin and created such longing in her that one part of her wanted to push him back on the bed and have her way.

"How long has it been?" he asked with his chest now brushing the tips of her breasts. "A little over a year? Do you miss me? Don't you miss how I make you feel?"

She closed her eyes and willed her knees to stop trembling.

"I can make you feel those things again." His voice held a note of promise. "Come to the apartment with me and the boys. Let me give you a *real* Christmas gift. All you have to do is unwrap it."

An image of her sister surfaced and all temptation disappeared. "I'm not interested in anything you have—gift wrapped or not." She stepped back and snatched her arm from his grasp.

Before the devil presented her with another apple, she rushed from the room. Downstairs, she helped her boys into their coats, all the while struggling to keep her tears at bay.

Kenneth played the comical role of a doting father and loaded everything into the car.

"Momma, are you sure you can't come with us?" Matthew asked one last time. "I don't want you to be by yourself on Christmas Day."

"Don't worry about me, baby." Birdie lowered herself onto one knee. "I'm going to be just fine." She kissed him. "Just remember to call me in the morning and tell me about the other toys Santa brought you."

"I will." Matthew's smile beamed. "It was awfully nice for Santa to take the other half of our gifts to Daddy's house."

Terrence rolled his eyes.

"Then we'll make sure we send him a thank-you note," she said.

Matthew nodded, and then his eyes lit up as if a lightbulb had snapped on over his head. "Do you think if we get a third house we would get even *more* presents?"

Kenneth laughed. "It doesn't quite work that way, son."

"Oh." Their son frowned.

"Kiss your mom goodbye," Kenneth instructed the boys.

Matthew gave her a quick peck but a long hug. "I promise to call you in the morning, Mom."

She smiled and then shifted her eyes to Terrence. He

still looked hesitant to leave. "You're going to be a good boy for me?" she asked because it was the only thing she could think of.

He nodded and leaned into her. It wasn't really a hug— more like he was giving her permission to hug him. And she did. She held him as tight as she could without causing any pain.

"I want you to have a good Christmas, too, Mommy," he said so softly she almost didn't hear him.

"I will, baby," she promised.

When he pulled back, he looked as though he didn't truly believe her, but he said nothing.

"Tell you what," Kenneth said. "Why don't I bring you guys by tomorrow evening around six so you can wish Momma a Merry Christmas?"

"That sounds good," Birdie said, smiling at her babies. "Do you want to visit me tomorrow?"

Both boys nodded eagerly.

"Then I'll see you tomorrow evening."

Birdie stood and watched her children march out the door, taking a good chunk of her heart with them.

"You know, my previous offer still stands," Kenneth said, lingering at the door.

"And my answer is still no."

Kenneth shook his head. "Suit yourself. But if the batteries run low, you know where you can find me."

With a final roll of her eyes, Birdie slammed the door in his face. She took several breaths to calm her racing heart. But, at the sound of Kenneth's car pulling out of the driveway, a fresh wave of tears flowed a well-worn path down her face.

The house was cold and quiet—too quiet.

In the living room the floor remained littered with ripped wrapping paper and empty boxes. It felt like the perfect metaphor for her life: ripped and empty.

The phone rang and Birdie nearly jumped out of her skin. For a moment she thought not to answer but then realized it was probably Kenneth telling her that they had forgotten something.

"Hello."

"Birdie!" Kimora shouted. "What the hell are you still doing home?"

Courtney nearly pulled a muscle trying to pry her artificial tree out of the box. When she finally succeeded, she wondered why in the hell she'd even bothered. The damn thing looked as if it had been run over by a Mack truck—several times—before being crammed into a Dumpster, as opposed to being stored in her attic.

Shaking her head, she walked over to the coffee table and poured herself another glass of wine. Even that was failing her tonight. When the heck was her buzz going to kick in?

She needed something to take her mind off Wyclef Onwu and little Tina Else. So far, she was failing. Her gaze drifted to the case file next to the wine bottle. As she sipped from the glass, she contemplated rereading the material—despite the fact she had most of its contents memorized.

The problem was emotionally detaching herself from her

cases. Over the years, she had successfully constructed a steel armor on the outside but was still at a loss on how to wear one on the inside.

Only Birdie and Kimora knew her secret: tough on the outside, soft on the inside.

Mr. Holloway would never believe it—and if she could help it, he'd never have the chance. She glanced at her wine. Maybe this stuff was working. Why on earth was she thinking about Patrick?

Courtney flipped open the folder, and an instant film of tears floated over her vision and blurred the photographs of Tina's bruised face. No matter how hard she tried, she couldn't wrap her brain around the evil that people possessed.

She quickly closed the folder, drained her wineglass and then returned her attention to her fiasco of a Christmas tree.

"What in the hell am I supposed to do with you?"

The phone rang.

She frowned and glanced over at the cordless unit next to the sofa. "Kimora," she guessed under her breath. Slowly she moved away from the coffee table to approach the phone.

"Ms. Brown?"

Courtney straightened at the sound of her assistant's voice. "Wendy?"

"Have you been watching the news?"

"Uh…no." Courtney glanced around the room in search of the television remote control. She found it buried beneath a box of Christmas decorations. "What am I looking for?"

"Channel five," Wendy said anxiously.

Courtney punched in the channel and then sucked in a

surprised breath at the image of Onwu. She turned up the volume and listened to the straight-faced female reporter.

"*Questions continue to swirl about the death of accused rapist Wyclef Onwu, who was found dead hanging in his jail cell. Police captain Travis Mobbs alluded to his suspicion of foul play....*"

"He's dead?" Courtney whispered.

"Can you believe it?" Wendy asked, her surprise still evident in her tone.

Courtney shook her head. Was it wrong to think this was some kind of Christmas miracle? She expelled a slow breath, but her heart continued to hammer.

After a long while, Wendy's voice filtered through. "Ms. Brown, are you still there?"

"Uh, yeah." She blinked and tried to clear her head. "It's over," she said, clicking off the television.

"At least it saves the taxpayers money for a second trial," Wendy joked awkwardly.

Courtney nodded. "Thanks for calling and letting me know," she said. "I appreciate it."

"I—I thought you'd want to know. Merry Christmas."

Courtney smiled tightly. "Merry Christmas." She disconnected the call and slumped onto the sofa. "Dead?"

Slowly but surely, a smile eased its way onto her lips. "Dead." She snatched up the phone again and this time dialed Patrick Holloway's home number from memory. This news should make his night. Her smile faded after the line rang four times. On the fifth ring, her call was transferred to voice mail.

"Mr. Holloway," she began, "I don't know if you've been

watching the news or if someone has already contacted you, but there's been a new development in the Onwu case. When you get a moment, just give me a call at home. I'll probably still be up." She heard herself start to ramble but couldn't stop. "I'm just getting around to putting up my Christmas decorations." She chuckled. "So, uh, just give me a call." She forced herself to hang up before she conveyed just how lonely she truly was on Christmas Eve.

"Get a grip," she counseled herself and jumped back to her feet. She had a tree to decorate.

The phone rang.

"Mr. Holloway?" she asked without looking at the caller ID.

"Coco," Kimora sang playfully. "You're late."

Courtney sighed in disappointment. "Look, Kimmy—"

"I have a special gift for you."

Courtney drew a deep breath and carefully folded her arms while still holding her empty wineglass. "What sort of gift?"

"You'll have to come to find out," Kimora baited.

"And if I don't?"

"Then I'll have to keep Patrick Holloway all to myself. You know what they say—once you go black, you never go back."

Chapter 5

"**M**erry Christmas!" Kimora shouted, showering Joel with glittering confetti as he entered through the doors of Club Sexy. Music thumped and laughter blared out to greet him.

Speech eluded the young twenty-two-year-old as his eyes roamed over the goddess draped in a tight red velvet dress that showcased a perfect hourglass figure. She wasn't as thick as he liked them, but damn if she didn't have enough to work with.

"Do you like?" she asked, spinning in a perfect pirouette.

"What's not to like?" he asked with nervous laughter.

"Baby, I like you already." She winked and hooked her arm through his. "I'm Kimora, your host for the evening and this is my place."

Joel smiled as he saw what looked like a sea of people chatting and dancing around in the room. "Nice place."

"Have we met?" the gorgeous hostess asked, her full, painted lips tempting him to steal a kiss.

"Well, actually, no." He glanced around the room again. "A friend of mine—"

"Say no more."

She placed a finger against his lips, and for the first time he caught the faintest hint of jasmine and vanilla. Now he wanted to taste every inch of her—and judging by the coveted stares in the room, he wasn't the only one.

"You're in luck. I have a couple of extra ladies coming tonight, and if the numbers hold out, there will be one woman for every man—or maybe a few ménage à trois will be in order!"

Joel blinked. He liked this woman's style.

The room roared with laughter and Joel turned to see what was going on.

"Sable!" she shouted. "Get this handsome young man a drink."

Sable, another hottie with a body that curved like a winding hypnotic road, turned toward them. Her eyes roamed over every inch of him, and it was clear that she liked what she saw. "What's your pleasure?" she asked.

"I'll have an orgasm," Joel replied with a wink.

Sable jiggled her eyebrows. "My favorite."

"Imagine that." Joel winked again and moved toward her.

"Oh, wait." Kimora caught him by the arm.

When he glanced at her again, she still had the same breathtaking effect on him.

"I need your keys." She held out a large crystal bowl.

He chuckled and deposited his keys into the bowl—all the while he couldn't believe his friend Derek had told him the truth about this Christmas party.

"Better hope I don't draw your name," she warned playfully. "I'll definitely put a little hair on your chest." She tweaked his nipples through his black turtleneck and then turned saucily back toward the door.

"Merry Christmas!" Kimora showered another invitee with confetti.

"You finally made it!" Derek shouted from behind Joel and pounded his back. "Didn't I tell you this party was going to be off the chain?"

"That you did." Joel turned with a wolfish smile and delivered his own blow to his buddy's arm. He drew a certain amount of pleasure at seeing his friend wince from the power behind his jab.

"Have you checked out the honeys in this place? I swear they all must have been special ordered from a Hot Chicks R Us catalog. I'm in heaven." Derek's head swiveled around just as a Gabrielle Union look-alike jiggled her hips past them.

The two men looked at each other.

"You don't think that was…?" Derek thought it over. "Nah, it couldn't have been. Could it?" He jerked back around in hopes of catching another glance.

She really did look like the famous actress.

Derek wasn't going to chance it. "Hey, I'll catch up with you later," he said and disappeared without waiting for an answer.

Joel shook his head and then turned his attention back to the partying strangers. He was more than a little awkward as he navigated through the crowd. As he moved, he tried to guess which woman would draw his keys.

This was absolutely the wildest thing he'd ever done. After

a long while, he wondered where the waitress had disappeared to with his drink.

"Merry Christmas," the robust bartender barked. "What can I get you?"

Something to calm my nerves. "The strongest thing you got."

That put a smile on the bartender's face. "I think I like you, son." He turned and reached for some mysterious bottles behind him. "This drink is guaranteed to make a man out of you." He set the drink down.

"What is it?"

"The strongest thing I got." The man winked. "Just what you ordered."

A few partygoers surrounding him smirked. Was he the butt of some joke?

The bartender's eyes twinkled and Joel was certain they also held a challenge. It wasn't like him to back down from anything. His hand wrapped around the glass before his brain registered what he was about to do. It wasn't until the scorching that trailed from his tongue to his toes that he even considered that the drink could be deadly.

A spasm of coughs racked his body and the air was suddenly in short supply. The ring of people around him laughed. A few took pity and pounded his back in aid. Soon it appeared his lungs forgave him and his breathing returned to normal.

Upon seeing the twinkling eyes of the bartender gazing back at him, Joel set his glass back down and barked, "I'll take another!"

The crowd cheered.

* * *

Patrick climbed out of his car and stared at the address listed on his invitation. He still didn't know why he'd come—other than the fact that he had absolutely nothing else to do on Christmas Eve and he felt like celebrating. Wyclef Onwu was no longer his problem. It was up to his maker now to judge him how He saw fit. Not even the mayor would argue with that.

He glanced up at the club and then down at his invitation. It intrigued him.

"Club Sexy." He wrinkled his nose, wondering for the millionth time whether it was smart for him to attend such a place. He was the district attorney. "Kimora." He still drew a blank. He'd searched his PDA, his address books and his dusty memory and he was certain that he didn't know a Kimora—but she'd made it clear that she knew him.

"C'mon, live a little," he coached himself as he marched up to the door. For the first time in years, he carried no cell phone, pager or beeper. That in itself was a liberating experience.

As he approached the building, the music and laughter grew louder. Suddenly he felt every day of his forty-two years and he wondered yet again why he'd come.

"Merry Christmas!" a woman shouted before throwing a sheet of glittering confetti in his face.

When his vision cleared, he was convinced the beauty standing before him had stepped out of a dream.

"Ah." The woman in red looked him over, and her smile widened. "I thought you were going to stand me up."

Patrick blinked. "I'm sorry, but do I know you?" His eyes

scanned past her to the dancing crowd. This was definitely not his scene.

"You don't know me *yet*." Kimora slid a hand down the side of her curvaceous figure while a blatant invitation glowed in her eyes. "But don't worry. The night is still young."

Patrick swallowed and pretended not to feel his arousal stiffen against his leg.

The beautiful woman laughed at the lame attempt. "Coco never told me you embarrassed easily."

"Coco?"

"Courtney," she said. "Assistant District Attorney Courtney Brown. I believe you know her?"

Patrick's gaze shifted to the crowd behind her again. "Is she—"

"Not yet." The woman's lips widened and her eyes danced. "But she will be soon." She picked up a large crystal bowl filled with keys. "Something tells me that I was right about you—but you'll have to play to win her."

He didn't understand.

"Trust me." She winked. "I'll need your keys."

Live a little. Patrick dug out his keys from his pants pockets and placed them in the bowl.

"C'mon in." She stepped back and allowed him to journey farther into the club.

He walked inside, catching a whiff of jasmine and vanilla. Damn, the woman smelled as good as she looked.

"I'm Kimora Evans." She extended a hand. "Coco's best friend."

"Coco, huh?" He struggled to keep his amusement under

wraps. "I would have thought that her nickname was something like 'ball breaker.'"

"Coco the ball breaker." Kimora smiled. "I like it."

Patrick chuckled awkwardly and crammed his hands into his pants pockets. Now what?

Kimora set the bowl down but plucked his keys out and studied the design of his leather key holder. "A four-leaf clover, huh?"

"I'm Irish," he said, realizing how stupid he sounded.

"You don't say?" She returned his keys to the bowl. "Can I get you anything from the bar?"

He laughed at the joke. "As a matter of fact, I think I could use a drink." Patrick glanced around, taking in the bevy of beauties. Damn, it had been a long time. Did he even remember how to pick up a woman?

Kimora laughed as though she'd read his thoughts and turned him around by his shoulders. "The bar is *that* way."

"Right."

"I'll bring Coco over as soon as she arrives."

"Oh, that won't be necessary." The last thing he wanted was for Ms. Brown to think he'd come to hook up with her. He was her superior, after all.

"Of course it is." Kimora laughed playfully. "You're the only reason she's coming to this party."

Sable stood at the back door, impatiently tapping her foot and anxiously puffing on a cigarette. "C'mon. C'mon." She glanced at her watch and cursed at the thought of all the tips she was missing out on and the action.

"I knew I could always count on you."

She glanced up just as Elijah stepped out of the inky blackness and into the globe of light from the lamppost. "I was just beginning to think you weren't going to show up."

He smiled as he approached, and Sable felt a stab of jealousy for her boss. Was he really dipped in gold? She didn't move when he'd entered through the door and his hard body brushed hers. Yeah, yeah, it was a cheap way to cop a feel of his muscular body. So sue her.

"Where's my girl?" he asked.

"Up by the front door, greeting the guests."

This was exactly the reason Elijah had used the back door. He wanted to surprise Kimora.

"Thanks again," he told Sable and planted a kiss against her cheek and slipped a hundred-dollar tip between her ample breasts. "Don't spend it all in one spot."

Sable sighed and then winked at him. "One day…" she promised him. And she meant it. If Kimora ever cut him loose, she would be right there to pick up the pieces. "Does she know how lucky she is?"

Elijah flashed the waitress a departing smile. "You got it all wrong." He shrugged. "I'm the luckiest bastard here."

Chapter 6

Everything Birdie tried on made her feel fat. For a party, it was probably best to stay away from anything with an elastic band, but damn if it didn't feel as if her best jeans were slicing into her stomach. She opted for a loose red-and-silver top, mainly because it came with a matching jacket and she could hide the slight jiggle of her upper arms.

Unlike her shoe-fetish friend Kimora, Birdie only had to dig through two types of shoes: flat and flat with arch support. When she had finally finished putting herself together, her critical eye hated everything she wore.

"I'm not going," she declared and threw up her hands. What was the point? Birdie stomped out of her room and made it downstairs to the refrigerator in record time. The doorbell rang just as she pulled out her favorite brand of double-chocolate-mint ice cream.

"Who in the hell?" She returned the carton to the freezer and went to answer the door. "Coco?" she asked when her friend blazed across the threshold.

"If I have to go, you have to go."

Birdie's gaze settled on her friend's smoking hot little gold dress and she blinked in surprise. "She called you, too?"

Coco nodded impatiently. "And she somehow managed to get an invitation to my boss."

"She didn't." Birdie felt a chuckle starting but then quickly swallowed it under Coco's murderous glare. She took another glance at her friend's attire and at long last she understood—just as Kimora must have.

"I thought you didn't like your boss," Birdie said, crossing her arms. Coco would go on and on about how the guy always got under her skin, and Birdie had chalked up her ranting to Coco's just being…well, Coco.

"I *don't* like him. And most likely he has no idea what kind of party Kimora has invited him to."

"So you're just going to go rescue him—in that outfit?"

Coco drew an impatient breath. "Are you going to help me or not?"

Birdie turned toward the foyer table and grabbed her purse. "Let's roll."

Kimora passed the duty of collecting keys to one of her employees and started flirting with a few potential "dates." Considering herself just shy of a professional dancer, she jiggled and popped her booty in time to 50 Cent's "Dance Inferno," and judging by how low her admirers' tongues wagged, it would be a good month before she had to mop the club's hardwood floors.

A hand blinded her vision, while a strong arm wrapped around her small waist and drew her back against a rock-hard frame. Instantly hot and wet, she knew the man's body well.

"Guess who?"

"Um…" She reached a hand behind her, pretending to be dumbfounded. But when she boldly slid her hands between his legs and felt the weight of her old familiar friend, she proudly announced, "Elijah!"

He laughed, uncovered her eyes and playfully spun her around. One glance at his strong, handsome features and Kimora licked her lips and felt her toes curl.

"Merry Christmas, baby." He tilted his head and kissed her plump, vibrant, red-painted lips.

She sighed, stroked his manhood through his pants and reveled in the feel of his hands grabbing and squeezing her butt. As their tongues delved into each other's warm mouths, neither of them cared they were in a crowded room—in fact, Kimora welcomed the guests' voyeurism.

"Now that's the kind of woman I want," a male's voice floated over to them.

Kimora broke the kiss and laughed in triumph at Elijah's dazed and confused look. "I feel like dancing," she admitted. "Care to join me?"

"If I don't, I have a feeling I'm replaceable."

"Damn right," the same male barked.

Elijah cut the man an annoyed look, while Kimora laughed and proceeded to lead her man through the crowd with her hand still firmly locked on to her favorite part of his anatomy.

Laughing, Elijah basked in the men's envious stares and the women's lyrical chuckles. However, it was obvious to him that people still assembled at the front of the club had never attended a Kimora party. They still held that deer-caught-in-headlights look, but he held no doubt in time their inhibitions would shed.

Across the club, down the corridor, they entered what was affectionately named the Champagne Room. Tonight it had been transformed into a miniature dance club—complete with a spinning disco ball. Dark, hot and ear-splittingly loud, the room was crammed with bodies pulsing to the stereo's infectious beats.

If it wasn't for her possessive claim on his iron-stiff hard-on, Elijah was certain that he would have lost Kimora, but soon enough they found a secluded spot and proceeded to get their groove on.

Dancing while Kimora did her thing was difficult. She had a way of moving her hips that made a brother want to break out the dollar bills and stuff them in every available spot on her body—and she knew it. Her dancing had nothing on what she could do in bed—and she knew that, as well.

Their hips bumped. Her ass grinded against his crotch, and her nails raked his chest and back. She was everywhere and nowhere and Elijah grew delirious with desire. *Just dance*, he told himself. This wasn't the time or place. But one glance to the bodies moving next to them and he suddenly realized a few of the other guests had abandoned notions of dancing and were actually…having sex.

The shimmering light from the disco ball faintly illuminated exposed hips, bare breasts and thrusting buttocks. He realized too why the music was so loud in the room: it drowned out the guests' groans and moans of pleasure. His gaze shot back to his dancing partner and he identified her cat-caught-the-canary smile and felt his member throb to the point of pain.

She crooked a finger at him, and he came to her willingly until she had backed up against the wall. He pressed his body against hers, loving the feel of her toned curves and soft mounds.

He took her mouth again, this time pouring everything he had into the kiss. In return, she gave him the same.

Kimora felt wicked and reveled in the feeling. She also knew if she didn't get Elijah into her soon, her body would explode with need. Accustomed to just going for what she wanted, Kimora brought her hands once again to the front of his pants, this time tackling the zipper. When she freed his hefty, throbbing sex, her body literally quaked.

Elijah, as if sensing her arousal, lifted her easily against the wall, hiked up her dress and pushed aside her thin lacy thong. His mouth slid from her mouth, scorched a trail down her throat and then finally his teeth peeled back the thin fabric covering her full breasts. He locked his lips around a dark tan nipple at the same time he thrust two fingers into her slick passageway, and Kimora's eyes rolled heavenward.

She just needed this quick fix, she kept telling herself. For the most part she knew it was a lie, but the lie still gave her the illusion that she was in control.

Elijah's hands worked their magic and robbed her of breath and thought until the first orgasm swept through every inch of her like a firestorm. When it was over, she kept her legs and arms wrapped around him as if he was her very lifeline.

Damn him for making her feel this way.

"I'm not through with you," he growled huskily into her ear.

I hope not.

"You're crazy if you think I'm going to sit back and watch you pull another man's set of keys. I have a big night planed for us."

She said nothing but smiled back. She had no intentions of spending the night with anyone else, either.

Elijah fumbled with his back pants pocket and produced a condom. "And you're crazy if you think I'm ready to leave this room."

Kimora took the condom from his fingers, and a couple of seconds later she glided the long latex over his steel erection and mentally prepared herself for a flight into the heavens.

Elijah did not disappoint.

He entered her slowly, giving her body a moment to adjust to his invasion. When she had done just that, she wiggled her hips and ground against him. Elijah moved her away from the wall and balanced her full weight in his arms while he bounced her tight body against his hips. As with all the other couples, the loud music drowned out their bodies slapping together.

Brief glimpses of the sexual activities going on around them proved to be a heady aphrodisiac, and soon Kimora and Elijah were set on proving that they could outperform everyone in the room.

Birdie and Coco pushed their way into the club. Neither knew what to expect but had prepared for the worst—at least they thought so, anyway. Laughter and music pierced and rattled their eardrums, while a thin layer of smoke drifted on the air.

When both realized that it wasn't tobacco, they glanced at each other and then slowly shook their heads.

"Let's split up," Coco shouted. "I'll look toward the back."

"Do you think he's still here?" Birdie shouted back. She scanned the crowd, taking note of the pencil-thin women walking around in clothes that left little to the imagination. Self-consciously she tugged at her jacket. "Maybe he's gone home."

Birdie glanced back toward her friend only to see that she had already disappeared into the crowd. She was on her own. "Great."

Sighing, she dropped her arms to her sides and resigned herself to search for a man she had only a vague description of. Christmas was getting worse by the moment.

"Birdie!"

She froze, momentarily surprised to hear her name shouted from the crowd. Finally she turned and glanced around to see if she could catch who was calling her. Then she saw him. "Stephen."

Kimora's cousin pried himself from a woman's spidery arms and made his way over to her.

"I was beginning to think that cousin Kimmy lied to me."

Birdie kept her smile together. "Actually, I'm not staying. I'm here helping Coco find someone."

"Well, that's the whole point of the party—singles who don't want to be alone for the holidays."

Joel splashed cold water on his face to help clear his head. *Moonshine. Hot damn.* What was he thinking? Then again, maybe that was the problem—he wasn't thinking. He stood before the bathroom mirror grinning to himself and enjoying his buzz.

When he returned to the party, three women dressed in scanty red-and-white Santa's-helper outfits—complete with matching caps—suddenly surrounded him. They also looked as if they wanted to ravish him for the evening.

A crooked smile hooked the corner of his lips and he easily slid into his best Mac Daddy impersonation. "Well, hello, ladies."

"Hello, yourself," one of the women greeted. She stepped forward, erasing the sparse distance between them, and brushed her large breasts against his chest. "Are you looking for a little three-on-one action?"

Hell yeah! Joel's gaze leaped to the other two women. He had never done such a thing, but he was more than willing to *rise* to the challenge. His eagerness must have shown in his eyes, because the sexy trio suddenly burst into giggles.

So was it a joke, a tease or—please, God—a legitimate offer?

Before he could give voice to the question, a stiff, cold breeze swept over him and alerted Joel that his bold Santa's helper had unzipped his pants. He looked around, trapped among walls of party people mingling. But that wasn't quite true, either. Off to the side, almost hidden by the bathroom door, a woman was bent over, her eyes closed, her head thrown back while her male partner thrust into her like a human jackhammer.

Hot damn!

The bold woman before him knelt, and when she did, Joel caught sight of another woman wandering the club's dance floor. When she turned her head, her eyes swept past him, and he instantly recognized his gorgeous peanut-butter beauty from Publix.

The night was getting better by the moment. He stepped back just as he was sure that his companion was about to wrap her mouth around his stiff hard-on. He reached down and carefully pulled himself back into his pants.

"Hey!"

"Sorry, ladies," he apologized and zipped up. "Change of plans."

Chapter 7

Coco was beyond shocked by the various sexual behaviors of Kimora's "guests." This party was just as she'd always suspected—one big excuse for an orgy. The farther she traveled through the club, the darker it grew and the more outrageous and uninhibited the attendees became.

A mysterious hand landed and squeezed her ass, and Coco whipped around, prepared to put her hours of Tae Bo to good use. Surprisingly, it wasn't a man at all.

"Whoa, girlfriend. I don't roll like that," Coco warned with a biting edge. "If you want to live to see Christmas Day, you'll back the hell up."

The hand released her and the woman gave her a casual, "Your loss."

Coco shook her head as she watched the woman turn away. In the next second, more uninvited hands invaded her personal space, and she hopped around like a Mexican jumping bean. After a few minutes of this, she decided suddenly that this rescue mission was just not worth it and bolted from the corridor as if the devil himself snapped at her heels.

So focused was she on her escape, Coco knocked the air from her lungs when she smacked into someone's solid back. "Damn it!" she snapped. "Get out of my way."

The tall man turned and settled his striking blue eyes on her. "Ah, Ms. Brown. I'd recognize that temper anywhere," he said with an uncharacteristicly goofy smile. "Or should I call you Coco?"

"Are you high?" she asked, narrowing her eyes with suspicion.

"I plead the Fifth on the grounds that my answer may incriminate me." He chuckled and smacked his lips. "Good Lord, I'm famished."

She rolled her eyes and locked her hand onto his wrist. "I'm getting you out of here. You're a district attorney, for God's sake."

"Well, I feel like celebrating. Onwu is out of our hair—"

"You heard?"

"Heard, danced a jig and came here to celebrate." He gave a loud whoop.

"Like I said, I'm getting you out of here."

"Wait, wait." He pulled his arm free and glanced at his watch. "They are going to be pulling keys soon." He leaned forward, looking as if he was about to topple over. "I have a feeling I'm going to get lucky."

His warm breath coupled with his overpowering nearness short-circuited Coco's alarm and suddenly she grew warm—hot, even. "Are you pulling keys tonight, Ms. Brown?"

Her gaze followed his small, plump lips. She didn't comprehend a word he'd said, but something had her wondering what it would be like to—

"Ms. Brown?" he asked, frowning.

"Y-yeah? What?" She shook her head. "Did you say something?"

He smiled and tipped up the rest of his drink that she'd been unaware he held. When it was drained, he flashed another lopsided grin. "I know I'm going to regret this in the morning, but here goes."

Maybe the clouds of smoke were affecting her thinking, because they were definitely affecting her reflexes. In one quick jerk, Patrick drew her slim body against his and crash-landed his small lips against her full ones.

A spark flared and immediately roared into an inferno. She could no more pull away than she could rip out her own heart. He tasted that damn good.

She melted against him, gave a moan—and he swallowed it hungrily. In the back of her mind—the very back—her inner voice screamed for her to snap out of whatever spell she'd fallen under and to get a grip.

She was kissing her boss!

Courtney fed from his lips long after her lungs had begun burning from lack of oxygen. Surprisingly she didn't care. She didn't care about a lot of things. When Patrick broke the kiss, it took everything she had not to snatch his head back down and feast again.

"I knew you would taste good," he declared triumphantly.

She didn't say anything. She couldn't.

"I wonder if other things I've been dreaming about are just as good."

His goofy smile returned and helped Courtney part the thick fog hovering above her brain. "Keep dreaming, Mr. Holloway. It's never going to happen."

This time his eyes followed her lips and she doubted he'd heard a word she'd said.

"C'mon." She tried for his hand again. "Let's get out of here before someone actually recognizes you—or worse, there's a raid on this place."

"Raid?" He perked up at that and glanced around. And for the first time, he seemed to notice a few questionable activities. "Are they doing what I think they are doing?" Patrick asked, nodding toward a couple near the corner of the room.

Coco followed his gaze and frowned when she spotted a hoochie mama leaning back against the wall with one leg over the shoulder of some dedicated brother's head buried beneath her dress.

"I'm afraid so," she shouted back to the district attorney.

"Then there's *no* way I'm leaving this party." He laughed and set his drink on a passing tray. "This is the best Christmas party I've ever been to. I'm not leaving until a lucky lady pulls my keys."

She stared at him and saw that he was serious. "Fine." She spun on her heel, her hand still clamped around his wrist while she tugged him through the crowd. When they neared the door, she felt Patrick pull back.

"Ms. Brown, I said I wasn't ready to leave."

Without looking back, she dropped his hand and approached the crystal bowl. "You want someone to pull your keys, then fine," she snapped and plunged her hand into the pile of keys.

Coco didn't know exactly what his keys looked like, but she vaguely remembered seeing a four-leaf-clover shape with green leather before, and now that was what she searched for. At long last, when she spotted the distinctive leather key chain, she pulled it out and pivoted to face him again.

"Are you happy now? I drew your keys, now let's go."

Patrick frowned. "No."

"No?" She blinked and then jammed her fists onto her hips. "Why not?"

He shrugged. "You don't exactly have the Christmas spirit. 'Tis the season to be jolly, you know." Laughing, he turned back toward the crowd and was immediately pulled into the arms of an attractive black tramp that had considerable more junk in her trunk than Coco.

"Talk about the luck of the Irish," Patrick shouted to the woman and tried to keep up with the latest hip-hop rhythm blasting from the speakers.

Coco grabbed a flute of champagne from a passing tray, downed it and reached for another.

"Whoa. Somebody's thirsty." A good-looking brother stepped forward and leered in her face.

Coco rolled her eyes. "Back off, homey. I'm not here for

you." She pushed the man out of her way, marched up and stepped into the minuscule space between Patrick and the tramp. "Excuse me, but he's with me," she told the woman.

"He looks like a free agent to me," the woman challenged and settled her hands on her hips.

"Girlfriend, don't try me. I'll snatch every bit of that two-dollar weave out of your head."

Ms. Tramp gave Coco a thorough glance over but then cut her eyes as she walked away. "Whatever."

"I thought so," Coco muttered and turned back toward Patrick. Tonight's wine, champagne and questionable smoke clouds buzzed in her brain.

Meanwhile, Patrick had already found another woman to lock lips with. In fact, the toothpick-thin redhead looked as though she was trying to tongue-wash his tonsils.

"Hey!" Coco jumped into action and pulled the two apart. "Back off."

"Why, Ms. Brown," Patrick said with wide-eyed amusement. "If I didn't know any better, I'd say you were jealous."

"I'm just thinking about your reputation." She shrugged beneath his twinkling gaze. Damn, it was hot in this place. "Kimora definitely has her fair share of questionable friends."

"And yet, here you are—" he inched closer "—in that wonderful dress."

"I came for you."

His smile widened. "Did you also wear the dress for me?"

A second alarm sounded as he lightly caressed her arm and waited for an answer. The buzzing grew louder in her head.

"Hmm?" Patrick shifted his hand and cupped her chin. "It's my favorite color on you. Did you know that?"

She didn't trust herself to speak, so she didn't.

Unsure whether he was getting to her, Patrick exhaled a frustrated breath. "I don't want to be alone tonight, Ms. Brown." He met and held her gaze. "I'm tired of being alone. Do you understand?"

Her voice still a faded memory, Coco nodded and then slid her hands up and around his neck. When she brought his head back down to her lips, she delivered a kiss that told him she had no intensions of sending him home alone.

"Hello, angel," Joel said in his deepest baritone. "When did you fly in?"

Frowning at the campy line, Birdie turned toward the jerk standing behind her. But she was thrown for a loop when she saw the young buck grinning back at her.

"You don't remember me, do you?" he asked.

"Actually, I think I do," she sassed. "Aren't you my son's playmate in kindergarten?"

He laughed at the joke but eased closer. "I may be young, but all my pieces and parts work just fine."

He licked his lips like a starving man placed before a feast, and Birdie was surprised to feel her legs weaken. It had to be his eyes—those hazel orbs surrounded by long, feminine lashes—that hypnotized her.

"The name is Joel. If you want to know, my key chain has a gold plate that reads 2pac."

She blinked in confusion.

"You know, the greatest rapper of all time," he added for clarification.

"Uh-huh. Actually, I'm not going to be participating in the key drawing. I'm just looking for someone."

"I was, too." He brushed the hair from her shoulder. "And now I've found her…again."

Birdie didn't know what to make of this pretty boy. He was unnervingly confident and sinfully sexy—the perfect combination for a one-night stand.

"Ah, there you are." Stephen's voice sliced like an iron gate between them. "Here's your drink."

Birdie turned toward Kimora's cousin and accepted the glass. Originally she'd sent Stephen for the drink as a way of ditching him. Now, since her body temperature had skyrocketed in Joel's presence, she bordered on dehydration.

"Thank you." She grabbed the glass and tossed back the drink like a seasoned sailor.

Joel and Stephen watched with wide-eyed fascination.

"I think I'd like to have another," she said, handing the glass back to Stephen.

"Yes, ma'am." He gave her a mock salute and scurried back to the bar.

"You know," Joel said, leaning so close that his warm breath rushed against her skin, "there are other ways to loosen up—some I'll be more than happy to help you with."

"Have a Mrs. Robinson fetish, do you?"

His eyes blazed with desire as he stepped forward and brushed his steel hard-on against her hip. "Do you have a problem with that?"

Where in the hell was that drink?

The young man grew bolder by the moment when he reached up to run his fingers along the opening of her jacket and in the process ignited a brushfire across her sensitive breasts.

"I—I have to go," she stammered and stepped back to break away from his touch. This was a dangerous game. She turned and waltzed straight into a thick cloud of smoke. She coughed and waved at the air. "Good Lord, that stuff is strong."

"The best out of the Caribbean," a man with a thick Jamaican accent said.

Birdie glanced over to the dark and handsomely chiseled man with long, ropy dreadlocks that hung past his shoulders.

"Wanna hit?" He offered her the blunt.

"No, thanks." Birdie stamped out the temptation. Just because Kimora behaved like an eternal sorority girl didn't mean that she had to.

The carefree Jamaican shrugged, took another hit and blew another long stream of smoke into her face. "Suit yourself."

Joel chuckled behind her and once again moved so that she was well aware of his arousal. "Quite a party, huh?" His strong arms slid around her hips. "Care to know what I asked Santa for Christmas?"

"A tricycle?"

"Close—since I'll *try* just about anything once." He chuckled again.

She laughed as well since the tension was magically seeping from her body.

"I asked for something nice and thick to hold on to." His

hands roamed the front of her thighs while his hips continued to bump against her butt—simulating sex though they were both fully clothed. "You have the face of an angel and curves in all the right places. I bet you're a tiger in bed."

He kissed the back of her head, and Birdie closed her eyes and fought for control, though she knew full well her mutinous body would win the war.

"Aren't you curious about what it would be like?" Joel asked, his hand now moving toward her crotch.

What the hell am I doing? Her eyes flew open in wild wonderment. "Don't." Her hand shot down to stop his from dipping between her legs.

He stopped his gyrating hips and his warm nuzzling, and Birdie immediately wanted to issue a countercommand. More smoke swirled, and she had to admit she was beginning to feel pretty damn good.

Then Stephen appeared in her peripheral vision.

"I gotta get out of here." She bolted in the opposite direction and quickly navigated toward the back stairs.

"Hey, wait up!" Joel called after her.

"I'll just go wait in the car for Coco," she told herself. She should never have agreed to come here. She should never have allowed a completer strange to touch her like that, talk to her like that.

"Hey!"

Joel's strong hand clamped around her wrist, and Birdie jerked around to demand release. However, when she turned, the young buck crushed against her lips with a kiss that obliterated her anger.

She couldn't remember ever tasting anything so intoxicating, dangerous and forbidden all at once. So far, he hadn't lied. All his pieces and parts *were* working. Did she dare find out just how well?

Chapter 8

Kimora was more than a little mussed up after her and Elijah's little performance on the dance floor—and she loved it. Hot and sweaty, she found it nearly impossible to comb her way through the crowd on her trembling legs to her upstairs office.

She removed the key from her silver loop earrings and then slipped inside. Before she could close the door, however, Elijah placed his foot inside.

"Mind if I join you?"

She hesitated. "I have to take a quick shower and change before the key drawings."

He shrugged with a boyish grin. "I know how to be quick."

"Since when?" she challenged with her own devilish smile.

"Since…well, never. But won't you give me a chance to try?"

Kimora knew that she had no intention of shutting Elijah out of her office. As far as she was concerned, that would never happen. But every once in a while there was no harm in letting him work hard for what he wanted. "All right. Just this once," she teased, stepping back from the door.

His grin transformed into a full-size smile as he moved into the room and locked the door behind him.

"Who are you looking for?" Patrick asked, opening his car door.

Now that they had stepped out of Club Sexy and away from the crazy party, the cool air had a way of clearing Coco's head. Maybe it wasn't too late to back off from this crazy thing. "I drove a girlfriend here. I don't think that I should just leave her."

His blue eyes narrowed suspiciously. "Are you trying to back out of tonight, Ms. Brown?"

"Did I say I wanted to back out?" she snapped. She didn't know why she was always so quick to get angry with him. Of course, being angry was easier than admitting she wanted to kiss him again.

Frustration pitched his handsome features. "What kind of game are you playing, Ms. Brown?"

"I'm not playing a game!"

"You could have fooled me," he snapped back, slamming the car door and marching toward her.

Courtney thrust her chin up and stood her ground. Yet she was still flooded with the same intense heat his body had exuded minutes ago at the party.

Damn it, she didn't want to be attracted to him. He was everything she couldn't stand. Plus, he was her boss!

"Look," Patrick growled. "I know that there is every reason why we shouldn't be attracted to each other. I'm your boss. Plus, you can't stand me and I can't stand you."

How the hell does he keep doing that?

"But I'm not going to lie to you," he continued, stopping within inches of her face. "Every day for the last two years, I've wanted you in my bed. I've wanted you in my shower. I've wanted you in places that don't seem humanly possible." He lifted his hand and it carelessly brushed across a breast on its journey to cup her chin. "You can't deny there's something…electric between us."

She could, but she would be lying. Damn him.

"I'm not going to force you to do something you don't want, but judging by your behavior in there a while ago, I'd say you want me, too. Am I wrong?"

"I don't know *what* it is I want," she finally admitted.

Patrick smiled and brushed a butterfly kiss against her lips. "I do." He turned, walked back to the passenger door and opened it. "Get in."

Courtney glanced back at the club. "But my girlfriend—"

"Get in," he commanded.

Normally she had a problem with authority—especially his—but Courtney *wanted* to go with him. Her head still tilted high, she moved toward the passenger door. "One night," she said, stopping in front of him.

He frowned at her stipulation.

"One night," she repeated. "I'm not saying that there is something between us—but if there is, one night is sufficient time for us to exorcise it out of our system. We tell *no one.*"

Her chin came up even higher as she stretched out her hand. "Deal?"

Patrick actually looked as if he was going to rebut the offer, but then he stared straight into her eyes and accepted the handshake. "Deal."

Birdie broke away from Joel, more than ashamed of her thoughts of adultery. Yet at the same time, her hazel-eyed dreamboat had done more for her self-esteem than she would have thought humanly possible. Then there was Stephen, who still appeared interested in her. He was more her age.

Stop it. She forced her thoughts to steer in another direction. All she needed was to go home, soak in a hot bubble bath and pull out her handy, uncomplicated, never disappointing Victor the vibrator.

A car door slammed, and Birdie glanced up among the metal sea of vehicles to see Coco's boss coming around a car and opening the driver's-side door. She hurried her footsteps, trying to catch him to let him know Coco was looking for him. But then her feet stopped all on their own when Patrick leaned over and kissed the woman next to him.

Coco!

"Oh, my God." Her lips widened into a smile. Kimora had been right about those two. Judging by the way they were kissing each other, Birdie almost expected the car to ignite. At the same time, she couldn't stop watching them. She couldn't stop the snake of jealousy curling into the pit of her stomach, nor the sparks of excitement.

* * *

Patrick dragged Coco over into his lap and pulled down one strap of her gold dress. His manhood throbbed at the sight of her large black nipples. He sucked roughly one into his mouth and loved the way her small body squirmed on top of him.

If he wasn't careful, he was going to come before they even got started. He couldn't allow that. He'd dreamed of this moment for too long.

Courtney squirmed against him again and he raked his teeth against her nipples. She drew in a sharp breath but urged him to continue. No doubt about it, Ms. Brown liked it rough.

He hiked her dress around her hips while she pushed up his turtleneck and T-shirt and then flung the clothes into the backseat. The contrast of their skin color was both striking and erotic. Patrick's need to get inside her only escalated.

Coco fumbled to unzip his pants while Patrick slid the seat back and down to give them more room. Hell, she had never done this in a car before—and never in plain sight.

This was what a Kimora party did to people.

In the back of her mind she was still looking for a reason to walk—any reason. She told herself if he was too gentle, she would walk. But it seemed the Irishman had a little roughneck in him. Next, she told herself if she pulled out a small penis, she would walk. But with what her hand discovered, she nearly stopped breathing.

Hot damn, I hit the jackpot.

"Back pocket," he said throatily.

Putting her own-mind reading ability to work, Coco knew exactly what she was digging for in the back pocket. When she pulled out the gold-foiled condom, she made quick work of sliding it on him.

Lips locked on his, Coco eased down onto his rock-hard erection. She gasped halfway down; her body was slow to adjust. But damn if he didn't feel good. Trembling, she opened her eyes and stared into a sea of passion-blue.

The intensity of his gaze should have frightened her or forced her to reconsider whether he could accept her terms of a one-night-only deal.

Shame to say, but Patrick grew impatient. He thrust his hips upward, completing the consummation and stealing another gasp from her trembling lips. For the briefest of moments they were still, breathing each other's breaths.

When she was ready, he slowly moved inside her. His mouth returned hungrily to her magnificent breasts. He nibbled and chewed while his thrusts became hard rams. She arched into him and begged him to make her come.

"Come on, white boy. You can do better than that," she challenged through gritted teeth.

Patrick accepted the challenge, and his hammering hips soon had her head bumping against the car's roof. So tight. So wet. So perfect. Just the way he always knew she would be.

Coco released a broken moan, then quickly another. As though their thoughts and bodies were in sync, pleasure ripped through the couple until they exploded with an earth-shattering shudder.

They clung to each other, hot and sweaty, though the December night was anything but.

"I better hurry and get you home," Patrick whispered.

Coco started to move from his lap, but he quickly locked his arm around her hips.

"Don't move." He slid the seat forward and finally turned the ignition key. "I want to drive with you just like this."

Coco's eyes glittered with mischief. "That could be dangerous, Mr. District Attorney."

"Not to mention exciting." Patrick shifted the car into gear. "Lucky for us, I only live two miles from here."

"Then you better hurry." She moved up and down on his shaft again. "I'm ready for another round."

Birdie stepped out of view and ducked behind a car when Patrick pulled from his parking spot. His headlights swept across where she had just stood and then disappeared.

Once her breathing returned to normal and she was certain the coast was clear, Birdie climbed up from her hiding spot. Her mind quickly reviewed what she'd seen. It had been beautiful to behold, inspiring to witness such passion. It had been so long.

She glanced back at the club. Inside she could still pick out a Christmas gift for herself, hopefully the one with the 2pac key chain.

Kimora whispered the name of her savior against the shower's tile while Elijah stroked her smoothly from behind and the hot water pounded their bodies. Their pleasure-filled moans had a loud surround-sound effect, given the bathroom's acoustics, and served as another heady aphrodisiac.

She realized as his gorgeous body injected her with what she needed that it was impossible to ever grow tired of him. They were made for each other—crazy lifestyles and all.

Elijah's hands clamped on her hips, and his thrusts hardened and quickened. Knowing that he was ready, Kimora aided him by squeezing her vaginal walls and rocking back against him.

One hand left her hip to entangle in her hair. She loved it when he did that—loved how he pulled and then loved the sound of his growled release.

"Ah, baby. You're the best." He nuzzled his face into the back of her hair and breathed in its fruity smell. "You're the best. You know that, baby?"

She did know it. She just didn't want him to ever forget it.

Their "quick" shower had lasted an hour, and Kimora returned to her guests wearing a short white dress that didn't quite reach midthigh, her wet hair pulled into a loose ponytail and a smile that stretched from ear to ear.

"Okay, it's that time," Kimora sang, jiggling a small gold bell to get everyone's attention and then turning on a microphone. A new level of excitement buzzed through the crowd. All music was shut off just as one woman's orgasmic cry ripped from the Champagne Room.

The guests ruptured with laughter.

"Remember—" Kimora rang her bell again "—what happens at the key party…"

"Stays at the key party," the guests chanted back to her, and another ripple of laughter washed over the crowd.

Kimora retrieved the bowl of keys. "Okay. Looks like a few keys are missing, so that must mean a few ladies have already left with a new Christmas gift."

More laughter.

"Ladies, line up. Men, stand against the wall." She set the crystal bowl down on a tall glass table. From the corner of her eye she spotted Birdie.

"Oh, my God. You came. I can't believe it." She rushed over to her friend and embraced her. "Is Coco here, too?"

Birdie felt her cheeks burn. "She, um, left." She glanced over Kimora's shoulder, locked gazes with a familiar pair of hazel eyes.

"Did she leave alone?" Kimora whispered.

"No."

"Patrick?"

Birdie nodded and then laughed. "Looks like you hit this one right on the head."

"Just call me Cupid." She took Birdie's hand and dragged her to the center of the room.

A wave of panic crashed within Birdie. "What are you doing?"

"Listen up, everyone," Kimora said into the mic. "The first bachelorette up is one of my *dearest* and best friends."

"Kimora, I don't think—" Birdie hissed.

"Shh," Kimora ordered under her breath and positioned Birdie before the bowl. "No matter whose keys you draw, nothing will happen that you don't want to happen. Take whoever it is out to Waffle House, have a cup of coffee, talk." Kimora shrugged and continued in a whisper, "*Or* you can take him to a cheap hotel and screw his brains out. The choice is up to you. I suggest you give yourself a Christmas to remember."

Birdie drew a deep breath and glanced around the room.

Stephen held up a drink, gave her a conspiratorial wink.

"All right. Here goes." Birdie dived her hand into the large bowl. A key chain with an American Liberty Bail Bonds emblem caught her eye, and her heart sank. She quickly released it and grabbed another, hoping no one saw her cheating.

"All right!" Kimora snatched the set of keys from Birdie's hand. "2pac is the winner!"

Chapter 9

Patrick turned wide onto his property, missed the driveway completely and ran over a few bushes before he finally brought the car to a halt just inches before crashing through the garage door.

"Oh, God. Oh, God," he gasped as Coco ground deliciously on his lap. "Don't stop. Don't stop." He gripped her hips to guarantee that she wouldn't.

"Who does it belong to, Patrick?" she asked, nibbling on his ear. "Hmm. Whose dick is this?"

"Y-yours," he rasped and banged his head back against the headrest.

"Louder," Coco commanded. "I don't believe you."

"It—it belongs…to you." Damn, he couldn't seem to get deep enough.

"If it's mine, then I can do whatever I want. Right? I can

have it anytime I want?" She slowed her hips while he desperately tried to speed up. "Hmm, Patrick?"

"Y-yes? Wh-what?" He struggled to follow the conversation. He just wanted the sweet release her body promised him.

Coco's smile reflected how much she was enjoying herself. "Can I have it anytime I want?"

Hell, at this point Patrick would gladly give her his house, his car and everything in his bank account—as long as she didn't stop. "Yes, baby. Anything you want. Anytime you want. Just let me…" All thought emptied out of Patrick's head as a glorious light exploded behind his eyes and he was finally granted the release he craved.

Drained, he clung to Coco as if she were the only life raft after a sinking ship. After a minute or two of labored breathing, Patrick became aware of the small kisses she rained across his sweaty brow, cheeks and lips.

"Did you like that, Mr. District Attorney?" she asked.

Was she kidding? "I loved it," he said, kissing her back. "And I want some more." He opened his door and gently turned in his seat.

Coco ducked down, but her head still bumped the roof when he climbed out of the car with her still connected to him.

"Oops. Easy," he chuckled.

She laughed and wrapped her long, shapely legs around his trim hips.

"Hey, Holloway," a male's voice shouted from somewhere. "Merry Christmas!"

Startled, Patrick lost his balance and spilled forward.

Coco gasped in alarm, hit the ground with a hard thump

and then had the rest of the air slammed out of her lungs when Patrick fell on top of her.

"Sorry. Are you all right?" He eased his weight off her rib cage.

She nodded and laughed. "Who was that?"

"I don't know." He looked up and saw they were shielded behind a bush. Across the street, his neighbor, Glenn Leavell, waved. "Hey, Glenn," Patrick shouted back. "Merry Christmas!"

"Is everything all right?" Glenn asked, walking down his driveway in his robe. "Nancy said your car nearly ran over your mailbox."

"Uh, yeah. Everything's fine." Patrick climbed to his knees. "Just had a little brake problem. I'll get it checked out."

Glenn continued walking toward Patrick's house.

"I'm fine now. No need to concern yourself," Patrick said, hoping to stop his neighbor from discovering what was really going on.

"Well, I can take a look at them, if you want," Glenn offered like a good neighbor. "I'm a pretty good weekend mechanic."

Coco walked her fingers up the flat of Patrick's belly.

"No! Stop!" Patrick shouted the command for Coco, but it was his neighbor who stopped in his tracks.

Glenn frowned. "Are you sure everything is all right?"

"Uh, yeah." Patrick had swatted Coco's hands away. "I didn't mean to snap." He smiled.

Coco carefully repositioned herself while still sheltered by the bush.

"What are you doing on the ground?" Glenn asked suspiciously.

"Well, I, uh…well, I…"

Smiling wickedly, Coco slowly brought Patrick's exposed sex into her mouth.

Patrick's eyes grew wide.

"You what, Mr. Holloway?" Glenn took another tentative step and was now in the middle of the street. "Are you sure you're all right?"

Patrick's breath hitched while he fought rolling his eyes to the back of his head. Damn if her mouth wasn't as hot as the rest of her. He instinctively moved his hips in perfect time with her rocking head.

"Mr. Holloway?"

"I—I dropped m-my keys," Patrick lied feebly and then swallowed a moan.

At any moment his neighbor was going to ask why he didn't have a shirt on. He just knew it.

Glenn's expression pinched, but he said nothing.

Blood roared in Patrick's ears while Coco brought him closer and closer to the brink.

"Well, all righty," Glenn said finally. "If you're sure everything is fine?"

"E-everything is w-wonderful," Patrick assured him, briefly closing his eyes. "Wonderful." He placed a hand behind Coco's soft Afro to hold her steady.

"Good night, then." Glenn stepped back. "Merry Christmas!"

"M-Merry—merry Christmas." He smiled and tried to wave.

Glenn turned and headed back to his house. When he reached the door, he glanced one last time across the street, waved and then went in.

Patrick finally closed his eyes and growled through yet another earth-shattering orgasm.

Coco collapsed in a fit of laughter.

"Oh, I'm going to get you back for that one," Patrick promised as he finally zipped his pants.

"Hey, you said I could have it anytime I wanted," she said in perfect wide-eyed innocence.

"Uh-huh." Patrick stood and easily swept her up from the ground. "Now it's time to do a few things *I* want to do."

Birdie's heart hammered in her chest as Joel stepped forward with a wide, magnanimous smile. While the crowd erupted into cheers, Kimora turned toward Birdie and mouthed, "Not bad."

Birdie's gaze performed a slow drag over her sinfully sexy "date," and her knees became Jell-O. No way was she going through with this. No way was she going to have sex with him.

"Hello, angel." Joel winked and accepted his keys from Kimora.

"Uh-uh." Kimora magically produced a spring of mistletoe and held it high.

A few chuckles and giggles peppered the crowd, while the blood drained from Birdie's face. Where had her earlier bravado gone? Had the alcohol and the smoke clouds finally stopped working their magic?

Kimora dangled the mistletoe directly above Birdie's head, and Joel eagerly leaned in for a kiss.

Stop him. Don't kiss him. You're not some hormonally charged teenager at the prom. You're thirty-five. Act like it.

Joel's thick, pillow-soft lips brushed against Birdie's, and her million-miles-an-hour thoughts came to an abrupt halt. His mouth quickly became more persistent, and she opened hers in time to feel the flicker of his tongue.

She leaned into him then, her knees seemingly gone on strike. A few whoops and a round of applause jerked her back to reality, and she pushed away from him, blushing.

"Ooh," Kimora said into the microphone. "Looks like we know what these two will be doing later on." She turned toward Joel, placed the mic behind her back and then warned, "Look, buddy. This is my best friend. No means no. If you step a toe out of line or try something she doesn't want, I'll come after you and skin you alive. Are we clear?"

Joel blinked.

"Are…we…clear?" she asked again, her tone hard.

"C-crystal," Joel replied, his gaze shifting questioningly toward Birdie.

The smile returned to Kimora's face as she brought the mic back to her lips. "All right, let's have a round of applause for our first Christmas hookup!"

Joel linked hands with Birdie and escorted her from the center of the room and toward the front door.

She should ask where they were going, but for some reason, she'd forgotten how to talk. Could she really go through with this? No, she didn't love her husband anymore. And, yes, it had been a long time since she'd had sex—Victor the vibrator excluded.

But an affair?

They had exited the club and were halfway across the parking lot before Joel finally spoke.

"My car is right up here."

Was that a tremor in his voice? Was he nervous, too?

"It's not a Mercedes or nothing, but you know a brotha is still trying to make things happen."

"I'm sure it's fine," she replied in a small, unrecognizable voice.

He stopped then and turned toward her. He didn't say anything for a long moment. He just drank her in—if that was the right term for it—taking in every detail of her face, breasts and curves. She didn't think he missed a single detail.

"We haven't been properly introduced," he said finally and thrust out a hand. "Joel Hawkins."

"Roberta Washington," she said, surprised she'd used her maiden name.

He nodded. "Nice to meet you. Though, I hope you don't mind me still calling you 'angel.'"

She blinked.

"It suits you."

She felt another blush coming on from the compliment.

"So," he said with a dramatic shrug. "What do you want to do? You want to go chill out at IHOP or something? Have a cup of coffee? Talk?"

She drew a deep breath and fluttered a smile. "I think I'd like that."

He winked and turned toward a powder-blue midseventies Chevy Caprice. He unlocked the door and held it open for her. "After you."

Demurely Birdie slid into the passenger seat and held on to her smile long after he closed the door, took his place behind the wheel and started the car.

The International House of Pancakes, open twenty-four hours a day, was a busy place even on Christmas Eve. For a few minutes she fretted over what she and Joel could possibly talk about. It didn't take a rocket scientist to figure out they were from different worlds, let alone different eras.

Surprisingly, Joel turned out to be easy to talk to. He was funny and animated. He even surprised her with his talent when he stood up in the center of IHOP and free-flowed for her and the early-morning patrons.

It was cruising toward two in the morning when the sandman sprinkled a little stardust in her eyes and she tried to stifle a yawn.

"Am I boring you?" he asked, concern clearly edging his voice.

"No." She waved him off. "I'm just not used to being up this time of morning."

"Should we go?" he asked, already signaling for the waitress.

A few wayward butterflies escaped her control to bat their wings madly in the pit in her stomach. Now what?

Did she ask him to take her home? End the night with a kiss on her doorstep or take him up to her bedroom—what was once her and Kenneth's bedroom—and have her way with him?

Joel took the ticket from the waitress, pulled a few bills from his billfold and tossed them down onto the table. "So what would you like to do next, angel?"

Birdie took a deep breath and said what was in her heart. "I want to go to your place."

Elijah

Christmas is officially my favorite holiday.

Just as I predicted, my baby's key party was off the hook. And now that the last couple from the lonely-hearts club has left to do only God knows what, Kimora is finally all mine.

We're already tearing at each other's clothes through the hotel lobby, the elevators and even as we tumble into my suite. I'm addicted to the smell, taste and feel of her. I just can't get enough.

Why haven't I asked her to marry me?

As her hand dives into my pants, the question loops in my mind. Why haven't I dropped to one knee?

I know earlier I bragged about how I like sowing my wild oats and how a brotha needs his space. But the truth is, I always boomerang to Kimora. There simply isn't another woman like her.

Suspicion flashes in Kimora's eyes as she pushes me onto the bed. "What are you grinning about?"

"Us." I land on my back. My pants and—hell, where did I leave my briefs?—anyway, the pants are pulled off me in record time.

Kimora giggles and turns toward the camera and tripod that's already set and aimed at the bed. She quickly hits a button, and the red record light appears above the lens. "Merry Christmas, baby." Kimora slides the dress from her shoulders. As it glides off her incredible body, all the blood in mine rushes to one area. It's enough to make a brotha pass out.

She winks and does a headfirst tumble onto the bed to land in the backward-cowgirl position. I love it when she does that.

"What about us?" she asks, rolling a new condom on me with her silky fingers.

Sighing, I caress her gorgeous back and squeeze her ample booty. When I don't immediately answer, she glances over her shoulder with a soft smile.

"You're not getting all mushy on me, are you?"

"I might be." I squeeze again.

"Don't," she says with a strange edge to her voice.

My hands still as our eyes lock. She means it, and I would be lying if I said it didn't feel like my heart was ripped from my chest.

"We have a good thing going, don't we?"

I nod, careful to keep my expression neutral.

Finally a smile returns to her face. "Then let's not ruin it by suddenly expecting more from each other than we're prepared to give."

She's right. I know she's right. But...damn.

"Hey, the only thing I'm prepared to give you is the best damn ride of your life."

"Yee haw!" She lifts her body and we finally get back to what we do best. But...damn.

Patrick

I can't stop watching her.

A part of me can't believe that she's really here—in *my* bed. It's probably why I can't sleep—I'm afraid when I open my eyes, she'll be gone. As moonlight spills through the bedroom windows and splashed across her earth-rich back, I'm struck dumb. I don't want to lose her, but I don't know how to keep her.

I laugh at the predicament and, in the next breath, curse myself for agreeing to a one-night-only deal. How can we ever go back to the way we were?

In my mind I imagine awkward scenarios at the office, both of us pretending this amazing night didn't happen. Can we keep this secret from our coworkers? Do I want to?

Coco sighs and stretches like a lazy cat beneath the sheets. I wait for her to open her eyes. I want her to open them. I also want to make love to her again.

That realization amazes me. The woman has turned me into a sex machine. Never would I have guessed that I could make love for so long and repeat the act so many times. Then again, fear had played a part in my mindset.

The fear of losing her.

Ms. Brown—or rather, Coco—never struck me as a woman who was interested in white men. And the last thing I want is to be some novelty act or, worse, some alcohol-induced party f—

"Can't sleep?" Her husky voice startles me.

"How can I when I have something this beautiful lying beside me?"

The pillow muffles her laugh, and I lie down next to her, still trying to memorize every detail of her luscious body. I smile and harden when she snuggles closer.

"You're kidding me, right?" she asks.

"Like I said, you're beautiful." I can't tell if she's annoyed or pleased with my body's response to her slightest touch. I can feel her gaze more than I can see her, and I wish I could hear what she's thinking. Has she already chalked this night up as a mistake?

I hope not.

She doesn't say anything. When she finally moves closer, she tilts her face toward mine. My mouth descends like a magnet toward her full lips. We moan at the same time, but my erection throbs at the feel of her hard nipples poking against my chest.

As I reach for another condom, a thought occurs to me. If I love her so thoroughly, maybe I'll make it impossible for her to leave, make it impossible for her to ever want the touch of another man. It's a desperate thought, I know, but one I'm willing to cling to when I enter and her body sheaths me.

She feels like a dream. She feels like heaven. She feels like home.

Joel

Damn, I should have cleaned this place up.

I have clothes, old pizza boxes and empty beer bottles discarded everywhere, and judging by the look on my angel's face, she's ready to bolt. "Please excuse the mess," I say, kicking a mysterious box out of the way so she can enter the apartment. "I've been meaning to, uh, hire someone."

Her eyebrows leap to the center of her head at that obvious lie. I shrug, undoubtedly making myself look goofier than necessary.

"Well, it's, uh, an interesting place you have here."

She smiles and I note she's a better liar than I am, but that's cool. At least she hasn't turned away screaming from the place.

"Uh, can I take your coat?" She hesitates, and for a frightening moment I think she's going to change her mind about all of this. Which, again, is cool. I ain't the kind of brotha that's going to make a woman do something she doesn't want to do. But, God, I hope she doesn't change her mind.

"Sure," she finally says with a sigh.

She turns and I take my time sliding the jacket from her shoulders. I lean over and place a kiss against one of her bare arms.

She freezes and closes her eyes, and suddenly I would give a million bucks to know what she's thinking. "Would you like something to drink?"

She turns and faces me. There's a question in her eyes, and without thinking I kiss her—and drop her jacket on the floor.

The kiss is soft—tender even—but then I get a little greedy. I can't help it. She tastes that damn good. I slide my arms around her thick waist and pull her close. I'm instantly turned on by the weight of her breasts against my chest. Oh, all the things I want to do with her race through my mind.

When she moans and presses even closer, I take it as a green light to sprint toward first base and I slide a hand up beneath her shirt.

Another moan tells me I've made it safely. Feeling a little cocky, I move under the bra and steal a quick pinch of her nipple. She gasps and lolls her head back, exposing her long neck to my greedy lips.

How we made it from the living room to the bedroom, I don't know, and in which order the clothes have come off is also another great mystery. All I know is, on my bed— which is a great deal cleaner than my living room—is a gorgeous, thick sistah with breasts and thighs that literally bring my eyes to tears and my pride to attention.

"Do you have a condom?" she asks.

I swear to goodness, I think the girl has said something in Greek. When she repeats the question, I finally come out my sex-induced thoughts to make sense of what she's saying.

"Oh, condom. Yeah, right. Hold on a minute." I can't remember where my pants went, but I am able to remember a new box I'd shoved in the nightstand next to the bed.

I rip open one packet and—no joke—the damn condom pings off my erection and smacks her in the eye. "Oh, I'm sorry."

She sits up, laughing and holding her eye.

I rush over to her, laughing myself, to see if she's okay.

"Yeah, yeah. I'll be all right."

When her laughter dies a bit, there's a look in her eyes, and I get nervous.

"You know, I think I would like that drink now."

I nod, not sure what that means, but I turn and walk back out to the kitchen. Four beers later, she finally admits, "I can't do this."

I knew this all along, I think, but a brotha should always cling to hope, right?

"It's okay," I say, stroking her hair from her face and smiling.

She nods at this, relaxes even. "Just because…he cheated doesn't mean that I…"

I draw in a deep breath and weigh my words. "Are you going to take him back?"

My angel hesitates. "No. My divorce is final…but two wrongs don't make a right."

I like this woman. She's a real class act. I try to convey this in my next kiss, but I think all I manage to do is transmit how much I still want her. We're both breathless by the time she breaks the kiss and, especially on my part, a little sad.

"Does he know how lucky he was?" I ask, stroking her face, still reluctant to let her go. To my surprise her beautiful eyes gloss with tears. "I may be young, but I know a good thing when I see it."

My angel smiles and tries to look away, but I cup her chin and force our eyes to meet again. "You're smart, beautiful and, judging by what I saw at the store earlier today, you're a good mom."

Hot tears leap from her eyes, and I smile as I brush them away. "You *deserve* to be loved. You shouldn't have to beg for it."

Hearing her soft sigh and watching her eyes lower to my lips, I recognize the permission her body language gives me to kiss her again. I lean forward and breathe in her sweet fragrance before tasting her lips. I find myself praying that it won't be the last time.

She moans and drapes her arms around my neck. The next thing I know, I'm leaning her back onto the bed. Once again her luscious curves have my erection throbbing well past the threshold of pain. But I can handle it. I just want to taste her for a little while longer. I'm not satisfied with just her lips, so I move to her neck, her collarbone and, of course, her spectacular breasts.

She tastes like honey and chocolate at the same time. For real, I feel like Charlie in the chocolate factory and I'm still praying my golden ticket isn't snatched at any second.

"We should stop," she breathes raggedly.

"We can stop anytime you want," I say, sliding farther down her body. She gasps and her hands slide through my hair. "Do you want me to stop?" I ask, arriving at the V of curls between her legs.

"Open up for me, angel."

She hesitates, and I kiss her thighs and wait patiently for her decision. Finally she parts her peanut-butter thighs to my watering mouth. I dip my head low to drink the very thing I thirst for. I run my tongue teasingly over her clit and I'm immediately pleased it tastes as good as the rest of her. My tongue dives deeper the next go-round, and deeper still after that.

My angel moans and squirms, and I have to hook my arms around her hips to lock her in place. I go in again, smacking and sucking as I make my way to her core. Her moans soon become orgasmic cries, and her legs tremble around my face, until at long last one drawn out cry fills the bedroom.

I kiss my way back up my angel's belly, chest and neck. I love the way her face glows in the moonlight and the way her breasts heave as though she's completed a marathon. After I reach for another condom, I hold it out to her. "Do you want to do the honors?"

I expect her to hesitate again, but she surprises me by reaching for it. But the feel of her fingers gliding down my erection is almost enough to do me in. When she lies back down, I hover above her hot, wet pussy for just a moment, waiting...

She finally croaks the magic word. "Please."

I smile, and without further ado I enter and sink all the way down until our bodies meet. I watch her, mesmerized by the ecstasy rippling across her face. I did that for her. She deserves it.

"Look at me, angel."

When she does, I begin to move inside her.

"You feel so damn good," I confess, straining to remain in control.

"So do you," she replies, holding my gaze and rocking her hips in sync with my own.

We started off slow, but in no time a hungry desperation grips hold of me, and soon our bodies are bumping faster and harder. The dizzying friction soon has me struggling for breath and spiraling out of control until a hot rush of pleasure juts from me like a geyser and I roar up at the ceiling.

Coco

I don't want to leave—but I have to.

I hate to admit it, but I can't think straight with Patrick looking at me, touching me and sexing me so good I can hardly breathe, let alone walk. I know I've been standing in this shower nearly thirty minutes and the water has long since turned ice-cold, but at the moment it's the only place I can string two thoughts together.

One thing is clear: I'm going to have to leave the district attorney's office. I can't imagine trying to carry on like business as usual after last night.

I just can't.

Flashes of us in the car and, good Lord, my behavior in the man's front yard—practically in front of his neighbor—send tidal waves of shame crashing in me.

I sigh and try to keep my teeth from chattering, but I'm still unwilling to leave the shower's solitude.

"Hey, are you all right in there?" Patrick's concerned voice penetrates the door and drowns out the water's steady flow.

"Uh, yeah. I'll be out in a minute." My words tremble through the space between us, and I realize a part of me wants him to come in and check on me—even join me in the icy waterfall—and the other part wants him to just go away.

I'm losing it.

As I stare out the shower's glass partition, I see the door crack open and his dusty blond hair standing at attention. When his striking eyes settle on me, I swear the water begins to heat up again.

"I'm making breakfast," he informs me with a smile.

At long last, I shut off the water and open the shower door. "It's lunchtime," I say, reaching for a towel.

He doesn't reply to this; he's too busy staring. His look caresses every inch of me and drives me absolutely crazy. "Stop that," I snap harder than I'd intended and stomp past him out the door. "Where in the hell are my clothes?"

Patrick doesn't say anything.

"I said one night, and the night is over." I search the bed, the furniture and the floor. Nothing. "First thing Monday, I'm turning in my resignation," I throw at him, hoping to finally elicit a response.

He still says nothing.

"What the hell did you do with my clothes?" I shout, whirling on him.

He glances up, and my eyes follows his to the ceiling fan. And there, like some cheap burlesque act, my gold dress is spinning around the room. I'm outraged, but at the same time it's incredibly funny. I glance back at Patrick, and the moment our eyes meet, the tension dissolves into laughter.

Undoubtedly feeling as if the coast is clear, Patrick approaches me with a confidence I should find disturbing. However, when his arms slide around my waist, it's hard not to notice my body melting into him.

"Merry Christmas, Courtney."

"Merry Christmas, Patrick."

We kiss. God help me. What's happening to me? This entire situation doesn't have a right angle in it, and yet I don't want to leave him.

And maybe I won't.

Birdie

I'm giggling like a sixteen-year-old after the prom and loving it. I actually bagged a bag boy. I don't want to psycho-analyze my behavior to death. Why did I do what I did, shouldn't I feel guilty and am I going to do it again? Well, I can answer that last part: hell yes!

Not only did I have the best sex of my life last night, I had some more this morning. And this afternoon. If I do keep this young pup around, I might have to send Victor into early retirement.

I glance over at him. He's like a double-chocolate cheese-cake to a diabetic. I have no business wanting him.

"You know, I have to leave," I say, crawling over him on the floor to find my clothes. "Kenneth is going to swing the boys by the house at six."

Joel groans and catches hold of my leg. "But I don't want to let you go." He pulls himself up and actually kisses my butt.

I giggle at his silly antics but close my eyes with a groan when he slides a finger into my sopping-wet kitty. At this rate, I'm going to be late.

"Joel, I have to go," I say, rocking back against his large hand. To my delight, he slides in another finger.

"Okay, angel." He kisses my back. "We can go in a minute."

I know how his minutes are—they turn into long half hours. When I hear the rip of yet another condom package, I wonder where in the hell all this energy I have is coming from. When he enters me from behind, I cry out in sheer pleasure. Then he pumps into me and his hands reach around to squeeze my breasts.

"Oh, hot damn," he croaks, pounding away. "Tell me when I'm going to see you again, angel."

Hell, I may never leave.

"I want to see you again tonight," he says.

I want to see him, too. The kids are only going to be there for an hour or two before going back to their father's.

"Angel?" His lips return to plant soft kisses across my back, while his hips remain on autopilot. "Can I see you again tonight?"

"Y-yes," I finally say, damning the consequences and then exploding from the inside out.

Joel's roar quickly follows, and I can feel the strength of his release and am awed by it. Once I catch my breath and Joel finishes bathing me with kisses, I climb from the floor and rush for a quick shower.

It's five forty-five.

I'll never make it home by six.

In the car, Joel can't keep his hands off me, and I playfully scold him right up until he gets pulled over for weaving on the road.

By the time he pulls up to the end of my driveway, it's six-thirty and Kenneth is pacing by his car. He stops in his tracks and glares at us.

"The kids must be inside." I exhale and glance over at Joel. "I'll see you in a couple of hours?"

"You got it, angel."

He leans forward and I meet him halfway for a kiss. Mmm…double-chocolate cheesecake. I inch closer and pray I don't go into a diabetic coma. Finally I turn toward the door.

Joel stops me. "Wait."

Before I can question him, he climbs out of the car and rushes to the passenger door and opens it.

"I'm young but a gentleman." He winks.

I blush as he takes my hand and helps me out of the car. I can actually feel Kenneth's heated gaze burn a hole through me. And just in case my kids are watching, Joel delivers a chaste kiss against my cheek. "Two hours," he whispers. "And you can leave the panties at home."

I giggle and head up toward the house…feeling like a Christmas angel.

Kimora

Competition is healthy.

Although, Elijah and I always take it to a ridiculous level. Neither one of us wants to be the first to say "I need a break" or "I need a moment to catch my breath." Now this would be funny if I wasn't so damn exhausted.

I have small bruise marks on my wrists, rug burns on my knees and a rash of hickies from my neck to my hips. I've never been more pleased in all my life.

I'm still smiling when I loll my head to the side and catch Elijah staring at me. He has that faraway look in his eyes again and it makes me nervous.

"I love you," he says.

My heart squeezes, but I manage to reply, "I love you, too."

His stare intensifies. "I mean, I'm *in* love with you."

Though the statement is meant to deepen this moment

of intimacy, in actuality it saddens me. "You're in love with someone else, too," I remind him.

Just like that, the light in his eyes dims. "You know we're getting a div—"

"Don't," I say, determined not to tumble into the dark abyss of regrets. But I fall anyway. "Untie me."

Elijah hesitates, probably regretting his words, but then finally unties me. I rub at my sore wrists and then untie the scarves binding my legs.

"Look, Kimora. Let's just forget I said that and go back to—"

"What? Go back to lying to ourselves?" The mood is irrevocably ruined, and I can't believe that I'm about to start crying.

"Look," Elijah starts in again, his agitation evident in his body language. "Sometimes I think that we're just playing this all wrong. We should be together. We're so much alike."

"That's right!" I shake my head and wipe at a tear before it dares to make a fool out of me. "We *are* alike. You're a playa and so am I! I *love* my life. I *love* my freedom. The last thing I need is someone like you rolling through, trying to change the program."

I know what you're thinking, and to tell you the truth I don't know why I'm reacting so strongly. I know his situation—I always have. And up until a few minutes ago, I was cool with it. But now I realize I'm *in* love with him, too, and that's just not acceptable.

"Someone like me?" He laughs as though he can't believe I went there. "Damn, girl. I just said I loved you, not that I wanted to marry you!"

"But you're thinking it." I snatch up my dress, though

without a bra I know my breasts are visible through the thin material.

He freezes for a long moment and then asks in a whisper that I have to strain to hear, "Would that be so bad?"

"You think I'm in some kind of hurry to be treated the same way you treat the current Mrs. Thomas? You got to be out of your *damn* mind."

He flinches as though I've struck him.

More tears surface. I wipe madly at them and then grab my purse and shoes before I stomp over to the door.

"C'mon, baby. Don't leave. It's Christmas."

He reaches for my arm, but I snatch it away. "I gotta go." I open the door and then stop. Turning, I march back over to the tripod and eject the tape. "I'll send you a copy."

"Kimora!"

I move past him.

"Kimora!"

I bolt out the door, blinded by a fresh wave of tears. "Damn it! He just *had* to tell me he was in love with me. Idiot!" I rush to the elevator bay and jab the down button. In the distance I hear a door slam, and my heart leaps in fear.

"Kimora! We need to talk!" I turn and see Elijah walking down the hall in the hotel robe.

Danger, Kimora Evans. Danger!

I jab the button again, and mercifully the elevator arrives. I quickly jump inside and Elijah's walk becomes a run.

"Kimora!"

I push the close-door button and then sigh in relief when the doors close just seconds before he reaches them. See what love does to you, girls? It makes you incredibly messy…and incredibly weak.

By the time the elevator arrives at the lobby, I've finger-combed my unruly hair and managed to get my shoes on. Unfortunately, at best, I look like an expensive hooker when I traipse out of the elevator with no underwear beneath a white dress.

All the men's eyes zoom toward me as I head out of the building. I hear a few women ask their men, "What in the hell are you looking at?" and even see a few of them get hit upside the head for staring.

It's a cheap high and an ego booster.

As luck would have it, a taxi driver is just finishing a drop-off and he nearly falls all over himself to offer me a ride.

"Thank you." I kindly pat the older gentleman on the cheek and climb inside and then give him my address as he settles behind the wheel. As I turn to give the hotel one last look, I do a double take at the sight of Elijah racing through the lobby still in his robe.

"Kimora!"

I laugh as the driver pulls off. I can't help it. It's funny.

"I trust you had a good Christmas," the driver says as a conversation starter.

Before I answer, I review my incredible party: Coco and her boss are finally doing the nasty; Birdie has hooked up with a hottie and hopefully gotten her groove back; and, of course, *my* incredible heavy-duty sex-a-thon. "It was pretty good," I admit with a smile. But New Year's is coming up, and of course there's Valentine's Day. "So many holidays—so many parties."

Who knows, maybe by then Elijah and I will have kissed and made up. If not, there's plenty of fish in the sea.

OUT WITH THE OLD

Donna Hill

Acknowledgment

Many thanks to all of the readers who have kept me in print for the past fifteen years. Your love and support is deeply appreciated. May this holiday season bring each of you your heart's desire.

Chapter 1

"Hi, Glen. A frozen apple martini and a Cosmo." Terri Wells slid onto the stool and put her black Kate Spade purse on top of the buffed-to-a-high-gloss shined bar. She took a quick inventory of the Chelsea hangout. For a Wednesday night, BARNONE was jumping.

The trilevel reconverted meat warehouse was the centerpiece of lower Manhattan. Philip and Lissa Tremont, the interior designers responsible for the homes often seen on *Lifestyles of the Rich and Famous,* had done the decor. *Opulent* was the operative word, with *lavish* running a close second.

"Nice crowd," Mindy Clarke purred as she took a seat next to her coworker and best friend in the whole world. She shrugged off her short fox jacket and let it hang loosely off her arms. Her short skirt rose accordingly when she crossed her creamy brown legs.

"Getting ready for the holidays," Terri groused. "Totally overrated." Colored lights and sprigs of mistletoe hung from the rafters and balcony railings and holiday wreaths hung from the doors.

Terri wasn't much for holidays of any sort—birthdays, anniversaries and especially any involving the gathering of friends and family to celebrate. Her father, Calvin Wells, had died right at the kitchen table on her tenth birthday, moments after he'd cut into her birthday cake. Her mother, Estelle Wells, passed away two years later on Christmas morning, right under the tree and on top of Terri's new Malibu Barbie doll. Her older brother, Sean had stepped in to take care of her, then up and disappeared right after Thanksgiving dinner a few years later. She was sixteen.

Pat, her mother's sister, took Terri in after that. Gave her the bare necessities of life: food, shelter and clothing. Pat, a devout Seventh-Day Adventist, didn't recognize any holiday, which was fine with Terri. Holidays and celebrations had a way of taking the things she loved away from her.

Glen returned with their drinks. "Running a tab tonight, ladies?"

"A very short one. Some of us have early hours." Terri winked and reached for her drink.

Glen covered her hand for a moment. "You free Sunday afternoon?"

Terri held his gaze. "This Sunday? Wow. No. Sorry."

A customer down on the far end of the bar vied for Glen's attention. He frowned and hurried off.

Glen had been trying to get next to her for months. He'd

done everything short of falling in front of her Benz. It wasn't that he was not good-looking. He was. But Terri Wells had a plan. A ten-year plan that she'd been working on since graduating from high school: go to Columbia University, graduate with honors, work in media relations, rise up the ranks, make a name for herself in the industry, marry someone rich and fabulous and never have to work again. Glen didn't fit the rich-and-fabulous part. And so what if she was almost three years off on her plan. At least she had one, which was more than she could say about Mindy.

She wasn't quite sure why she and Mindy were friends. It just sort of happened. Mindy had latched on to Terri like bait on a hook. And Terri, for all her efforts, hadn't been able to shake her loose. That was more than a decade ago. When Mindy decided she wanted to be your friend, it was a wrap.

Terri, on the other hand, preferred her solitude. She had a plan. And friends and family and business associates were not going to stand in the way or distract her from her ultimate purpose—landing Michael Blac, co-owner of Sterns & Blac. Her fine, fabulously wealthy, sexy boss.

Mindy sipped her Cosmo and rocked her leg to the beat of Mary J's latest cut.

"I don't know why you don't give that man a play," she said in her slow Southern drawl over the rim of her glass.

"Come on before he gets back," Terri hissed while snatching up her purse.

Mindy placed a twenty on the bar. "You are such a tease and you owe me ten bucks for the drink."

"Yeah, yeah. Come on. I see a table in the back."

"In the back!" Mindy squawked. "No one can see us in the back." She puckered her glistening lips.

Terri ignored her protest and zeroed in on the table. She had no intention of standing for the rest of the evening. And if someone got to the table before she did, they would have to fight. Her feet were already howling from standing for hours earlier in the day. She'd done three presentations for some potential new clients and conducted a seminar on marketing strategies at her old alma mater Columbia University. She was beat, but she knew a Wednesday night at BARNONE was a must. It was celebrity hangout night, and any manner of celeb, accompanying posse and shutterbugs could be found on "hump day." This was where she got all the inside scoops, found out who was doing who and what rising or falling stars might be in need of her incredible spin skills.

While Sterns & Blac, the company where she worked, handled a variety of clients, Terri specialized in entertainment. And with one scandal trying to outdo the other, she always had plenty of work.

Mindy put her apple bottom in the chair first. "You know how much I hate being in the back," she grumbled.

Mary J blocked out the rest of her complaint.

Terri scanned the crowd, rocking to the beat and sipping.

A popular recording artist, dressed in all white, surrounded by his crew, made an entrance. They went straight to the private banquettes that overlooked the dance floor.

"Would you like to order?" a young waitress shouted over the din.

Mindy looked up at the skinny woman who couldn't

weigh more than seventy pounds wet with all her clothes on. "I'll take the honey wings and a side salad."

"Make that two," Terri said.

The waitress jotted down the orders on her pad and was quickly engulfed by the pulsing, gyrating crowd.

Radio diva Wendy LaMont was holding court on the far side of room with several familiar faces, Terri noted. She took off her teal-colored Donna Karan jacket and draped it on the back of her chair. She finger-fluffed her full head of shoulder-length hair. Since she'd known she would be hanging out, she'd opted for a camisole in eggshell-white to rock beneath her jacket, rather than her regular office attire of starched blouse and designer suit. If there was one thing that Terri Wells knew, it was how to wear clothes, and she had the perfect figure for it. She was as relentless at keeping her size-ten body in pitch-perfect shape as she was at developing award-winning PR campaigns. *If you wanted to be a winner, you had to look the part* was her motto.

"I knew I'd find you two here," Josh Bishop, one of their office colleagues, said as he pulled up a seat and sat down uninvited.

"Hey, Josh," Mindy shouted, bobbing her head to the new one by Kiesha Cole.

Terri gave him the benefit of ignoring him and sipped her drink.

"So the skinny is that there's going to be a big announcement made at the staff meeting tomorrow," Josh was saying.

Terri cut her eyes in his direction.

"Any ideas what it's about?" Mindy asked, tucking her strawberry-blond weave behind her ear.

"Not a clue. It's all very hush, hush. I'm figuring it has to do with the Christmas bonuses."

Every year Sterns & Blac held its annual competition. Terri had won the honor two years in a row and was the reigning media queen. She had every intention of making it a three-peat.

"Think you can win again this year, Terri?" Josh asked, peering at her through thick black-rimmed glasses. He ran his hand through his equally thick black hair.

She shrugged her bare shoulder in a nonchalant gesture. "It's anyone's game. There are a lot of talented people in the company."

"You're so modest," Mindy cooed. "You know you're the best. You'll probably make partner."

That's why she liked Mindy, she realized. Good for her ego. Terri offered a slight smile.

"Anybody feel like dancing?" Miles asked.

Mindy jumped up almost before the request was fully out of his mouth.

He grinned, flashing a row of overcrowded bottom teeth, and took Mindy's hand.

Mindy sashayed onto the floor, shaking her behind as if she'd hit lotto. Terri shook her head and smiled.

There was something almost childlike about Mindy, Terri mused. She was guileless and took the world at face value, never looking beneath the murky surface. She rarely had a bad day, and her sunny disposition could almost be irritating if you let it. Terri often wondered how anyone could be that damned happy all the damned time. It was the one mystery she couldn't crack.

She spotted Liberty Wagner, the day-before-yesterday pop icon, making her way across the floor. Word on the street was that Liberty was looking for new PR management to jump-start her floundering career. Terri smiled before finishing off her drink, keeping her eye on Liberty. A few of the guests recognized her, but the general population paid her no attention. Terri saw her opening. She pushed back from the table just as the waitress returned with their food.

Good. The food would serve as a placeholder. She snatched a tangy wing from the plate, took a couple of bites, wiped her mouth and headed off to meet her prey.

Chapter 2

"You did?" Mindy's hazel eyes—courtesy of expensive contacts—widened in admiration.

Terri stirred her coffee, blew gently over the steamy brew. "We're going to schedule a meeting." She set her coffee down on the counter.

"You are amazing. Right in the middle of all that noise and madness last night you land a new client—and Liberty Wagner at that! You are definitely the best," she fawned, her expression a road map of happy exclamation points.

Terri shrugged. "I just want to do a good job for her—if she'll have me," she added in the self-deprecating way that she'd mastered. She ran her tongue over her lips.

Mindy clasped Terri's forearm. "Of course she will. She'd be a fool if she didn't." Mindy smiled wide as the Hoover Dam, her pearly whites—courtesy of an incredible dentist—sparkled against her almost-too-perfect face.

Terri straightened her black Dior jacket over her well-defined but toned hips, then rested her right one against the counter. She crossed her panted legs at the ankle—the sleek look of sophistication just the image she wanted to project as she spotted Michael Blac enter the employee lounge.

She'd pulled her shoulder-length curls up on top of her head today in a carefully calculated casual look that revealed her slender neck and her new diamond studs.

"Good morning, Mindy, Terri," Michael greeted as he approached.

"Morning, Mr. Blac," Mindy said, the syrup in her words so thick it oozed with sticky sweetness—courtesy of her Georgia upbringing.

Although the entire company was on a first-name basis, Mindy stuck by her Georgia roots and called Michael "Mr. Blac."

He turned his megawatt smile on Mindy and wagged a finger. "One of these days I'm going to get you to call me Michael," he teased.

Mindy actually batted her eyes, and if Terri didn't know better she'd swear Mindy blushed.

Terri cleared her throat. "Good morning, Mike." She handed him a cup of coffee just the way she knew he liked it—black and strong.

His gaze slid in her direction and took her in with a long, slow swoop. He reached for the mug with his name on it. "Thank you, Terri. I can always count on you to anticipate the next move."

"Always," she reiterated.

He took a sip, his dark eyes still trained on Terri. "Mmm, just the way I like it."

Terri smiled with no teeth. Letting the comment do what it will.

"I'll see you two ladies in the staff meeting." He nodded to them both and strode off.

"Dreamy," Mindy sighed.

"I beg your pardon?" Terri's neck jerked at a ninety-degree angle.

Mindy folded her hands demurely in front of her. "I was only saying how dreamy he is. A woman would be lucky to land Michael Blac." She turned to Terri, the epitome of innocence plastered on her face. "Don't you think so?"

Terri blinked several times. Was that a predatory look she saw forming in Mindy's store-bought gaze? She straightened her shoulders.

"It's not something I'd thought about," Terri said in her best and-you-better-not-be-thinking-about-it-either voice, with an arched brow for added effect.

"Hmm." Mindy pursed her lovely glossed lips. "Oh, well, better get ready for that meeting." She took her cup and walked off, her skirt just skimming her knees.

Terri wasn't quite sure what to make of what had transpired. All she knew for sure was that she didn't like it.

The senior staff of ten publicists and marketing specialists sat around the obese conference table with Michael Blac at the head. Once everyone was settled, he stood and addressed the members in the room.

Michael was model-handsome. At six foot three, he carried his height and his solid one hundred and ninety pounds with the grace and power of a panther. Never a five-o'clock shadow could be found on his Hershey-chocolate-colored skin. Everything about him was meticulous, from the sleek trim of his mustache to the precision cut of his close-cut hair to the manicured nails on long piano-player fingers. He was known to be as equally ruthless as he was charming. A master in the art of spin, Michael Blac was a walking advertisement for his multimillion-dollar company.

"As you know, each year I issue a corporate challenge." Nods all around. "This year I want to tie the challenge into the holiday season." Terri cringed. "The challenge is to create the most elaborate and media-catching campaign geared specifically toward men. You have a budget of ten thousand dollars."

Everyone shared a look.

"The winner will receive an all expense paid trip for two to Rio to bring in the New Year."

Oohs and aahs rippled around the room.

"You have two weeks to prepare your proposal and get them in to me for consideration in the competition. Those that are selected will get the ten-thousand-dollar budget. The campaign must be ready to launch the week before Christmas. And, as always, I'll be the judge." He smiled magnanimously. He looked at everyone in turn. "The one to beat is Terri." His gaze dropped and settled on her for a moment. "She's been the undisputed winner two years in a row."

She poked her chest out just a little but not enough to appear pompous. She linked her fingers together atop the table.

"Good luck, everyone." He walked out. Class dismissed.

Everyone was buzzing and humming about the latest challenge. Terri's fertile imagination was already in full swing, ruminating over the possibilities. She knew the majority of the staff was envious of her, the deals she'd landed and the string of high-octane clients she'd brought in. Her list was without question the most impressive. She knew she'd have her hands full trying to beat out the competition this year. They'd all be going after her.

She'd have to set aside her ambivalence about holidays and celebrations. She couldn't let that be the reason why she lost this challenge.

"Have any ideas?" Mindy whispered, sidling up next to her as they walked back to their offices.

Terri looked at her from the corners of her eyes. "Not that I'm willing to discuss."

Mindy pursed her lips. "You won't even tell me? I'm your best friend."

"That has nothing to do with it. This is a competition, remember." Terri jerked her chin upward.

Mindy's cherub face wrinkled like crushed paper. Terri almost felt bad. She shrugged it off.

"Meet you for lunch?" Mindy asked when they approached her office door.

"I'll call you and let you know. Not sure when I'll be able to get away."

Mindy stared at her for a minute, and Terri would have sworn that Mindy looked as if she didn't believe her.

"Sure," Mindy said and walked into her office.

Terri twisted her lips, then walked off to her office down the hall. She went straight to her computer.

She scrolled through her media library files. They contained all the gossip columns and legitimate headlines that had made the major newspapers and wire services. She'd created the file herself about three years earlier. A nifty little search program that she'd developed. She'd set the program to search for certain words from a designated list of newspapers, magazines and newscasts. With a few keystrokes she could put her finger on any tidbit of information on just about anyone. It was her little secret weapon.

She took her time and went through the items, using the keyword *men*. Tons of stuff turned up, of course, most of which she quickly discarded. Then she hit pay dirt.

Earlier in the summer a day spa for men had opened in Harlem to rave reviews—Pause for Men.

Terri leaned back in her seat and grinned. She almost rubbed her hands together in glee. Pause for Men, a ready-made entity.

She keyed in the Web site address for the spa. The contact person was Stephanie Moore. She frowned in thought. The name was familiar. She wondered if it was the same Stephanie Moore that once worked for H.L. Reuben and Associates, the hotshot PR firm.

Terri added the phone number to her Rolodex. She

needed to map out her plan first before she approached the owners. She grinned. It was a win-win situation.

Less than an hour later Terri had sketched out a preliminary plan that featured the spa, specifically the Pause for Men spokesperson. He would have to be a member, good-looking, relatively articulate and willing to get in front of a camera and speak to reporters. It would be an in-house competition. Ideally the idea of notoriety, designer perks and travel will entice sign-up as well as promote good health among men. From everything that she'd read so far on Pause, they promoted a holistic approach to good health and offered specialized health foods and drinks. It was perfect.

The next thing she did was compile a list of potential sponsors, from clothing designers to hotel chains, magazine outlets to computer manufacturers and travel agencies.

She carefully reviewed her information and ran her pitch in her head several times, pacing in front of her desk as she did so.

Finally she was ready. She crossed the room and closed her office door. There was no accounting for eavesdroppers when it came to the annual competition.

She returned to her desk, spread her notes out in front of her and dialed Pause for Men.

"Good afternoon. Pause for Men. Barbara Allen speaking."

"Hello, my name is Terri Wells of Sterns & Blac. May I speak with your publicist, Stephanie Moore?"

"Ms. Moore is unavailable at the moment. Can I help you or take a message?"

Terri quickly scanned her notes. One of the articles

mentioned the names of the owners, one of which was Barbara Allen.

"Yes, perhaps you can. Are you Barbara Allen, one of the owners?"

"What is this about?"

Terri heard the slight shift from cordial to skeptical. "I'm sorry," she soothed. "I work for Sterns & Blac, a corporate marketing firm. I've been doing some research on your new business and I'd hoped that I could meet with the owners to discuss and project that I'm sure you'd be interested in."

"What kind of project?"

She was going to be difficult. "I have some promotional strategies that I'd like to share with you."

"We already have a publicist, as you know," Barbara said. "And we don't have a budget for another one. Thank you for—"

"Ms. Allen," she interrupted before the dial tone cut her off. "Actually, I have ten thousand dollars in *my* budget to work with." A little white lie.

Silence.

"Ms. Allen?"

"Give me your number. I'll have to get back to you."

Annoyance pinched her lips into a tight line. She counted to five.

"Sure," she said full of fake cheer. She gave Barbara the number. "When should I expect your call today?" She tapped her fingernails on the desktop hoping that Ms. Allen understood her blatant hint about *today*.

"Before the end of the day."

"Great. I look forward to it. Have a wonderful day and thank you for your time."

"No problem. Goodbye."

Terri slowly hung up the phone. Her hand lingered on the receiver. Maybe this wasn't going to be as easy as she'd thought. If the other three were as difficult as Ms. Allen, she may have to rethink her project.

She'd give them until the end of the day. If she didn't hear from them, she'd move to plan B. But first she'd have to figure out what plan B was.

Terri opened her search file and starting exploring other options.

"Hey, Steph," Barbara called out.

Stephanie stopped en route to the spa's café and turned. She smiled as Barbara approached.

"Hey, yourself. What's up? I was going to grab a bite to eat really quick. I have two interviews coming in."

Barbara's dark eyes brightened. "Great. If the applicants are as good in person as they are on paper, hire them!"

Stephanie chuckled. She tucked a stray lock of her champagne-colored hair behind her right ear.

It never ceased to amaze Barbara how much Stephanie looked like the model-turned-talk-show-host Tyra Banks. She shook off the thought and got to her reason for stopping Stephanie.

"I took a call about an hour ago from a Terri Wells. She asked for you."

"Me? Why? Who is she?"

"She said she works for Sterns & Blac."

Stephanie thought for a moment, then her brows rose. "Oh, yes," she dragged out. She nodded her head. "I definitely know the company. They were one of our big competitors when I was with H.L. Reuben. And her name came up quite often." She leaned on her right leg. "What did she say she wanted?"

"She said she has a proposition and wants to talk to us about it."

Stephanie twisted her lips to the side. "Hmm. Well, it's fine with me. You want to check with Ellie and Ann Marie?"

"Not a problem."

"I'd be really curious to hear what her proposal is and what it could possibly have to do with us."

"She did mention that she had a ten-thousand-dollar budget and it wouldn't cost us anything."

Stephanie grinned. "Now that's a proposition I want to hear. Let me know when she wants to come in. I gotta run. Catch you later." She hurried off.

Barbara shrugged. The whole publicity-and-marketing thing was totally over her head. Her role as massage thera- pist was to keep the string of men supple and in shape, which was fine with her. She headed off toward the steam room to get ready for her next client. But if there was someone out there willing to invest in their business then she was all for it. As soon as she was done with her client she'd bring Ellie and Ann Marie up to date.

Terri looked up when the knock on her door interrupted her plan B. She exited from her computer file.

"Come in."

The door eased open. Mindy poked her head in. "Hey girl. Busy?"

"Yeah, kinda. But you can come in."

Mindy closed the door behind her and sauntered in. She came across the room and plopped down on a chair and crossed her legs. She folded her hands atop her thighs and leaned forward.

"We've been friends for a long time, right?" Mindy began.

"Yes…" Where was this going?

"In all the years we've known each other we've never spent the holidays together."

"You know I don't do holidays," she cut in.

"Exactly. That's why I wanted to tell you that I'm really going after this competition this year, Terri," she drawled in that syrupy-sweet twang. "I want to win in the worst way." Her cheeks flushed. "I have every intention of taking Mr. Blac to Rio when I win." She smiled as if she'd just seen heaven. Her eyes rolled upward and her color heightened from her throat up to her hairline. She started rocking her leg up and down.

If Terri had been standing, she would have fallen down face-first. She knew this heffa hadn't just said that she wanted to take Michael Blac—*her* Michael Blac—to Rio. Oh, hell no!

Terri's skin grew taut around her chiseled features, making her large eyes even larger. A slow, dangerous smile moved across her mouth.

"Oh, really?" She rose from her seat, then came to stand in front of Mindy. She looked down on her before bracing her hands on the arms of the chair. She was an inch away from Mindy's too-pretty face. "You want a competition? Then you have it," she said with deadly calm. "Bring on your best game."

Mindy's lids fluttered furiously, as if trying to dislodge something from her eyes. She drew in a breath, then pushed up from her seat, forcing Terri to step back. She put on her best Southern-charm smile. "This little ole Southern gal is no backwoods hick. But my mama always told me to put my cards on the table. So since we're friends and all, I thought it best to let you know that I intend to play to win." She stepped around Terri and rocked her hips as she walked to the door. She turned and looked at Terri over her shoulder. "May the best woman win—*the man.*" She winked and walked out. Once she was on the other side of the door, she released a breath of relief, then drew herself up. Damn that had been hard, but it was for Terri's own good.

Terri's eyes closed to near slits. She wanted to throw something but knew better. Friends—ha! Who needed them. If Mindy wanted a fight, she had one. It was on now!

Chapter 3

Friends were totally overrated, Terri thought bitterly as she maneuvered her BMW around the rush-hour traffic of midtown Manhattan. She stopped at the light and absently rubbed the center of her chest. All day it had felt tight and her stomach hollow.

She blinked, surprised to find her eyes burning as if she were about to cry. *Ridiculous.* What was there to cry about? The fact that her supposed best friend had stabbed her in the back? *Silly.* So what if Mindy was the only person she'd ever confided in about anything? So what if Mindy knew that the only thing Terri wanted in the world other than a fat paycheck was Michael Blac? She sniffed and blinked faster. So what if she'd taken all of Terri's secrets and tossed them down like a gauntlet at her feet? She swallowed over the hard knot in her throat. She'd just get over it, that's all. The same way she'd gotten over all the other hurts, slights and ills in her life.

Toss it up to experience, she decided and pulled across the intersection, only to come to a halt on the other side by a line of traffic held in place by a stalled delivery truck.

She tapped her fingers on the steering wheel. It was just as well, she ruminated, reaching for the radio dial to tune in to the last segment of the Wendy Williams Experience. She didn't need friends. She didn't need family. She didn't need anyone. Simple as that. She'd win this competition and land a sweet deal and Michael Blac in the process.

The traffic inched along. At this rate, it would take her an hour to get uptown to Harlem instead of the reasonable twenty minutes. Thankfully she'd scheduled the appointment with the owners of the spa for six-thirty.

Barbara Allen had called back about four-thirty, just when Terri had been on the verge of moving full steam ahead to plan B. Barbara had said that all of the owners were excited and eager to hear what she had to say. That was a big relief, Terri thought as the traffic finally began to move. She knew her plan had the potential to be seriously major in every way. It would put her, the spa and Sterns & Blac in front of everyone. She was really eager to put her ideas together with Stephanie.

She'd done her research on her, as well. Stephanie had been a heavy hitter during her tenure at H.L. Reuben and then she'd just disappeared.

Terri finally made it to Broadway and continued uptown until she reached her turn on One Hundred and Twentieth

Street. She cruised along until she spotted the brownstone that housed the spa. She drove onto the next block and parked, then hurried back. She checked her watch: six twenty-five.

"Good evening. Welcome to Pause. How can I help you?"

Terri came to the front of the horseshoe-shaped reception desk. "Hello. I have an appointment with the owners. I'm Terri Wells." She handed the woman behind the desk her card.

Elizabeth's smiled bloomed in welcome. "Yes, of course." She stood up and extended her hand. "Elizabeth Lewis. I'm one of the owners."

"Nice to meet you." Terri shook her hand, glanced briefly around, then settled her attention on Elizabeth. "Looks like a really nice place. The newspaper clips don't do it justice."

"We worked really hard. As a matter of fact, Raquel, the daughter of one of the co-owners, worked on the decor." She handed Terri the brochure that had been done by Stephanie's new boyfriend, the photographer Toni. "This will give you a better idea of the facility."

"Thanks."

"I'll call Stephanie." She picked up the phone, said a few words, then hung up. "She'll be here in a minute. Barbara is with a client, and Ann Marie had a last-minute outside appointment. And I have to hold down the front."

"You could use a few extra hands around here."

Elizabeth laughed. "That's an understatement. Actually, that's what Stephanie is doing now—finishing up an interview."

Terri nodded, then stepped away as a new arrival approached requiring Elizabeth's attention. She wandered over to the café and took in the soothing atmosphere. Soft music played in the background. The muted sea-green colors and ergonomic furniture lent themselves to a sense of relaxation and tranquility.

"So sorry to keep you waiting."

Terri turned to face Stephanie. Wow, she looked so much like Tyra Banks is was disconcerting.

Stephanie smirked. "I know. Don't say it…Tyra Banks. I get that a lot."

Terri was totally embarrassed for staring with her mouth halfway open. "I'm sorry. Really."

"No problem. There are worse people I could resemble." She extended her hand. "Stephanie Moore."

"Terri Wells. Your reputation precedes you."

"Yours as well. You've done some really great work."

"Thanks. The PR world is small, and the number of black females doing their thing in it is even smaller."

"How true. Well, let's get to it. I'm eager to hear what you have to say. We can talk in the café if you like."

They walked into the café and found two empty lounge chairs away from the traffic. Terri placed her portfolio on the short tree-stump table that was varnished and stained in the same soft shade of sand as the floor.

Terri leaned back and actually put her feet up, following Stephanie's lead. "This is like lounging on the beach."

"Yep, right smack in the middle of Harlem."

Terri reached for her portfolio and flipped it open. She

took out two sheets of typed paper and handed one to Stephanie. "Just to give you some background…" She went on to explain about the yearly competition at Sterns & Blac, her wins two years in a row and what this year's competition entailed.

"What I want to do is create an exclusive campaign to establish the 'Pause Man.' He would have to be a member, in good shape and health, which you all would determine. I'm partnering with clothes designers, travel agents and technology gurus—the works. The winner of the campaign would be deemed the Pause Man and win a trip, get a spread in a major magazine, along with an assortment of gifts and prizes, but specifically become the spokesman for men's health and fitness. We can bring in nutritionists, men's-health experts to give classes during the course of the campaign, provide screenings—the whole nine yards."

Stephanie was nodding slowly as she listened. It was a brilliant idea, one that she may have thought of herself if she'd had the time. Pause could become the premiere outlet for men's health and fitness, more than just a spa.

"I love it. And I think my partners will love it, too."

Terri blew out a sigh of relief. "Great! I guess you and I can work out some specifics, like the application, media announcements, requirements, things like that."

"Fine. I'll definitely have to step up my game in hiring some more help. We are already up to our eyeballs. And with a new campaign on the horizon we'll definitely be overwhelmed."

"Then why don't you let me work out all the little details. I'll run them past you for your approval, and you can keep doing what you need to do here."

"That makes sense. I'd hate for anything to fall through the cracks because of me."

"Don't worry, with the two of us on the job, this project is going to fly." A big old grin spread across her mouth.

"My sister, I must agree."

Terri collected her belongings and stood. She extended her hand to Stephanie. "Thank you so much for agreeing to the project. I'm really looking forward to working with you."

"Well, as I said, it's not all a done deal yet. I still have to talk to the ladies to make it official. But I'm sure it will be fine. I'll get back to you in a day or so. Is that good?"

"The sooner, the better. We're already moving into October. So we have two months to get it together and pull it off."

"Your boss must be something else to come up with these challenges every year."

"Yeah, he's something," Terri said a bit wistfully.

They started walking out.

"I've never actually met Michael Blac. I've seen pictures and read up on all of his accomplishments. What's he like live and in living color?"

Terri chuckled. "He's…dynamic, highly intelligent, driven for excellence. He's fair to all of his employees, but he only expects the best."

"And he's not bad to look at," Stephanie added, snatching a sidelong glance at Terri. There was no mistaking the admiration in her voice for Michael Blac. Stephanie knew the look, the tone. There was more going on. She'd traveled down that rocky road of having a thing for her boss. It nearly cost her everything. She only hoped that Terri wasn't on that path, as well.

They reached the exit door.

Terri stuck out her hand. "Great to finally meet *the* Stephanie Moore. You know, your name is still uttered in reverent whispers," she said tongue in cheek.

Stephanie chuckled. "That and two dollars will get you on a New York City train." She shook Terri's hand. "Good to meet you, too. You'll hear from us no later than tomorrow. I'll give everyone the rundown when we close tonight."

"Sounds good. I'll look forward to hearing from you."

Terri floated to her car. What she wanted to do was the happy dance, having crossed the goal line with no interference. This campaign was going to be huge, bigger, better and badder than anything she'd ever done. And when she won those two tickets to Rio, she'd march right into Michael's office and hand him his flight to paradise—with her. After all, he did say a companion of your choice.

For once, the impending holiday season was taking on new meaning.

Chapter 4

Michael turned off the late-night news. The room became bathed in moonlight streaming in from the terrace windows overlooking the Manhattan skyline.

His condo on the Upper East Side of Manhattan was an eclectic mixture of ultracontemporary with a cool urban flair. Near-life-size black-and-white photos of hip-hop artists graced the stark white walls right next to renderings from Elizabeth Catlett and Cynthia Saint James. Low-slung glass-and-wood tables played host to a white leather sectional that comfortably sat ten. Music was piped in from hidden speakers strategically placed in every room of the luxury two-bedroom duplex.

His custom-designed Japanese kitchen was always the conversation piece when he had guests. Built-in woks sat in the center island of stainless steel and black marble. The kitchen looked out onto the terrace garden that wrapped around to the living room. The garden—an actual replica of a Japanese garden—was dotted with exotic plants, miniature bonsai trees and a man-made pool that housed the rare and very expensive koi fish.

But his bedroom was his haven. It was where he worked, where he played and where he rejuvenated after a long day. Quiet as it was kept, for all of his playboy accoutrements, he was far from it. Beneath the *GQ* exterior, he was a boy from Alabama who knew all about hard work and family values. He was the last of six children, all preceding him being girls. And "thank you, Jesus," his father's famous words at finally having his one and only son.

"Boy, you have no idea what it's like being the only man in a house full of women all these years," his father had repeated to him the instant he was old enough to understand.

He loved his sisters dearly, but he had to agree with his dad. Living with a woman was hard on a man.

Michael turned on the lights that ran along the upper moldings of the ceiling, washing the earth-toned room in a warm butterscotch glow. With a flip of the dial the intensity could be lowered or increased, and alternate bulbs turned off and on cast inviting shadows in the room.

In all his forty-four years he'd had no desire to take up residence with a woman either temporarily or legally. He preferred the luxury of change. Maybe one day he'd change his mind and settle down, passing along his thriving empire to his heirs. But until then there was always his little black book if he got lonely.

He pulled back the faux suede coverlet and hopped into bed, bringing his laptop with him.

He checked his e-mail for any late developments. Often members of his staff would send him updates or queries regarding major ongoing projects or his assistant would send him an e-mail alert to remind him of any early-morning plans. He was a bit surprised to get an e-mail from Mindy.

He frowned. To his knowledge, she wasn't assigned to one of the teams. As far as he knew, she was handling the basic client caseload, nothing that would require his supervision, input or a late-night e-mail. He clicked the read button and his surprise rose several notches. She wanted to meet with him privately in the morning.

Mindy had spent hours after work the previous day searching for the perfect outfit and getting her weave redone. She wanted to look the part of the highly successfully overachiever even if she wasn't one. It was, after all, about appearances.

Hard work was not Mindy's forte. As the only daughter of a land developer and a busy socialite, Mindy grew up in the rarified world of the black Southern elite. She'd never had to do much more than ask and it was hers. It wasn't that she lacked intelligence. Actually, she'd graduated at the top of her class at Columbia. That's when her life of privilege had changed.

Upon graduation, her parents had deposited fifty thousand dollars into her savings account, paid the rent on her apartment for two years and sent her out into the wide world.

That had been more than a decade ago. She'd long since exhausted her nest egg and had been forced to find work. She was a natural charmer, so publicity was a no-brainer. Little did she know that she'd actually be forced to work at it.

Fortunately she had connections, and blood was thicker than water—thank goodness.

Mindy turned from side to side, admiring herself in the full-length mirror. The designer jeans and hip-length hand-painted jacket looked too good to be true on her, Mindy thought. Casual but classy. She didn't want to look as if she was trying too hard when she met with Michael later that morning.

She hoped he'd read his e-mail, she thought as she peered closer at the mirror to apply her lip gloss. But even if he hadn't, as long as he was in the office she knew he'd be willing to see her. He maintained an open-door policy with the entire staff.

She admired herself for a few more minutes. Satisfied, she picked up her shoulder bag and headed out.

When she arrived at the office, it was already full of activity. There was a barely contained energy running through the floor. It didn't take Mindy long to realize what all the excitement was about. At the end of the long, wide corridor she spotted Michael, Terri and Liberty Wagner. Michael was smiling and laughing, periodically touching Liberty's arm.

"Did you hear?" Josh said, easing up alongside Mindy.

"Hear what?"

"Terri landed Liberty Wagner. She's going to be doing a full-out campaign for her. Liberty just signed a new contract with Harmony Records and she wants a top-notch PR effort to ensure the success of her comeback. I hear Michael is ecstatic."

"Ecstatic, huh?" She forced a smile. "That's really nice for Terri."

"If anyone can put Liberty Wagner back on the map, Terri can. She sure has a way of landing the big fish."

"Yes, she does." She kept her eyes glued on the trio. "Well, I knew all about it anyway," she said in an offhand manner. "Terri tells me everything."

Josh looked at her askance. "She happen to tell you what she's working on for this year's challenge?"

Mindy shifted her shoulder bag. "Not yet. She's still working on it. But I'm sure I'll be the first one to know."

Josh pushed his glasses up on the bridge of his nose. "I'm sure you will. And maybe some of Terri's star power will rub off on you while she's at it." He chuckled, shook his head and walked away.

She wanted to tell four-eyed Josh just where he could stick his sarcastic comments, but that wouldn't be ladylike. She lifted her chin and marched down the hall to her office.

Mindy immediately turned on her computer and printed out her preliminary concept for the challenge. Her goal wasn't so much to win as it was to point Michael in the right direction.

For years she'd lived in Terri's shadow, always on the fringes. Terri thought nothing of squirreling herself away for hours or days on a project, leaving Mindy all alone. She'd been alone all her life. Her parents were too busy to pay her any attention, so they gave her things to occupy her. It wasn't *things* that she wanted. She wanted a friend, someone to truly care about her for once. And if she got Michael's attention, she was sure she'd get Terri's, as well.

Her inside line rang just as she finished printing up her report.

"If you're free, Mr. Blac will see you now," Carmen, Michael's assistant said.

"Thanks, Carmen. I'll be right there."

She drew in a breath before gathering up her paperwork, then headed toward Michael's office. Just as she turned the corner she ran right into Terri.

"Oh, sorry," Terri said. She looked Mindy over. "Where are you headed to in such a rush?"

"So you got the Wagner deal, I hear," she said, changing the subject. She held her folder tight to her chest.

Terri grinned. "Yeah, that's going to be major. I'm going to have to put in a lot of hours to pull it off, but that's the rules of the game."

Mindy flashed her pearly whites. "If anyone can do it, you can."

"I'd better get busy," Terri said, apparently having forgotten her earlier question.

"See you later." Mindy hurried off before Terri remembered what she'd forgotten.

Terri watched Mindy hurry down the hallway. She was up to something, Terri thought. Not a day had ever gone by that Mindy didn't ask to meet for lunch or drinks after work, even if they weren't speaking. Hmm.

Terri spun away and walked toward her office. Whatever Mindy's agenda was, she had one of her own. She smiled. She knew she had this competition in the bag and she'd have Michael at the end of her rainbow. Friends—ha! Highly overrated.

Mindy stole a glance over her shoulder before she knocked on Michael's partially opened door. In a tiny corner of her soul she felt a twinge of guilt for what she was about to do.

She steeled herself, shook off her angst and knocked.

"Come in."

"Good morning, Mr. Blac," she said, poking her head in.

Michael, always the gentleman, stood and waved her in. "Come in. Have a seat. Would you like some coffee or tea?"

"No, thank you, sir. I'm fine."

Michael's smile was indulgent. "Please, I've swallowed the fact that you refuse to call me by my first name, but I have to put my foot down with *sir*."

Mindy lowered her gaze the way she'd seen the women do in *Memoirs of a Geisha*, then looked up at him. "It's just my upbringing."

"I can appreciate that. Now what can I do for you?"

They'd kept up this front and had been doing this dance for years.

She took a seat and opened her leather portfolio on her lap. "I've never been much for competition. As you know, I haven't entered any of the previous contests."

"Yes, I know." He walked behind his desk and sat, folding his hands on the desktop. He looked her in the eyes.

"But this year is different." She smiled expansively. "I have an idea that I want to present for your consideration."

Chapter 5

Michael walked out of his office and stopped at Carmen's desk. "I'm going out for a couple of hours. You can reach me on my cell if anything urgent comes up."

"Sure. And don't forget your four o'clock."

"Right. Thanks." He walked toward the bank of elevators.

"Michael."

He turned.

"Can I speak with you for a moment?"

"Sure, Terri. I'm on my way out, but I have a few minutes. What's up?"

"I'll ride down with you. I don't want to hold you up."

"Come on, then."

The elevator doors opened and they stepped in.

"What's on your mind?"

"I know this may be an awkward time, but I wanted to run

my project idea past you." Her heart was racing faster than Jesse Owens at the Olympics.

The elevator descended, then stopped on the next floor. A lunch crowd got on and Terri had to squeeze next to Michael. His arm was pressed firmly against hers. Her nipples stood at attention. She struggled to stay focused.

"Sure. I was thinking that you might have decided against entering this year after the coup you pulled with Liberty Wagner."

She inhaled his scent. Her stomach fluttered. "Yes, I, uh, well that won't stop me. I love hard work."

"That you do." He grinned at her. "So let me hear your idea."

"Well, what I was thinking…" They stepped off the elevator.

By the time they'd reached the lobby doors she'd succinctly pitched him her idea and informed him that she'd already spoken to the owners of Pause.

"Sounds like another winner. All I'm hearing is good news today. First the Wagner deal. Then, of all people, Mindy comes in with a dynamite idea. And now you again."

She stretched her lips into a tight smile. Mindy had pitched her idea? That's where she must have been going when Terri had seen her earlier. That little… Well, all's fair in love and war.

"Get all of the particulars on my desk. I'll take a look at it, but it sounds stellar, as always." His gaze lingered on her face for a moment.

A furnace lit inside her. "Thanks."

He nodded. "Have a great day." He pushed through the revolving doors out into the brisk October air.

Terri stood for a few minutes watching him until he soon disappeared among the rush of human traffic on Fifth Avenue.

She should have been elated at this point. Instead she was seething inside. All this time Mindy had pretended to be her friend. Well, the hell with friendship. And the hell with Mindy Clarke.

She spun around and stalked back off toward the elevators. She would win this competition and she would win Michael, too. A new year was on the horizon. What was that saying—out with the old, in with the new? Yeah, well, Mindy was now old news!

Michael caught a cab on the corner. He'd made it a policy to steer clear of any relationships with his employees. He frowned upon office liaisons. If he'd had his way and could find the slightest justification, he would fire Terri Wells in a heartbeat. But day after day, year after year, she'd only gotten better at what she did. Her contribution to the company had been paramount to its impeccable reputation. She had the magic touch. If only she could touch him. But if everything worked out as planned, she would. He smiled and sat back against the tattered leather of the yellow cab. The new year couldn't roll in fast enough for him.

Terri returned to her office with a new fire in her veins. This was going to be the best campaign she'd ever put together. She'd make whatever Mindy—or anyone else, for that matter—did look like child's play.

She went over all of her plans, making sure not to miss

any details. She included graphs and charts and demographics and she was pretty sure with endorsements and sponsorship she would come in under budget. She saved the document, then printed out her ten-page proposal.

Holding the document in front of her, she should have been elated, excited about her next major accomplishment. But she felt empty, as if this was all just an exercise in futility. So what if she won more accolades at the job, put the spa on the map and won a trip? She truly had no one to share all of her joy with.

Her life had been a struggle. Everything that she had, all that she'd accomplished had been hard-fought. She had to be the best at everything she did. It was the only way to keep the fear out of her heart—the fear of loss. If she worked hard, proved herself, maybe the people that she loved and cared about wouldn't leave her. But by the time she'd turned sixteen and been forced to go and live in the loveless house of her aunt, she'd known that attaching herself to people only led to heartache. So she attached herself to objects and achievement. Those things could not be taken from her.

To anyone looking at Terri Wells, she personified stylish, intelligent, easy on the eye and successful. Who wouldn't want to be just like her? She'd guaranteed her success through determination, hard work and single-mindedness. But for all she had on the outside, it did nothing to fill the emptiness of her insides, which she struggled daily to camouflage. And the one time she even dared to dream of having a *someone* instead of a *something*, it remained an elusive fantasy. Michael Blac was the one variable that she couldn't guarantee.

With a new breath of resolve, she pushed the disparaging thoughts to the back of her mind. She collected her papers and put them in a folder with the intention of taking them down to Michael's office.

On her way down the hallway she spotted Mindy. Her chest tightened for an instant, but she lifted her chin and kept going.

"Hi, Carmen," Terri said, stopping at the assistant's desk. "I wanted to leave this for Michael."

Carmen removed her headset and took the folder. "I'll make sure he gets it."

"Thanks." She walked back to her office, hoping to avoid Mindy. No such luck.

"Good morning, Terri," Mindy chirped. "Missed you in the employee lounge this morning."

"I was busy."

They faced each other like gladiators waiting for the signal to do battle.

Mindy offered up an olive branch of a smile. "Get your proposal done?"

Terri snickered. "I noticed that you didn't waste any time."

Mindy folded her arms beneath her enhanced breasts. "I thought it was about time that I stepped up my game. I've been coasting here for a long time."

Terri looked her up and down. "You got that right. I'm surprised you haven't been kicked to the curb long before now. If I didn't know any better, I'd think you had some kind of inside hookup."

Mindy flinched.

"Now, if you'll excuse me, some of us have work to do." She brushed past Mindy and continued down the hall to her office.

Mindy turned slowly and followed Terri's course. Her heart ached. She missed her friend. Even though it often seemed as if the friendship was all one-sided. Hanging her head, she went back to the office, wondering if her brilliant idea was so brilliant after all.

When Terri returned to her desk, the message light on her phone was flashing. It was from Stephanie Moore. They were eager to get started on the proposal.

"Yesss!" Her eyes narrowed in determination. If it was a fight to the finish that Mindy wanted, she would get it.

She knew that once Michael read her proposal, his approval would be in the bag. He'd already told her how innovative it was. If only his eyes would light up about her instead of about the possibility of a new acquisition, she thought. Michael Blac was all about business. He kept everything at work strictly professional and insisted upon that among his staff, which was why she'd never considered making a move to get his attention until now.

She'd saved a sufficient amount of money. She had solid investments and had successfully built up a rapport with her client base that she knew she could take with her anywhere she went. During the past year she'd been investigating striking out on her own, starting her own PR business—and meeting Stephanie Moore had cinched it for her.

With all of the pieces in place, she could walk away from Sterns & Blac. And then there would be no earthly reason why she and Michael couldn't pursue a relationship. When she won this challenge, she planned to lay her cards on the table: *Michael, I quit. I'm in love with you and I want you to come with me to Rio and see how things go.*

Michael was a businessman. It was a business move with an emotional catch.

She stared at the phone. A catch is right. What in the world made her think that Michael Blac was the least bit interested in her other than as an outstanding employee?

Nothing.

Chapter 6

Michael finished up his four-o'clock meeting. It had taken much longer than he'd planned. It was already after six. No sense in going back to the office now. At least he didn't have to worry about picking up his car from the company garage. He'd opted to leave it home today, knowing that he had a lot of running around to do.

He stood at the corner of Fifty-Sixth and Madison Avenue debating his next move—go home alone or treat himself to dinner alone. He could call any number of his women friends who would probably be happy to join him, but he wasn't in the mood for idle chitchat.

He hailed a cab and gave the driver the address for BARNONE. He'd heard it was one of the city's hot spots on any given night, but he'd yet to make an appearance. Tonight was a night he felt like getting lost in the crowd.

When he entered the lounge, he was surprised to see so many people already filling the space. The music was pumping and happy hour was definitely in full force.

He was shortly escorted to a table and placed his dinner order. Settling down, he gazed around at the crowd and quickly noticed several members of the New York Knicks in a banquette on the upper level. And if he wasn't mistaken, Mos Def was at the bar chilling with Busta Rhymes.

Michael smiled as he sipped his drink. This was certainly all that he'd heard about and then some. He put his glass down and turned to his left, and that's when he caught sight of Terri Wells. She was with Liberty Wagner.

He stood and wove his way around bodies and in and out of tables until he reached them at the hostess counter at the front of the lounge.

"Good evening, ladies."

Terri turned and her heart did a little dance. "Michael." She blinked several times. "I didn't know you came here."

"Heard this was the place to see and be seen, so I figured I was long overdue in checking it out for myself." He turned his charm on Liberty. He extended his hand. "Ms. Wagner. It's a pleasure to see you again. We at Sterns & Blac are thrilled to work with you. I owe it all to this dynamic woman here." He cast a smile in Terri's direction.

"I've been hearing about your agency for a while. When Terri came up to me the other night, it was like karma," the singing diva said in her trademark sultry voice. Her spiked platinum-blond hair looked stark white beneath the lighting of the lounge, but it was perfect for her heart-shaped face and periwinkle eyes.

"Do you have a table already?" He directed his question to Terri.

"No. Actually, we were hoping to get lucky." Her heart was racing so fast her knees began to shake.

"Well, why don't you join me. I have a table on the other side." He lifted his chin in the direction of the table.

Terri looked to Liberty for confirmation.

"Sounds fine to me," Liberty said. "It will give me a chance to get to know you better—outside of the office." She flashed Michael a cover-girl smile and slid her arm through his. Terri inwardly cringed.

"These ladies will be joining me at my table," Michael said to the hostess, who'd just returned to her station.

"Wonderful." She pulled out two more menus and led the way to the table.

Michael held the chairs for Liberty, then Terri, while they sat down.

"Would either of you ladies like something to drink?" Michael asked.

"I'd love a glass of Cristal," Liberty said before batting her long lashes.

"What about you, Terri?"

"Oh, nothing for me." The last thing she needed was to get all loopy in front of her boss.

"At least have a glass of wine," Michael insisted. "After all this is a celebration of sorts."

Terri blew out a breath. "Hmm, okay, a white wine spritzer will be fine."

Michael signaled for the waitress and put in their drink orders.

"So, Liberty, tell me all about your upcoming project. Although Terri will be handling everything, I do want to remain in the loop." He shot Terri a short smile.

Liberty leaned forward, exhibiting her deep cleavage as an appetizer as she rested her elbows on the table and tucked her palms beneath her chin.

Terri drew in a breath and sat back, laughing at all the appropriate places while Liberty regaled them with ribald stories of her tours.

She'd never felt so out of place in her life. She was accustomed to controlling every situation she was in, being on center stage without as much as her heartbeat elevating. But when it came to Michael Blac she seemed to lose her poise and her focus. In business matters she was fine. She could handle him in the boardroom, passing in the hallways and chatting in the employee lounge. But this was different. This was a social setting. Drinks were flowing, the atmosphere was casual and she was out in a public place with her boss.

"You're pretty quiet tonight," Michael said when Liberty excused herself to chat with a friend she'd spotted.

She shrugged slightly. "I'll have plenty of time to talk with Liberty."

"I'm sure you will. She's an interesting woman." He looked her square in the eyes.

Terri's face grew hot. She forced a smile. "That she is."

Michael lifted his glass to his lips and took a swallow. "Other than work, I don't know much about you."

She blinked several times. What did he just say?

"Is this where you spend your off hours?"

Was that a trick question? "Um, actually, it's an ideal place to catch up on what's happening in the entertainment world." She laced her fingers together. "Other than that, I don't make it a habit to hang out, if that's what you mean."

"I wasn't implying anything. Just wondering, that's all." He paused. "What else do you like to do when you're not working and landing megaclients?"

Was he just making small talk or was he really interested? "I, uh, like to belly dance. I take classes on Saturdays." Was that the only thing she could come up with? She was starting to feel ill. Must be the wine spritzer.

The right corner of his full mouth curved upward. "Belly dancing. I would have never thought that about you." He chuckled.

Now he was making fun of her and probably thought she was some kind of…

"I think that's great."

"You do?"

"Yes. Most women would say something like, 'Oh, I like to garden or relax and curl up with a good book.'"

Terri lowered her head and laughed, then looked up at him. "Is that what most women tell you?"

He shook his head. "You'd be surprised at the things I hear."

Terri began to relax. "So what do you like to do?"

"This is really gonna sound strange. I cultivate exotic fish."

Her eyes widened. "Really? Now that's different."

He told her about his collection of koi and how he'd gotten interested in fish and fishing as a young boy growing up in Alabama.

"You grew up in Alabama? You'd never know it."

"Oh, I can turn the accent on when need be," he said. "Much of it got stripped away by my years of schooling at MIT."

"I had no idea you went to MIT. That's impressive." Not only was he handsome and charming, he was brilliant, too.

"My dad wanted me to go into engineering, so I went to make him happy. But marketing and PR are my true passions."

He talked some more about his youth, mentioning his five older sisters and his overwhelming need to get out of the house full of women.

Listening to him talk about his childhood made him more human, more accessible. But she couldn't let her thoughts carry her away. He was just being nice and killing time until his apparent real interest returned from doing her diva thing.

"But enough about me. Tell me some more about Terri Wells."

"There's not much to tell. I grew up in Queens, lived with my aunt after my brother disappeared. He'd been taking care of me after I'd lost my mom and dad. My father died on my birthday and my mother on Christmas morning. Been kind of turned off holidays and celebrations ever since."

"Wow, I'm sorry. I had no idea." He studied her for a moment. "I supposed I'd be turned off, as well. So you don't celebrate the holidays at all?"

She shrugged. "Just another day to me." She drew in a breath and put on a beaming smile. "All water under the bridge."

"Whew! Sorry I took so long," Liberty breathed, plopping down into her seat and cutting off any further conversation. "Did you all order yet?"

"No," Michael said, speaking up. He cut a look at Terri. "We were so busy talking, totally forgot about dinner."

Liberty slid a glance in Terri's direction. She raised a brow in question. "Really?" She pulled her chair closer to the table and scooted nearer to Michael. "I'm sure whatever you had to say was intriguing." She ran her gaze over his face before running her tongue over her lips.

Michael cleared his throat. "Ready to order, ladies?"

"I'm famished," Liberty cooed, pushing her breasts in his direction.

Michael signaled for the waitress, and the moment—or whatever it was between Terri and Michael—was lost.

"This has been a real treat, ladies," Michael said once they'd stepped outside into the brisk October night.

Terri pulled up the collar of her coat as a stiff wind whipped by, stirring up the debris on the street.

Michael stepped around her and adjusted her silk shawl around her shoulders.

She looked at him over her shoulder. He smiled and

gently pressed the shawl in place. "Can't have my star player getting cold," he said in a voice that bordered on too personal.

"Thanks."

"Can I give you two a lift?" Liberty offered. "My car sits plenty."

"I appreciate the offer," Michael said. "But I'm going to get a cab."

"My car is in the lot," Terri said.

Liberty shrugged. "Terri, I'll give you a call in about a week. I'm in the studio for the next few days, working out the kinks in the CD. By then you should have some things to show me?"

"Absolutely."

"Great." She turned to Michael with her back to Terri. "It was really special getting to know you, Michael." She lowered her voice. "Maybe we can do this again, just me and you."

Liberty's driver stepped out of the car.

"Uh, your driver is ready."

She smiled. "Next time." She sauntered off and was helped into the car.

"She's really something," Michael said. "I think we'll have our hands full."

"I'm sure we will. But I can handle it." *Can you?* she wanted to ask but didn't.

"Where are you parked?"

"Right down the block in the lot."

"I'll walk you."

"That's really not necessary. I—"

"I insist." He took her arm. "Lead the way."

They walked about a half block. Every few feet their shoulders bumped and Terri felt a little thrill. Here she was walking down the street, near midnight, under the stars, with the man of her dreams. At least she could fantasize.

"I'm in here," she said and came to a stop in front of one of the park-and-ride lots.

"I'll wait here until you get your car."

She nodded and walked up to the attendant with her ticket stub. Moments later the attendant brought her BMW to a sharp halt in front of her.

"Nice ride."

"Thanks. Have to look good for the clients."

"That you do."

She wasn't going to read anything into that. "Well, good night. Thanks for taking care of dinner."

"Save you the trouble of putting in the voucher." He smiled.

"Yes."

They faced each other for a few more awkward moments.

"Well, I'd better go."

"Right. Good night."

"Good night, Michael."

He opened the door for her and she slid in behind the wheel. She dared not look up at him or she was certain she would ask him if she could drop him off somewhere.

He leaned down into her open window. "Get home safely. I'll see you in the office tomorrow."

Terri nodded. "You, too."

He stepped back and she slowly pulled out of the lot and into traffic.

For several moments Michael stood on the sidewalk, watching her car until it turned several blocks down. He stuck his hands in his pockets and began walking down the street.

Yes, if this plan didn't work out, he was definitely going to have to fire Terri Wells.

Chapter 7

The next few weeks flew by. Terri was consumed with work, which was fine with her—less time to think about Michael.

When she'd come into the office the morning after they'd met up at BARNONE, he'd been back to his business-as-usual self. So apparently the looks, the interest and the double entendres had all been in her imagination after all. Michael had been simply being nice, nothing more.

At least he'd officially approved her proposal, so she was going full steam ahead on it.

She ran into Mindy in the hallway.

"Hey, haven't seen much of you lately," Mindy said, almost sounding a bit hurt.

"Been really busy. Besides, it seems that we are on opposite sides of the fence."

Mindy tipped her head to the side. "That's just business,

Terri. Since when does business have to interfere with friendship?"

Terri wanted to tell her since she'd decided that part of the prize was the man she wanted, but she wouldn't give Mindy the satisfaction.

"I'm really busy. I've got to run."

"How about lunch? You have to eat, don't you?"

"I was planning on ordering in. See you later."

Mindy watched her walk away. She'd never known Terri to be so cold. She was used to her being distant when she was involved in a major project, but it had never interfered with the two of them.

Fine. If that was the way she wanted it, then so be it. The gloves were coming off. She was going to whip Terri's stuck-up ass royally.

Michael had made a point of staying as far away from Terri as possible since that night at the lounge. It wouldn't do anyone any good to show any interest that could be construed as favoritism. It was bad enough that Terri had won the competition hands down two years running. If anyone even got an inkling…well, he couldn't let that happen.

He grabbed his coat, deciding to take a stroll during his lunch hour, when he was waylaid by Mindy.

"Mr. Blac, I need to speak with you a moment."

"Sure, what is it?"

She pushed out a breath. "All bets are off. This is going

to be for real, and may the best woman win!" She spun away on her heels before Michael could respond.

Michael frowned. What was that about? He didn't want to know. He shook his head and continued on his way.

Terri desperately needed a break. She'd been working nonstop since she'd arrived at eight. Liberty was being a real diva, piling on demands by the hour. Terri was starting to regret her little coup already.

She pushed up from her desk and stretched her arms high above her head to get out the kinks. Maybe some fresh air would help. She reached for her coat on the rack behind her, grabbed her purse, then walked out.

She was about a block away from the office building when it started to flurry. She looked up at the sky in disbelief. It was barely November, and snow already?

She took her shawl from around her shoulders and draped it over her head and continued down the street. She peeked into one of the deli windows and saw Michael standing on line. Good sense told her to keep going, but it must not have kicked in fully. She pulled the door to the deli open and walked inside, looking in every direction but his.

"Terri?"

She acted duly surprised. "Michael. Hi."

He walked up to her. "I almost didn't recognize you, all incognito." He chuckled, pointing to the shawl over her head and shoulders.

She laughed. "It started snowing on my way over, and I didn't feel like going back for my umbrella."

"Snow?" He peered outside. "Can Christmas be far behind?" He turned to look at her. "Oh, sorry. I know how you feel about the holidays."

"Not a problem. No reason for others not to enjoy it on my account."

"Can I buy you lunch?"

"Excuse me?"

"Uh, I can put it on the company account. We can talk business."

"Well…if you're sure."

"Positive. Get what you want. I'll grab a table in back and meet you at the cashier."

What am I doing? he thought as he went to find a table. The last thing he needed was to spend any time alone with Terri. But he couldn't seem to help himself, and it was only getting worse. How was he going to remain impartial if she was always crowding his thoughts?

He met her at the cashier counter and paid for her lunch, then escorted her to their table.

"It's really starting to come down now," he said as he helped her into her seat.

"Out of the blue," she murmured. *In more ways than one.*

"How is everything going with Liberty?"

Terri groaned. "She is seriously trying to run me ragged."

Michael chuckled. "I'm sure it will be well worth it in the end. What about your competition campaign—how is that going? Or should I ask?"

She smiled. "Going extremely well. I got a major electronics company to sign on and I have a meeting with the head of a hot hip-hop clothing line tomorrow morning. I've gotten confirmation from a few incredible sponsors, and we are guaranteed a spread in a national magazine."

Michael slowly nodded as he took it all in. This was definitely a dynamite campaign. But he had to admit, barring the caveats of Mindy's proposal, they were running pretty tight.

"Sounds as if you might really need a vacation when this is all over—not to say that you will automatically win," he quickly clarified.

"I don't take anything for granted," she said and wished that he didn't smell so good. It was interfering with her meal. She was close enough to him to see that his dark eyes were encircled by a lighter shade of brown and his skin, the color of toffee, was flawless, not a nick, not a bump. His mouth was moving, but she wasn't really paying attention. She was imagining what his lips would feel like on her own— or better, on other parts.

"So what do you think?"

Terri blinked several times, feigned a short coughing spell and said, "Excuse me?"

"I was asking what you thought about my offer?"

"Your offer…"

"I know it's a bit unorthodox, but since Carmen can't go, and you have been working so hard, I thought it would be great if you could accompany me. You have a great ear for BS, can see things in a project that no one else can. And you'll get the chance to relax a little, get out of the cold and enjoy some sun."

Damn, she wished she'd been paying more attention. What in the world was he talking about?

"So how 'bout it? An all-expense-paid business trip to Florida for the weekend."

This time she choked for real.

Michael jumped up from his seat, rushed to her side and began patting her on the back. "Are you all right?"

"Oh…goodness," she sputtered, trying to pull herself together. "Must have gone down the wrong way," she croaked.

Confusion knitted his brow. "You haven't eaten anything, but…you never know." He gave her one last pat on the back. "You okay?" He looked down into her eyes.

She nodded and reached for her bottle of Sprite. She took a long swallow. Now, had he just asked me to go with him to Florida?

Michael took his seat. He stared at her for a couple of minutes. "Well, what do you think? I know it's short notice…"

"Um, I think I can manage." She gave him a shaky smile. "Actually, it sounds like fun."

"Great!"

"Who are you meeting with?"

"The owner of the Orlando Magic. They want to put together a literacy campaign featuring their team members."

"Excellent." Her mind was already running full blast.

"I can see the engine running," he teased.

Terri focused on him. Her face grew hot. "Sorry." She

shrugged. "You can take the girl out of the office but not the office out of the girl."

"That's what I love…like about you, Terri." He cleared his throat. "You are always so focused on the goal."

Did he say *love*? But he'd quickly cleaned that up. "I try."

"I'll arrange for your ticket and book you a room at the Orlando Hilton. Uh, I think it would be best if…you didn't mention this around the office. I would hate for the other staff members to get the wrong idea."

"Of course. I totally understand. And I really appreciate your confidence in me and this opportunity."

He checked his watch. "I have to run. I have an appointment." He stood. "You go ahead and finish your lunch. I'll see you tomorrow."

"Sure. Thanks again."

"My pleasure." He turned and hurried out into the building snow.

Terri sat at the table, stunned. Michael Blac had asked her to accompany him on a business trip. They would be staying at the same hotel. Her heart ran at an alarming rate. *It's just business, nothing more.* Stay focused. Mindlessly she finished off her lunch and returned to the office dazed and excited.

By the time her day ended at four-thirty, there was at least an inch or two of snow covering the ground. But that didn't deter her from doing what she must—shop!

If she was going to Florida in three days and meeting with potential new clients, she had to look the part. And of course her repertoire had to include some fun-in-the-sun clothing, as well.

As she wandered through her favorite boutique, for once she was grateful that the fashion world was always two seasons ahead of the prevailing one. Summer attire dotted the racks. She picked out two lightweight linen suits for her meetings, a cocktail dress in a soft salmon color for dinner and an assortment of T-shirts and capri pants for her jaunts around town. Her last stop was for shoes. She found a pair of kitten-heeled slingbacks that would work well with any of her outfits. She had a bathing suit that she'd purchased last summer and had never had a chance to wear. She'd be sure to tuck that baby in her suitcase.

Satisfied with her purchases, she headed home. Slipping and sliding her way to her car, she realized this trip couldn't have come at a better time.

Michael paced the floor of his living room like a man possessed. What in heaven's name had gotten into him to blurt out something like that to Terri? An unsanctioned trip with him to Florida? He pressed his palm to his forehead.

Hey, he was the boss and he could do what he damn well pleased—in the event anyone should ask. This was business and a business decision. Terri was the best at what she did, and he knew he could use her help in sealing this deal. Right. That's all there was to it.

Then why was it a secret? Why had he paid for her ticket and her room with his personal credit card? *You know why,* that wicked little voice in his head chanted.

He stalked across the room and into the kitchen. He pulled open the fridge and hunted around for a cold beer. Finding a Coors tucked in the back, he pulled it out, twisted off the cap and took a long swallow. Maybe the icy beer would cool his head. It didn't. And the more he thought about it, the more it sounded like a really bad idea. He was going to have to find a graceful way to make some excuse why she couldn't go, that's all there was to it. Yes, he'd tell her first thing tomorrow.

Chapter 8

Terri could barely contain her excitement. When she ran into Mindy in the employee lounge, it took all she had to hold her tongue and not shove her news right up Mindy's perky little nose. Grrr, how could she have ever thought that they were friends?

She crossed the room and went straight to the coffee-maker. "Good morning," she mumbled.

"Hi." Mindy angled her body toward Terri. "Listen, about what I said in the office that day..." She blew out a breath. "We've been friends for a long time."

"I *thought* we were friends," Terri corrected. "Until you chose to stab me in the back."

Mindy's face pinched. "Everyone on staff is eligible to go for the annual competition, Terri. You don't have a lock on it, you know." She desperately wanted to tell her what was really going on, but she couldn't. She needed to see this through to the end for both of their sakes.

Terri snorted. "Fine. Then there's really nothing to talk about."

"I'm sorry you feel that way. Can I make it up to you?"

Terri slashed a look in Mindy's direction. As much as Mindy got on her nerves, she did miss her. What was going on between them was silly. She missed the gossip, the hanging out, the having a friend. And Mindy actually looked hurt.

Terri blew out a breath. "How are you going to make it up to me?"

Mindy immediately brightened. "I was having some friends over on Friday, just dinner—buffet-style—music, talking. You know…just hanging out."

Friday! Yikes. She was leaving with Michael on Friday. "Wow, I wish I could. But I have plans for Friday—"

"I could easily switch it to Saturday if that works better for you," she quickly cut in.

This was getting worse by the minute. "Mindy, I really appreciate the offer. Really. But this is the one weekend where I really can't change my plans. I'm sorry."

Mindy would not be moved. "What have you got going on this weekend? If you have a date or something, bring him along. It will be—"

"Mindy, I'm sorry, I can't," she blurted out a bit more harshly than she'd intended. "Maybe another time." She took her coffee cup and started to walk away.

"Yeah, another time," Mindy murmured as she watched her leave.

* * *

Terri returned to her office and shut her door. She really felt awful having to lie to Mindy. As much as Mindy's blatant challenge rubbed her the wrong way, she knew that Mindy had a good heart. After all, her fleeting comments to Mindy about Michael had been vague at best. But Mindy was her best friend. She should have been able to read between the lines. What else could she have possibly meant when she said things like she wanted a man just like Michael Blac one day, that Michael was the epitome of sexy, that most men she'd dated paled in comparison to him. True, she'd never actually come right out and said *I want Michael Blac*, but it didn't take a mind reader to get her drift.

So for Mindy to look her square in the eye and tell her that she was going after Michael herself…well, that was the height of betrayal.

She plopped down in her seat. Maybe one of these days they could be real friends again—after she was married to Michael. She smiled at the thought. As a matter of fact, she'd even be gracious enough to invite Mindy to the wedding. A slow smile slid across her mouth. *Mrs. Michael Blac*. That had a really nice ring to it. And maybe, just maybe, if she worked it right, Michael would be the one thing she cared about that wouldn't be taken from her, too.

Michael had been rehearsing his speech to Terri all morning, but he couldn't seem to get the words right. How could he look her in the eye and tell her that his invitation had been a mistake, a spur-of-the-moment mistake because he was totally consumed by her and couldn't think clearly? What if by some freak twist of fate someone on staff found out? That would be ugly and embarrassing for both of them, and all the hard work that Terri'd put in over the years would become suspect.

Ever since Mindy had come to him with her idea and her alleged inside information, he'd finally allowed himself the possibility to dream that attaining Terri Wells was within reach. Yet he had to be rational, as well. He knew Mindy in a way that many others didn't, so he had to take the silver platter she offered him with quite a few dashes of salt.

He sighed and turned to face the window. All night he'd dreamed of walking along the Florida beaches with Terri, seeing her out of the office element, breaking down those walls that she'd put up around her. He suspected that beneath that cool, in-control and well-put-together exterior was a woman of fire waiting to be unleashed. The throbbing in his pants grew uncomfortable the more he thought about her, visualizing her in his mind's eye.

The quick knock on his door had him drawing in a sharp breath as the vision of Terri slipping out of her business suit under a moonlit sky scampered away to the recesses of his fertile mind.

He glanced at his hardened member. "Down, boy," he murmured and tried to think about trucks as he quickly sat down behind his desk.

"Yes, come in." He flipped open a file and feigned concentration.

Terri peeked her head in. "Sorry to bother you, Michael.

I was wondering if you have a few minutes to go over this budget for the Liberty Wagner campaign."

"Sure. Come in." His hard-on grew in intensity as he watched her long legs cross in front of him before she sat down. He pushed his seat closer to the desk.

"I put all the numbers together and I really believe it to be fair. And we can get all of the things she wanted without breaking the bank." She opened her folder and handed him her spec sheet.

Her lashes are incredibly long, he thought as he took the papers and tried to pay attention to the dancing numbers on the page. He cleared his throat and concentrated harder even as the soft scent of her clouded his head. He ran his finger around the collar of his shirt. It was strangling him. "They must have the heat on full blast today." He chuckled. "They look good." He glanced up at her and she was staring at him. Really staring at him. She blinked rapidly and looked over his shoulder.

"Yeah, it's getting pretty cold out there," Terri said inanely.

"Uh, Terri, about the Florida trip—"

"Oh, yes!" Her eyes lit up. "I've been thinking about some really innovative campaign strategies that would be just perfect for athletes. I've already put some of the ideas down and I'd love to go over them with you, see what you think."

He swallowed and fixed a smile on his face. He didn't have the heart to tell her what he should. "Sounds great. I knew you would be right on top of things." He shifted uncomfortably in his chair as images of her on top of him filled his head.

"I try. I want this to go well for you. You won't be disappointed."

Okay, that was enough. She had to go. "Great. I look forward to seeing you…what you have."

She nodded. "I'll have everything for you by the time we leave."

Terri hesitated for a moment, her chest rising and falling in anticipation of actually being alone with Michael on the beaches of Florida. Then, as if suddenly stirred from a dream, she drew in a short breath and her vision cleared. "Well, I better let you get back to work."

Michael couldn't speak, watching the swell of her breasts reach for him, then teasingly retreat. He was suddenly as thirsty as a desert refugee. And the heat had definitely gone up another notch. Was she breathing like that and licking her lips like that simply to torment him?

"Uh, yes…I better get back to work."

Terri pressed her polished lips together and nodded her head before turning to leave.

"You can leave the door open," Michael said, savoring a few more minutes of watching her walk—from behind.

In the few minutes it took for Terri to get to her office, she was one mess.

This is crazy, she thought, tugging on her thumbnail as she paced in front of her overstacked desk. She'd worked with Michael for years. True, she'd silently lusted after him, but recently… She shook her head in despair. Now it was beginning to interfere with everything she did. When she was anywhere near him, she started to lose focus. And Michael never gave her an inkling that he felt the same way.

She'd spent the better part of her time at Sterns & Blac working so hard, taking on new projects and bringing in new clients to keep her mind off of her life. Work was the healthy substitute for love and family.

But day after day her admiration for Michael slowly morphed into something more. She began to see him as part of her life, something she'd never done before with anyone. She'd never dared. She was afraid of Michael seeing her as a woman, a needy woman. Instead she showed him how well she worked that no challenge was ever too big. The wall of work shielded her from her emotions. If she never became attached, she couldn't lose. Until recently, until Mindy's challenge, the way she'd lived and what she'd believed had been fine. Now, for the first time since she was sixteen, she was afraid of losing again. She couldn't let that happen—at any cost.

Before heading home for the day, she had to make a stop at Pause For Men. She was scheduled to meet with Stephanie Moore to go over the details of the promotion.

She really liked Stephanie, she mused as she battled the rush-hour Manhattan traffic. She had her program totally together. What impressed Terri most was that Stephanie had the confidence to step out on her own, leaving a major corporation behind to do her thing. That was admirable.

Maybe she could do the same thing one day. It would certainly quell her dilemma of working with Michael and not being able to fully pursue him.

She smiled to herself. Tomorrow she would be on a plane to Florida to spend three whole days with Michael. Every time she thought about it, she felt all giddy and girlie inside. It wasn't that she was expecting anything to happen. But it offered the perfect opportunity for her to showcase her womanly wiles outside of the office. If Michael didn't get the hint, then he never would. But if he did…well they'd just have to work it out.

Terri cruised around for a few minutes until she found a parking space, then hurried back to the brownstone where Pause was located.

When she stepped inside, it was as busy as when she'd first visited, if not more so. These women had certainly come up with a brilliant idea.

As she walked to the reception desk she also noticed some new staff faces. Stephanie must have been successful in finding the staff that she needed.

"Hi. I'm Terri Wells. I have an appointment with Stephanie Moore."

"Yes. Good evening and welcome to Pause. I'll have Ms. Moore paged."

The young woman picked up the phone, and seconds later Stephanie's name was announced on the PA system.

"So how long have you been working here?" Terri asked.

The young woman smiled. "Today is my second day."

"How do you like it so far?"

"Everyone is great." She lowered her voice. "And what red-blooded female wouldn't want to work in a place where she can look at gorgeous men all day long?"

Terri grinned. "You have a point there."

"Hey, Terri," Stephanie said, walking up to the front desk. "Sorry if I kept you waiting. I was tying up a few things. We can talk in my office." She turned to the receptionist. "Maya, if any calls come in for me in the next half hour or so, please just take a message."

"Sure thing, Ms. Moore."

"Love that suit," Stephanie said, admiring the trim-looking Vera Wang pantsuit in midnight-blue.

"Thanks."

"So how are you?" Stephanie asked as they went down-stairs to the offices.

"Great! Better than great."

Stephanie opened the office door. "Well, you'll definitely have to tell me what put that extra spark in your eyes." She stepped inside and pointed out the empty chair to Terri. "So where are we?"

Terri sat down and opened her portfolio. She pulled out her notes and gave Stephanie an update on the sponsors that had been secured. "How are you making out with the application?"

"All done." Stephanie swung around in her seat and pulled it up on her computer, hit the print button and handed the copy to Terri.

Terri nodded slowly as she reviewed it. "Looks good." She blew out a breath. "Now that all the major details are in place, we can launch the campaign."

"Absolutely. I'll have Maya be sure to give an application to all of our clients. Our graphic designer, Toni, will be doing the brochure and in-house posters based on the information from you."

"We want to have all the candidates signed up by Thanksgiving."

"Once all the candidates are in, I'll get them to you so that you can make the selection. I want the choice to be totally impartial."

"Works for me." She handed Stephanie the application.

"No, you can keep it for your files."

Terri stuck it in her folder and stood. "This is going to be fabulous. I can feel it."

"I know." Stephanie got up, as well.

"I've really got to run. Heading to Florida in the morning."

"Business or pleasure."

Terri grinned. "Both."

Stephanie's brow rose. "Really?"

"Yes, I'm going with my boss."

"I see." She pressed her lips together, thinking about the right way to broach the subject. "Terri, I realize we don't know each other very well and I may be totally out of line, but…I've been down that road—and it's an ugly trail."

"What are you saying?"

"I'm saying that getting involved with your boss is always bad news."

Terri jerked her chin upward. "It's not like that," she insisted, but she didn't sound convincing.

"Okay," Stephanie conceded. "I'll walk you out." She went to the door and opened it.

"Is that why you left H.L. Reuben?"

Stephanie stopped cold. She stole a look at Terri from over her shoulder. "Yes." She closed the door and faced Terri. She pressed her palms to the back of the door. "I did it for all the wrong reasons. Thought I was in love." She laughed sadly. "The money was great and the perks were even better. But no one in a position of power should ever become involved with a subordinate. Because when it turns ugly…it gets just that—ugly."

Terri lowered her gaze. "He doesn't even look at me like *that*." Her voice had suddenly lost its bounce. "He thinks of me as a dynamo worker with a brilliant mind for spin." She sputtered a laugh. "For a long time I thought that was enough. But lately, at least for me, it's turned into something more. I want more. More than just a pat on the back, a plaque on my wall and a raise. I want him." She looked Stephanie deep in the eyes. "It may never happen. Michael is a stickler for company protocol and he'd never cross that line as long as I was working there."

"Hmm. Maybe *not* working there is your option."

"But until I get him to at least notice me as a woman and not just a worker bee, I can't leave."

"Sounds like you're caught between a rock and a hard place."

"Who you tellin'?"

"All I can say is be careful what you wish for. Think about what you're doing and how what you do will affect your tomorrow."

Terri pushed out a breath. "I will. And thanks."

"For what?"

"For being a real sister and putting another sister in check. I appreciate it."

Stephanie stepped away from the door, then opened it. "Anytime." She walked into the corridor. "And listen, if you ever get it in your head to leave Sterns & Blac, I could definitely use a whiz partner like you."

"Do you mean that?"

"I don't say anything I don't mean. I'm independent now. This project, getting Pause up and operational, has been the first for me under my own banner, and more offers from corporations and individuals are coming in every day from all the media attention we've received. I know I won't be able to handle them all the way I want."

Terri listened, letting Stephanie's words and vision sink in. "It's certainly something to think about. Thanks for the offer. Depending on how things go in Florida, I just may take you up on it."

Stephanie gave her a crooked grin. "Good luck, girl."

Chapter 9

Terri tried three times to put on her mascara, but her hand was shaking so badly there were black joggers running down her right cheek and her left eye was bloodshot from having poked herself in it earlier. She was a mess. What she wanted to do was cry. She was exhausted. If she'd slept an hour during the night, she'd slept a long time.

She had fifteen minutes to get out of the house in order to arrive at the airport the requisite hour early to battle the barrage of security checkpoints.

Bordering on hysteria, she threw water on her face, added cleanser, then took her washcloth and scrubbed off all hints of makeup. She grabbed her bottle of moisturizer and spread some evenly on her face. She peered closer at the mirror. The red splotch in her left eye was growing less angry—nothing that a pair of designer sunglasses couldn't temporarily cure.

She put on some lip gloss and tossed the tube into her makeup bag, then put the bag into her purse. She quickly surveyed her apartment, feeling that she had forgotten something. Never in her life had she been jittery about going on a trip. She traveled so often it was second nature. But this time she felt like a kid on her first flight. She knew the reason. This trip was different. This trip she would be spending with Michael. Should be no big deal. The trouble was, in her mind she saw it as a romantic getaway. But her imagination warred with reality. To Michael, it was business and nothing more. Somehow over the next few days she'd have to reconcile the two.

She heard the car horn of the taxi outside. She took one last look around, grabbed her rolling suitcase, her purse and her trusty laptop and headed out. Whatever happened would happen, she thought as she shut and locked the door behind her. She was determined to make the most of it, even as Stephanie's words of warning echoed in her head.

Michael spotted her the instant she entered the airport terminal. The muscles in his stomach tightened and his heart beat a little faster. She looked great, classy yet casual in jeans, brown suede ankle boots, white turtleneck sweater and brown suede jacket. Her lips, as always, looked lush and so very kissable. And with the dark shades she looked like someone famous trying to avoid the probing eyes of the paparazzi. But no one could miss Terri Wells. Even on a bad day she was stunning to look at.

He'd lost count of how many times he'd picked up the phone to call her and tell her the trip was canceled. But every time he'd reached for the phone an inner voice had told him no. Business sense warred with the man in him. On one hand, there was no doubt that she was ideal for the job at hand. On the other, he had no business being alone with her. Not the way he was feeling about her. And that troubled him. He truly was not certain that he could avoid mixing business with the pleasure that his mind and body craved.

When he saw that she was finished checking in, he made his presence known.

"Hey, there." He came up beside her.

She glanced over her shoulder, and he'd swear her eyes lit up behind the dark glasses.

"Hi! Have you been here long?"

He shrugged. "Only a few minutes. All done?"

She nodded and tucked her e-ticket into the top pocket of her jacket. "Yep. All done."

He took the handle of her luggage. "Right this way."

They headed off toward the winding line that led to the security checkpoint.

"Our first appointment is later on this evening, so we pretty much have the day to relax and go over the pitch."

He was so close behind her she could feel the heat of his breath brush her cheek as he spoke and vibrate through her body. A shiver ran along her spine as a moan slipped from her mouth.

"You say something?"

"Uh, no." Gosh had she really moaned out loud!

"Oh. Thought I heard you say something."

They passed through security without incident and shortly after boarded the plane.

Terri looked at her ticket as she stepped on and for the first time realized that they were traveling first class. *Whoa.*

"I think we're right over here," Michael said, pointing to the two seats in the third row. "You want window or aisle?"

"Window, if you don't mind." She put her carry-on bag in the overhead compartment and sat down.

Michael slid in beside her. Even though there was more room in first class, there was no getting away from how close they sat to each other. His nerves were popping. She smelled too good, almost edible. That thought made his penis jerk in response. He fastened his seat belt and tried to relax and think about trucks and not how soft her right breast felt each time it brushed against his arm. Damn, this was going to be a long, excruciating flight.

Could he feel her trembling? Maybe he'd think it was the vibration of the plane. Oh, God, this was torture. She glanced down and looked at his hand that held the arm of the chair. He had long, slender fingers, hands that could be as strong as they were gentle. She couldn't look. When were they going to turn on a movie or something? She rested her head back and closed her eyes, but that only made the vision come alive. Now that hand wasn't holding the chair arm, it was stroking her. Those long fingers were unbuttoning her blouse, his thumbs brushing across her nipples until she wanted to scream with delight. She gripped the armrest as the plane took off. Then nearly leaped out of her seat when she felt the warmth of Michael's hand cover her own.

"I know you aren't afraid of flying."

Her eyes flew open. She swallowed. "No. Takeoffs and landings are not my favorite things, though."

He patted her hand. "You're safe with me." He smiled at her, his eyes lingering on her face.

She pressed her lips together and nodded, afraid to squeak.

"Sit back and relax. We'll be there in no time."

"Good idea." She breathed in deeply and closed her eyes, willing her runaway imagination to focus on the facts and figures, projects and plans and not—repeat, not—the feel of Michael's hand still resting on hers.

At some point exhaustion kicked in and she must have fallen into a deep sleep. The next thing she knew, she was being gently shaken awake.

"Hmm." She snuggled deeper into her pillow.

"We're here," came a rich voice in her ear.

Her lids fluttered open. When she looked up, Michael was looking down at her. *Down at her?* When she focused, she realized that she'd actually fallen asleep on his chest. *Ohmigod.*

"I didn't have the heart to wake you." He gently lifted strands of hair away from her face.

At least he was smiling, she thought, misery settling in the pit of her stomach. She wiggled her body and sat up. "I am so sorry."

"No need to apologize." He paused a bit and his voice dropped two notes. "It was really quite nice."

Her nipples stood at attention. Her ears must be clogged from the flight—she hadn't heard right.

Michael cleared his throat. "We better get moving before we wind up heading back to New York."

She laughed nervously and fumbled with unfastening her seat belt. "You're right." She looked around quickly. They were the last ones on the plane. *Ohmigod.*

They took a car service to the hotel, and all Terri wanted to do was get in her room and recoup. She couldn't begin to imagine what Michael must be thinking and wasn't sure if she wanted to know.

Once they were checked in and on the way to their rooms, Michael said, "It's still early. So why don't you rest or do whatever and let's say we meet down in the hotel lobby at one-thirty for lunch?"

"Sure. Sounds fine."

They stepped off the elevator. "We're right down this hallway." Michael led the way, then stopped in front of her door. "I'm right across the hall if you need me."

You have no idea. "Great. I think I'm just going to unpack and review the proposal."

"And I think I'm going for a swim." He grinned. "See you later."

He turned and pulled his luggage to the room directly opposite hers. She quickly turned around and stuck her card key in the slot. The green light flashed and the door popped open. She ducked inside, not even wanting to give herself a millisecond to imagine him in swimming trunks.

She'd felt so good resting against me, Michael thought as he unpacked his clothes. It had taken all of his self-control not to wrap his arms around her and draw her closer. He hung up his shirts and glanced down. Before he took his swim, he needed a cold shower. He undressed, tossing his discarded clothes on the bed, and took a long, cool shower.

Terri decided that the best thing she could do was stay in her room, get her head together so that she would be able to put on a good show for the owners of the Orlando Magic. She was just stepping out of her boots when the phone rang.

Frowning, she hop-stepped across the room with one boot on and one off. Who in the world could that be already? Probably the front desk. She picked up the phone on the third ring.

"Hello?"

"Hi. Listen, I was thinking, why don't we hang out at the pool for a while? We can have a lunch there, kick back and relax and go over the pitch. That is, if you're not too tired."

"Uh, sure. If you want. That's not a problem. I just need to change."

"Great. I'll meet you down there in, say…a half hour?"

"Sure."

The phone disconnected.

Terri plopped down on the bed, then fell back across it spread-eagle.

"Damn, damn, damn."

* * *

Michael stood in the middle of his room with the phone still in his hand. What in the world had he done that for? The last image he needed burned into his brain was Terri Wells in a swimsuit.

"Damn, damn, damn."

Chapter 10

At least she'd remembered to shave her nether parts, she mused as she put on her two-piece suit. Last summer she'd seen a beautiful orange floral-print sheer duster that went perfectly with her solid orange swimsuit and she had to have it. Last year she'd never gotten a chance to wear it, but she was overjoyed that she'd have the chance now.

She slipped the weightless duster over her suit, stepped into her white sandals with the orange bow and grabbed her sunglasses.

It's only an impromptu meeting for lunch at the pool with my boss, she chanted while waiting for the elevator. Nothing more, nothing less.

The elevator doors opened on the lobby level and she followed the signs leading to the outdoor pool. As she swished down the winding hallways, she caught the attention of several of the male guests along the way. The appreciative looks and innuendo-laced comments like, "The afternoon is certainly looking good," made her only wish that Michael would feel the same way.

She stepped out into the hot Florida sun and wished she'd remembered to bring her floppy straw hat. Her sunglasses would have to suffice. She put them on.

Terri looked around at all the bodies in various stages of repose, some stretched out on deck chairs and others jumping into or swimming in the cool water.

She saw him the instant he emerged from the water. Her entire body grew hot. He was gorgeous. There was no other word for it. And as he crossed the deck with water dripping off his chiseled frame, the women he passed thought the same thing. He grabbed a towel from one of the striped chairs and ran it over his face and head. Then, as if he sensed her presence, he looked in her direction. *Thank goodness for dark glasses.*

Better than I'd imagined, he thought when he saw her standing there. She was incredible to look at, and if she thought for a moment that the little robe thing she had on hid what lay beneath, she was mistaken. If anything, the see-through wrap only magnified her assets, made them more desirable. He quickly took the towel from around his shoulders and wrapped it around his waist.

"Hey, you made it."

"Yeah. Uh, pretty crowded out here."

"Florida is the fun-in-the-sun capital." He chuckled. "Come on, I reserved us two lounge chairs under an umbrella."

Terri followed him to the other side of the expansive deck, alternately watching his calf muscles and his broad back.

"Here we go."

Terri gingerly sat down on the edge of the deck chair.

"Hey, stretch out, relax, this is the vacation part of the trip. We'll have plenty of time to work later today and tomorrow."

She angled her body and lifted her legs up onto the chair, then eased back. Her wrap fell open, fully exposing her goods all the way up to her bikini top, where the robe was held in place by a delicate bow.

Michael's mouth dropped open. The texture of her skin looked like silk, and he was pretty sure it felt like it, too. Her legs were long, honey-brown and shapely. The tiny bottoms that she wore should be illegal. He averted his gaze before he did or said something totally inappropriate.

He cleared his throat and reached for his sunglasses. "Uh, would you like something to drink to cool off?"

"Some iced tea would be great." What she really needed was a cocktail but she couldn't risk her head getting any more cloudy than it already was.

Michael signaled for a passing waitress and ordered two iced teas and requested the lunch menu.

"I've stayed here before," he said once the waitress was gone. "The food is really good. I'm sure you'll like it."

"I'm really easy to please." *Ooh, that had not come out right.* "What I mean is, I'm not picky when it comes to food. I like pretty much anything."

He grinned. "Yeah, me, too. Do you eat out a lot?"

"Only for business. I actually like to cook."

"Do you? That's refreshing. Most of the women I've run across—especially women in the corporate world—would rather eat out. Or should I say, be taken out to eat."

"I guess it comes from having to take care of myself for so long. I had to have a bookcase put into my kitchen to hold all of my cookbooks." She laughed.

Michael chuckled. "Now that is impressive. What's your favorite dish?"

She pressed her lips together, thoughtful for a moment. "I really like Thai food. I make a dynamite duck with stir-fried vegetables over spicy rice." She smiled proudly.

"You're making me hungry." His eyes, shielded by his sunglasses, rolled leisurely up and down her legs.

The waitress returned with their drinks. "Are you ready to order?"

Michael turned to Terri.

"I'll have the grilled chicken with a side salad."

"And you, sir?"

"I'll have the same."

The waitress took the menus. "It should only be a few minutes."

"Want to go for a swim while we wait on the food? It's never good to swim on a full stomach."

"Okay." She stood with her back to Michael and untied her wrap, dropping it onto the chair. She reached up and tucked her hair into a knot on top of her head, then turned to him. "Ready when you are."

For a second too long he stared at her. He swallowed over the knot in his throat. She was exquisite. "Uh, okay, let's go."

He undid the towel wrapped around his waist and practically ran toward the cool water, praying that it would temper the heat that was building.

They frolicked in the water like children, laughing and splashing each other and even having a mock race that Michael let Terri win.

"The waitress just brought our lunch," Michael sputtered, wiping water from his face as he held on to the side of the pool, bobbing in the water.

"You let me win," she puffed, shaking water from her hair.

He pushed up onto the deck and looked down at her glistening face. "I would never do that." He winked and stretched out a hand to help her out.

She took his hand, and both of their eyes widened in momentary shock. He gripped her palm and pulled her from the water with ease. She was nearly flush up against him when she emerged. Her breath expelled hard and fast, her chest rising and falling, brushing tantalizingly against his.

"Uh, we should get some towels and dry off," he muttered, but he was unwilling to move.

Terri nodded numbly.

A passerby bumped into Michael, and the movement disconnected them.

They tried to look everywhere but at each other as they made their way back to their chairs and settled down to eat.

Terri could have been eating straw for all she knew. She chewed and swallowed by rote. When he'd touched her and pulled her to him, their bodies almost naked, she'd thought she would lose her natural mind. Her whole body was vibrating from something as simple as that. She couldn't even imagine what the real thing would be like.

This was not good, Michael thought as he methodically chewed on a piece of chicken. Terri was an employee, and no matter what Mindy may have said, it was unethical for him to cross the line. She'd been nothing but professional, and here he was thinking constantly about seeing her totally naked...and more.

"What time is our meeting tonight?" Terri asked, breaking into his erotic thoughts.

"Seven-thirty. I've made reservations in the hotel restaurant."

Terri pushed the rest of her food aside. "Well, I think I'll go back to my room, go over the pitch and take a nap. I'll meet you at the restaurant later."

Michael watched her get up. He stood. "Why don't we meet about fifteen minutes earlier to go over our strategy?"

"Sure." She fastened her duster. "Thanks for lunch. I'll see you later." She hurried away.

Once inside the security of her room, Terri broke down and wept. Everything she'd gone after, she'd succeeded in obtaining—material possessions, recognition for her work. It had been enough. Until now. What she wanted most was within reach but forbidden, and the fear of wanting and then losing what she desperately desired was more than she could handle.

For so long she'd kept emotions and connections to people at bay, building up an invisible wall that she allowed no one to cross. It had been safe that way. If she kept her feelings in check and didn't allow herself to care or feel, she would never experience the pain of loss ever again.

She was afraid. There was no way to put a positive spin on that. She was scared. Scared that she'd somehow allowed feelings to creep under her skin and awaken that need that she'd sworn she buried a long time ago. She needed more than material things, a fat bank account and pats on the back for a job well done. She needed to be loved. And that petrified the hell out of her.

What was worse—now that she'd finally allowed herself to admit that she had needs, the one thing she needed was off-limits.

Chapter 11

Terri dressed meticulously for the dinner meeting. This was her element. This was something she could deal with. She stood in front of the full-length mirror that hung on the back of the bathroom door.

She'd chosen an off-white Chanel suit with three gold buttons down the front of the cropped, high-collared jacket. The wide-legged pants hugged her at the waist, then cascaded downward to flow like an ankle-length skirt. Her accessories were simple: gold studs in her ears and two gold bangles on her left wrist. Satisfied, she went into the bedroom and put on her slingback shoes in the same color as the suit. She checked the time on the nightstand clock: seven-ten.

She went over her notes one last time and checked to make sure she had enough copies, slipped them into a plain manila folder, grabbed her clutch purse and headed out.

Michael was waiting for her in the lobby when she emerged from the elevator. He couldn't help but stare. First the swimsuit and now this.

"Hope I didn't keep you waiting," she said, sounding very formal.

Michael straightened, put on his business face. "Not at all. I just got here myself. Let's go inside and get our table."

They'd barely been seated when their dinner guests arrived. Michael stood and extended his hand.

"Mr. Long, Mr. Peterson. This is my associate, Terri Wells. She'll be doing the presentation."

Terri reached out her hand and shook both of theirs.

The men sat down.

"We're really excited to hear what you have to say," Peterson began.

"I'm sure you will be impressed," Terri said with confidence. "Why don't we order and we can discuss the proposal while we eat."

As Terri laid out her strategy, the men nodded continuously in agreement, periodically punctuating her ideas with "excellent," "I like it," "perfect."

Michael sat back and relaxed, watching her do her thing with more and more growing admiration.

"My thought is, why break a mold that already works? The Mets have been doing it for years, setting up events to read to kids in a variety of venues. But the added attraction of this program will be that the kids will be part of the training camps and the reading will be incorporated into the program."

Peterson sat back, wiped his mouth with his linen napkin, then placed it atop his empty plate. "I think your idea is perfect." He turned to Long, who nodded his head in agreement. "Of course, we'll take this back to the board for final approval, but I don't see that there will be any problem."

"Once approved, how long will it take to implement?" Long asked.

"We can get started the minute you all are ready," Michael said.

"Very good. We hate to eat and run, but there were some last-minute plans and we have a plane to catch." Peterson stood. He looked down at Terri. "Thank you for all of your hard work, Ms. Wells."

"It was my pleasure."

Peterson turned to Michael. "You'll hear from me sometime next week."

Michael stood and shook the men's hands. "I look forward to it."

Once they were gone, he sat back down and turned a spotlight smile on Terri. "That was pitch-perfect. I know it's in the bag."

Terri grinned. "Glad you approve. I think it's a great plan."

"So do they. Now it's only a matter of signing on the dotted line. I knew I'd made the right decision when I asked you to do this. You're the best in the game, Terri."

"Thank you very much. That means a great deal to me."

"I think this calls for a toast." He signaled for the waitress, and when she arrived, he ordered a bottle of their best champagne.

"To continued success," Michael said, raising his glass.

Terri touched her glass to his. "To success and all the things one deserves."

Michael looked at her over the rim of his glass as he brought it to his lips.

They sat in the restaurant for nearly an hour talking about everything under the sun and getting slowly light-headed from the champagne. Michael lifted the bottle to refill Terri's glass and it was empty.

"Wow, we actually knocked off a full bottle of champagne."

Terri chuckled. Her head felt foggy but her spirit felt light. "That we did," she was able to say. Michael was looking more tempting by the minute, so the best thing to do was to excuse herself, celebrate her victory in her room and sleep off the alcohol. "I think I'm going to go to my room." She started to get up, and Michael hurried around to her side to help her up.

His arm was on her waist. His breath blew against her ear. She sighed softly. It felt so good. Her eyes almost closed as the need to snuggle against him rose at an alarming rate.

"I'll walk you to your room," he said, his tone suddenly hot and husky.

Terri looked into his eyes. "Thank you," she whispered.

They stood in front of her hotel room. She fumbled in her bag for her access key. He was so close she couldn't think. She held her breath.

"Here, let me get that for you." He took the card from her

hand and slid it into the slot. The green light popped and the lock disengaged.

Terri pushed the door.

"Terri…"

The heat of his body was all over her. She dared to look at him, and when she did, he leaned in and kissed her.

Her heart slammed against her chest as she drew in a sharp breath. His arms wrapped around her waist and pulled her to him. He kissed her desperately, like a man dying of thirst.

This can't be happening, she thought as she felt his tongue enter her mouth. Her body trembled as she gave as good as she got.

She stepped backward into her room, taking him with her. He shut the door.

The room was dim, the furnishings silhouetted by the light shining in from the moon that hung in a cloudless sky.

"I want you," he said against her mouth. He brushed her hair away from the sides of her face.

Terri stepped out of his embrace and slowly began unbuttoning her jacket in answer to his unspoken request.

Michael ran his tongue across his lips, relishing the taste of her on his mouth as he watched beauty unfold in front of him.

Terri let her jacket fall from her shoulders to the floor. She reached for the single button on her slacks. Michael reached out and stopped her.

"Let me." He unfastened the button and unzipped her pants, then pushed them down over her hips. He took a step back in order to gaze at her.

She drew in a breath, hoping that he liked what he saw.

"I knew you would be beautiful," he whispered.

She stepped out of her pants, came forward and kissed him lightly on the lips as she worked the buttons of his shirt. "Let me," she said in a smoky whisper and slowly undressed him.

Michael reached around her and unsnapped her bra, slid the straps from her shoulders, his fingers like blades of fire as they trailed down her arms. Her head spun and her heart pounded when he lowered his head and placed hot, delicate kisses along the rise of her breasts before taking one, then the other nipple into his mouth.

Terri gasped, clasping his head in her hand to draw him closer. Her legs grew weak as Michael sucked and teased, groaning with need. He hooked his thumbs in the band of her panties and pushed them downward, then cupped her in the palm of his hand, the juice from her rising excitement dampening his palm.

This is crazy, he thought as his fingers found their way inside her. It shouldn't be happening, he reasoned even as his fingers moved in and out of her in a steady, sensual rhythm. *So wrong but so right, so wrong but so right*, his mind chanted. But he couldn't stop. He didn't want to. What he wanted was more. He wanted all of her. He wanted to feel her wet heat wrapped around him, sucking him in. That's what he wanted, and he knew he would never be satisfied if he didn't have it, couldn't feel it—no matter what tomorrow may bring.

In a tangle of limbs and unleashed desire they clamored onto the bed, kissing, touching, moaning, feeling. He was on top of her now, her legs spread wide on either side of him, her wetness beckoning him.

Michael snatched a pillow from the top of the bed and pushed it beneath her hips. He shoved his hands beneath the pillow to raise her higher, then pushed himself deep inside her.

Terri cried out in surprise and delight as he filled her all at once. The surreal feel of Michael inside her was an indescribable sensation. He was so hard she was sure that if she moved the wrong way, he'd break. But she wanted to move, she wanted to feel him move inside her—slow, faster, hard, soft, more, more, more. She clung to him, afraid that if she let go even for an instant, this incredible feeling he'd created would cease.

But Michael took his time. He wanted this to last until neither of them could stand it anymore. The fit was perfect. Our bodies were made for each other, he thought as she rotated her pelvis, meeting him thrust for thrust. If he died right at this moment, he'd know that he'd found heaven inside of Terri.

Then she did something that had him calling God. She was working her muscles to grip and free him each time he pushed inside her. He'd heard some women could do it, but he'd never experienced it until now. It was driving him mad, and he felt the surge for release begin to burn from the bottom of his feet, move up his legs, settle in the pit of his stomach for an instant before he splashed inside her with such force white light shot before his eyes.

His building climax set hers off. Her entire body shuddered as if electrified. Her mouth opened to scream, but no words, no sound could substitute for the blinding sensations that ran like supercharged currents through her veins.

Michael licked her neck, nibbled her ears and kneaded her breasts while whispering, "Let go. Come to me. Give it to me."

Her body was no longer her own. Her head pounded. Her heart raced. And she came with a power so forceful all she'd become was pure sensation. She gave in to it, letting it consume her, like fire set to kindling.

They held each other, their bodies still moving and grinding, holding on to the last vestiges of delight until they were drained.

Michael reluctantly slid out of her and rested his head on the cushion of her breasts. Neither of them spoke. Each was caught up in the vortex of what had just transpired and the reality of the line they had crossed.

Chapter 12

Terri's eyes fluttered open. She felt damp and sticky. She pressed her hands between her thighs and sighed softly. A slow smile tilted the corners of her mouth. Then she frowned and sat up in the bed. She looked around the darkened room, pulling the twisted sheet up to her chin. She was alone.

Her breathing escalated. *Michael.* She'd slept with her boss. It wasn't a dream, it was real. But now the nightmare began.

"Oh, God. What have I done?" He must think I'm a real slut. Just get me drunk, screw me and leave. How can I face him again, especially knowing that he didn't even care enough to hang around until the sun came up? "Damn, damn, damn! Fool, you stupid fool."

She wrapped herself up in the sheet that still held his scent, buried her head in the overstuffed pillow and wept.

* * *

It was easier this way, Michael rationalized as he sat in the airport waiting for the first flight out. With him gone, they wouldn't have to pretend, go through all those awkward moments and try to act as if nothing had happened. They'd have a little space, time to cool down and think before they had to see each other again at work on Monday.

Maybe he was being a coward by walking out and leaving a note. But he knew if he stayed a moment longer, he would have made love to her again and again, compounding an already ugly situation. There was no way he could fire her now without the possibility of a lawsuit. And he certainly didn't want her leaving because of what had happened and ultimately jeopardize the deals she'd brokered that were still in the works.

Be for real, man, he thought as he heard his flight being called. You don't want her to leave because you don't want her to leave, plain and simple.

Whatever doubts he may have had about his feelings for Terri were no longer doubts. He was in love with her. And in their situation, that was no good for either of them.

Terri had never felt so defeated, so humiliated in all her life. Even with all the losses and heartaches she'd endured, nothing could compare to this.

As she walked down the corridor to her office, she kept her eyes straight ahead. She felt as if everyone knew, everyone could see straight through her facade of cool control.

The words in Michael's "Dear Jane" note burned in her

head. *Sorry I had to leave. Didn't want to disturb you. Something came up and I had to get back to New York. Stay and enjoy the rest of your weekend. Everything is taken care of. Great job on the Orlando deal. Michael.*

Not a word about what had happened between them, nothing incriminating. That riled her even more. Not only was he going to act as if nothing of importance had happened, he wasn't going to make even the slightest reference to it in writing.

She'd been laid and paid, simple as that. She blinked away the tears that threatened to ruin her makeup as she opened her office door. She was a big girl. She'd handle it. Loss was her specialty anyway. She'd simply do what she'd always done—bury herself in her work. At least she was assured of success.

For the better part of the morning Terri stayed holed up in her office, not even venturing to the employee lounge for a cup of coffee. She made a series of phone calls to all of her sponsors for the spa and got the confirmations she needed. She spoke briefly with Stephanie to confirm that the applications were getting into the hands of the clients and was advised that the response had been overwhelming. Stephanie would be sending over the first batch via FedEx to arrive at Terri's office first thing the next morning.

"Is everything okay?" Stephanie asked once they'd ended the business portion of the conversation.

"Sure. Everything is great. Why?"

"Hmm, you don't sound like yourself."

"Probably the connection," she said a bit more harshly than necessary. "And I'm just really swamped today."

She heard Stephanie breathe heavily into the phone.

"Okay. Just checking." She paused a beat. "Listen, if you ever want to talk…"

"Thanks. But it's all good. Have a great day."

She hung up before she burst into tears and spilled her guts about her sordid encounter with her boss.

Pulling herself together, she moved on to Liberty Wagner, who'd left a bevy of "urgent" messages over the weekend. After soothing the diva and assuring her that the press materials were being put together, that Terri was working closely with her recording company and the release party was going to be a megasuccess, that the invitations were being printed and everything was going to be fine, she was finally able to hang up and catch her breath.

When she looked up it was nearly one o'clock. Most of the staff would be out to lunch. Maybe she could sneak out for a minute and grab something to eat. She was starving.

Like a thief in the night, she crept out of her office with her coat draped over her arm and made a beeline for the elevator.

When the doors opened, Mindy and Michael stepped off. Her muscles froze and for a moment she couldn't react. Her gaze shot to Michael's, but she couldn't read his innocuous expression.

"There you are." Mindy beamed, showing all her teeth. "Haven't seen you all day."

"I've been busy."

"So have I. We were just discussing the challenge."

"I'm planning on making my announcement in the morning."

"So soon?" Terri asked, fighting to hold herself together.

"To be honest, the entries this year weren't as high as last and the content of many of them was not of the caliber that I'm looking for."

Terri licked her suddenly dry lips. "I see. Well, I'm going to lunch and I have an appointment outside of the office, so I won't be back for the rest of the day," she added. She looked from one to the other, then stepped onto the elevator before the doors closed. She turned to face front, and Mindy finger-waved a goodbye while Michael continued down the hall without so much as a backward glance.

She forced a tight-lipped smile as the doors swished closed.

Terri wandered up and down the streets of Manhattan, her appetite all but gone. She didn't have an appointment, but it sounded good at the time and gave her an excuse for not having to run into Michael—or Mindy, for that matter—at least for the time being. Tomorrow was a different story, however. She couldn't keep hiding in her office indefinitely.

Stephanie was right, she thought. Starting up an affair with your boss, even an abbreviated one, was bad news. No good could ever come of it. Absolutely none.

She hailed a cab and gave directions to her apartment. Maybe she'd wake up tomorrow and this would have all been a terrible dream.

* * *

Michael stood on his terrace in nothing more than his shirtsleeves, even as the chilly November wind whipped around him. His hands gripped the ice-cold railing as he gazed out onto the twinkling lights of the city.

He couldn't get the look in Terri's eyes out of his head when she'd faced him at the elevator. There had been such pain and disappointment. The fire that was always there seemed to have been snuffed out, and he was sure it was his fault.

Never in a million years should he have gone to bed with her, no matter what his body had been saying. Good sense should have won out. He should have walked away when that door opened.

That night in the hotel had not been part of the plan. He should never have listened to Mindy. Her confession had opened the door to a room that should have remained shut. It had given him the opening that he'd kept tucked away, that thing he didn't want to think about, didn't want to indulge—Terri Wells.

Maybe by some miracle, if he hadn't alienated Terri entirely, it would work out. Somehow.

Snow began to trickle down from the sky. Michael looked up to the heavens, turned and went inside.

Josh knocked on Terri's office door about ten o'clock the following morning.

"Come in," she said with great reluctance.

"Hey, staff meeting in the conference room," he said, sticking his head in the door.

Terri nodded. "Thanks. I'm on my way."

"Ready to walk away with the prize again this year?"

She sighed and pushed back from her seat. She looked around her desk and picked up her notepad. "It really doesn't matter, Josh."

"Doesn't sound like you. You're the one whose coattails everyone wants to grab on to." He chuckled.

Terri didn't comment but walked toward the door, keeping her gaze averted. She wanted to get this over with. She walked past Josh. "See you inside."

When she walked into the conference room and took a seat at the end of the long table, Michael had yet to make his appearance. Fortunately, from where she was sitting, he wouldn't easily be able to look her straight in the face and she could ignore him totally.

She concentrated on jotting down useless notes on her pad as the room slowly began to fill. Mindy came in, rounded the table and sat directly opposite Terri.

Michael walked in looking sharp and in charge as always. Terri's stomach fluttered as she surreptitiously watched him take his place at the head of the table. He cleared his throat. The room quieted.

"Good morning, everyone. The past few weeks have been challenging. Although I didn't get the volume of entries that I anticipated, some of the ones that I did receive were stellar." He glanced around the room, letting his gaze drop on each of the seated staff members. It lingered for an instant longer on Terri before moving away. "The decision of selecting a winner this year was extremely difficult. And I am pleased to say that this year is an absolute first for the five years that the challenge has been in effect."

Murmurs and looks all around the room.

Michael reached for the remote, dimmed the lights and turned on the projection equipment. For the next few minutes the staff was treated to a PowerPoint presentation of the ten entries that ranged from athletic competitions to public service announcements to the Everyday Man campaign of Mindy's to Terri's spa project.

It was the first time that Terri had an inkling as to what Mindy had put together. She had to admit it was fun, sexy and quite ingenious. It was a yearly calendar campaign. Each month featured a different everyday, eligible bachelor with a short blurb on what he did for a living, vital statistics and what he was looking for in a woman. Terri could already see the phenomenal sales on the calendar.

The presentation came to an end and the room filled with sincere applause.

Michael looked downward for a moment, pursed his lips, then looked up. He clasped his hands in front of him. Terri's mind sprinted to how those hands had felt on her body, the places his fingers had been. She felt as if she was choking—and nearly did when Michael made the announcement.

"This year, for the very first time, we have not one winner but two."

Mindy's eyes widened.

"The winners are...Mindy Clarke and Terri Wells."

The news got worse for Terri from there.

Michael held up his hands to quiet the applause. "In light of having two winners, the all-expense-paid trip to Rio for two will go to the two of you." He looked from one winner to the other.

Mindy was delighted. Terri looked ill.

"Congratulations, winners. And, as always, all of the entries are deserving of recognition and there will be an extra holiday bonus included with your check." He took a breath. "That's it, folks. Thanks as always for your hard work. Have a productive day."

Everyone started to leave, passing Mindy and Terri to share their congratulations.

"Wow, Terri, how does it feel to share the glory?" Josh whispered in her ear.

"It's a great project," she said, tucking her notepad beneath her arm.

"Mindy, Terri, can I see you both in my office?" Michael called out.

Terri gritted her teeth. "Sure," she murmured. "Gotta go," she said to Josh.

This was probably the best thing, Terri thought as she took the hesitant walk to Michael's office. At least she didn't have to worry about asking Michael to join her and be told she was crazy. It was a stupid idea to begin with. What was most surprising in all this was that Mindy had actually won. She'd obviously underestimated Mindy all this time. Maybe she was losing her edge. Maybe it was time to move on.

She knocked lightly on Michael's partially opened door. "Come on in."

Terri stepped inside. Mindy was already seated. She looked over her shoulder and up at Terri. Her smile was tentative.

Terri lifted her chin and took a seat next to Mindy in front of Michael's desk.

"Ladies, congratulations to you both. You presented outstanding campaigns and I'm excited about both of these projects." He opened a leather folder and extracted two packets, handing one to each of them.

"Inside are your airline tickets, hotel information and an American Express card with two thousand dollars available to you for expenses."

"Thank you so much, Mr. Blac," Mindy enthused.

"You're quite welcome. Your campaign is clever and has unlimited potential." He turned to Terri. "As is yours." He sat back and cleared his throat. "I know that the two of you are friends both inside and outside the office, so I'm sure this will be a good experience for both of you."

Mindy reached over and touched Terri's cold hand. "I think so, too." She tried to get Terri to make eye contact, but she wouldn't. She seemed to be staring at someplace beyond Michael's shoulder.

Michael drew in a long breath and exhaled slowly. "Well…" He slapped his palms against the table. "Congratulations again. You'll each get an intern to assist you in any way necessary to get your projects launched. Time, as you know, is of the essence. We want to make the official media announcements at the end of the week, with a kickoff the week before Christmas. That's coming up fast."

Terri knew the drill. She'd been down this road before. But she felt so hollow and dirty inside. All of her usual enthusiasm was missing.

Terri stood and took her packet. "Thank you, Michael…for everything. I think I'll get back to work." She turned to Mindy. "Congratulations," she said quietly.

"One more thing," he said before she walked out. "I'll be on vacation beginning today. I'll be back after the first of the year. However, I'm always available by phone or e-mail if needed."

"I'm sure that won't be necessary," Terri said, her words as cold as the air outside.

Nothing in Michael's controlled demeanor changed save for the momentary tightening of his eyes as if he'd been stung by surprise.

Terri straightened her shoulders and walked out, shutting the door firmly behind her.

As she made her way back to her office, she knew that she could no longer stay with Sterns & Blac. There was no way that she could continue to face Michael day after day, knowing what happened between them, knowing how she felt about him and how he *didn't* feel about her.

All of her projects were in place, the wheels were in motion. She could easily train an intern to pick up any loose pieces. Her major work had been done.

She sat down at her desk and began to write her letter of resignation.

The you-have-mail icon flashed on her computer screen. She slid her chair closer to her screen and clicked on the icon.

From: mblac@sternsblac.com
To: twells@sternsblac.com
Terri, I failed to mention that since I will be leaving until after the new year, I am leaving you fully in charge of handling the Orlando deal. After all, it was your idea that got us in. I am forwarding all of your contact information to our new partners. They were totally impressed with you…as am I. I know they will be more than happy to work with you. Again, thank you for the incredible work you've done. Enjoy your trip. You deserve it.
Michael.

Terri tilted her head back and squeezed her eyes shut. When she opened them and looked down at the pad in front of her, the words blurred on the yellow page. She snatched up the sheet of paper, balled it up in her fist and tossed it in the wastebasket.

Chapter 13

The following weeks were a whirlwind of activity. Terri was busy nearly twelve hours per day, which was fine with her. By the time she dragged herself to her apartment, she was too tired to think or feel. The trip to Rio was looking better each day.

She opted to skip the office holiday party, as she did every year, and spent it instead in her apartment. She sat in her lounge chair on Christmas Eve, sipping on a glass of white wine as snow fell in white waves from the heavens.

All around her she could hear the sounds of children's laughter, Christmas carols and jingle bells. Friends and families gathered to share the joy of the season. Tears slipped from her eyes.

Terri arrived at JFK Airport on the morning of December thirty-first more eager than ever to get away, clear her head and figure out what she was going to do with the rest of her life. She looked around the airport terminal decorated with red-and-green garland with holiday music playing intermittently over the speaker system. She didn't see Mindy among the crowd of holiday travelers. They hadn't spoken since the day of the announcement, so she had no idea what flight Mindy was on. Maybe she'd finally chased away her one friend, as well. Funny thing was, after all that had transpired and all the energy she'd put into building her career, being the best, winning at all cost, she would trade it all in to have her friend back.

Her flight was called and she headed through security. In a few hours she'd be in sunny Rio and for five days she could put this all behind her.

Terri arrived at the hotel in Rio and was taken to her suite. It was absolutely fabulous. It looked out onto the beach for miles. She could see beachgoers already partying below. Fireworks lit up the twilight sky.

She grinned, starting to feel better. Tonight she would join a bunch of strangers and bring in the new year on the sandy beaches of Rio. No one knew her, no one knew what was in her head and in her heart. She could simply blend in and pretend to be happy. She unpacked her bags and picked out an outfit.

When she came down to the lobby several hours later, partying was in full effect. Champagne and mixed drinks flowed like the ocean. The lobby sparkled from the chandeliers that looked like stars that had descended from the heavens. Everyone was smiling, laughing, embracing each other and total strangers. She had yet to see Mindy.

She walked through the lobby into the hotel restaurant and peeked inside. It was packed, with nearly every table filled. The dance floor vibrated to the beat of the music from the live band. Colored lights flashed from the ceiling, making the revelers look surreal. Terri rocked to the music as she stood in the doorway.

"I knew you could move, but not like that."

She drew in a sharp breath that stuck in her chest. Slowly she turned around. Michael was standing in front of her.

"Hi," he whispered, his eyes trailing slowly over her, setting fires everywhere they landed.

"Wh-what are you doing here?"

"It was Mindy's idea." He cocked his head over his shoulder. Mindy peeked her head out from behind Michael.

Mindy stepped up to Terri and took her hands. "For as long as I've known you, the hardest thing you've worked on is keeping yourself from caring. When I started getting inklings that you had feelings for my cousin Mike…"

"Your cousin!"

"Distant, very distant," Michael chimed in. "Through marriage, not blood."

"Anyway, I went to Michael and I told him…how you felt."

"What!" She wanted to sink through the floor.

"And that's when I decided to enter the competition. I wanted you to see that work isn't everything, that there are people who care about you and that it's okay to care back.

I wanted to see what you valued more. We've both been looking for the same thing, Terri. You wanted to be able to love again and not be afraid, and I wanted a friend. If your mighty throne was pulled out from under you, then maybe you'd see what was really important—love and friendship."

"What's even more important," Michael said, stepping closer, "is that when Mindy came to me and told me that she was planning to enter and her belief of how you felt about me…well, that opened the door that I'd kept shut since the day you walked into my office to interview for the job." He paused and looked deep into her eyes. "That night in Florida…it wasn't a mistake. It was the best night of my life."

"Night in Florida?" Mindy squawked. "You mean you two…already!"

Michael winked at Mindy over his shoulder. "Can I have a little privacy, cuz?"

Mindy pouted but stepped to the side.

"I've been struggling for the longest time on how I could justifiably fire you."

Terri's eyes widened. "Fire me? Why?"

"I didn't want anyone to know how I felt about you. And I certainly couldn't break my own cardinal rule by dating my employee. Then, after Florida, I knew if I fired you…well you'd really get the wrong idea, and I'd never have a chance with you."

"How *do* you feel about me?" she asked, holding her breath.

"I'm in love with you," he said without hesitation. "And to answer your unasked question, no, you didn't skyrocket up the corporate ladder because of my feelings. You're damned good at what you do. Don't ever doubt that."

Her heart banged again and again in her chest. A smile as brilliant as the fireworks that exploded outside bloomed across her face. She stepped up to him, wrapped her arms around his neck and kissed him, long, hard and slow.

As they stood there locked in each other's embrace, the buildup to the countdown for the New Year began.

Five, four, three, two, one!

"Happy New Year" was screamed, bellowed and shouted. Confetti and balloons fell from the ceiling. The band played a calypso version of "Auld Lang Syne" while revelers kissed, hugged, danced and made merry.

"Happy New Year, baby," Michael whispered against her mouth.

Terri opened her eyes and stroked his cheek. She glanced over, and Mindy was smiling and crying.

"Can I get some love?" she whined.

"Come here, girl." Terri stretched out her hand, drawing Mindy to her. "Thank you," she whispered.

"That's what friends are for."

"How 'bout we go party and bring in the new year right?" Michael said, looking from Terri to Mindy. "I think we have some real celebrating to do."

"Lead the way," Terri said, giddy with happiness.

He crooked his arms, and each woman took a side. They walked onto the beach and joined the party.

What more could I possibly want? she thought as she danced with Michael on the beach. She had a man who loved her, a true friend at her side and—little did Michael know—a dream job working with Stephanie when she got back to the States. Yeah, the new year and her future were looking real good. And the best thing was, she wasn't afraid to face it.

MERRY CHRISTMAS, BABY

Monica Jackson

Her First

"They said they were sending out a new physical therapist today," my mother said.

I looked across the kitchen table at Mama sitting in her wheelchair. "What happened to Melissa?"

"She broke her fool leg skiing." Mama rolled her eyes.

"That's too bad. I know she's going to hate being off her feet. She's so active."

"Humph. Silly heifer strapped sticks of wood to her feet to slide down a mountain in ice-cold snow, and for what?"

I hid my smile behind my cup of coffee. Mama was working herself up to rare form this morning.

"For what, girl?"

"I don't know, Mama."

"To climb back *up* the cold-ass, snowy mountain and slide

down it again. It's insane, I tell you. Back in the day, black folk had more sense."

"Times change."

"And not for the better," Mama grumbled. "Lord knows what sort of fool I'm going to get up in here to replace Melissa."

"I'm sure whoever they send will be fine." At least I hope they'll be fine once Mama gets done with them.

Mama had been staying with me ever since she'd had her stroke. I wished Mama would have sold the house in Eskridge and come to Atlanta sooner. But Mom was stubborn.

Damned if I live off my children. Besides, y'all get on my last nerve, she'd say.

Mama was a mess. Like she thought she didn't get on my last nerve, too.

"What day are you off work this week?"

"I'm off next Friday."

"I can never tell when you're coming or going. I see why there's a nursing shortage if they put all of y'all through this hoo-ha."

"My schedule is regular, Mama. I work every other weekend and I have every other Monday and Friday off."

"How are people supposed to keep track of what's every and what's other?"

"It's on the calendar on the refrigerator."

"Humph. There's a sale at JC Penney this weekend. I have some Christmas shopping I have to finish. I wanted you to go and get me some things."

"Why not have May do it?"

"May is one of the ones I need to shop for. Besides, I never see you since you hired that other part-time aide."

I had to guard my off days. Otherwise, I know Mama'd drive me stir crazy. I needed time to escape to my room, read a book, get on the computer or simply get away from the house.

"We see each other all the time. I got the other aide so I could have a bit of breathing space."

"A waste of money is what I call it."

"Do you want more coffee, Mama?"

"I'm all right."

"I'm going to shower and dress."

"Hurry up, I need you to help me to the bathroom soon."

A few minutes later I was in the shower, warm water sluicing over my skin. I wished it could wash the fatigue out of my bones, too.

I didn't know how I was going to get in everything I needed to do. I needed groceries and I had Christmas shopping to do. The season was closing in on me, and I didn't feel even a little bit festive.

There was no way I could get anything done before I had to be at work at 3:00 p.m. I'd been working second shift ever since I graduated from nursing school.

But now I wished I worked day shift. It felt as if I put in a full shift at home before I went to work and put in another. I was up early every morning to get my mother up, get her dressed and feed her breakfast. I got up at least twice during the night to turn her so she didn't get bedsores.

But despite everything, I appreciated the opportunity to

pay back the love. Mama got up more than twice a night for me, once upon a time. She'd woken early to feed me breakfast and get me dressed for years.

My brother helped supplement Mama's limited income and paid for the nurse's aides, but he had a growing family and he lived in California, so the physical help he was able to give was limited.

"Sharyn!"

Ah—Mama bellowed. I turned off the water and hurried out of the shower. "You all right?"

"I need to go to the bathroom now."

I pulled a robe over my damp body and hurried to take care of my mother.

I'd just gotten Mama settled into the wheelchair when the doorbell rang.

"Let the new girl in. I can't wait to see what kind of fool they sent me this time."

I pitied the physical therapist, whoever he or she was, that had to work with my mother. Mama was always cantankerous at best, but she was impossible now that she was wheelchair and home bound.

I pulled my robe a bit tighter and wished I'd had time to get dressed before the new therapist had arrived.

But when I opened the door, instead of the therapist, a handsome white man stood on the doorstep. He didn't look the salesman type, but I supposed the better ones didn't. He looked like a movie star, all sun-streaked hair, blinding white teeth and expensive everything. "Can I help you?" I asked.

"My name is Nick Cohen. I'm here to see Betty Silvers."

"She isn't interested." I wondered what he was selling. What kind of door-to-door salesman could afford a slammin' suit like he was sporting?

"What?"

"She isn't interested in anything you have to sell. Thank you."

I started to push the door shut, but to my astonishment, he blocked it with his foot.

"Take your foot out of my door!"

"I think Mrs. Silvers is interested in what I have to offer."

"Take your foot out of my door before I knock it out."

Was I gonna have to call 911 on this fool? I'd heard of persistent salesmen, but dang.

"You misunderstood."

Misunderstood what? Did he think he was talking to a child?

"I have an appointment with your grandmother. I'm going to be doing her therapy."

Oops.

"Betty Silvers is my mother," I said, contrite. "You don't look like a therapist." That was an understatement. "How are you going to do therapy in a suit like that?"

I knew suits, and that one cost more than a dime.

"Would you like to see my badge?"

"Please."

He dug out his wallet and handed me a card. His hands weren't Hollywood though. They were the hands of a man who worked—rough and callused, although clean—rather than the suit-wearing fancy-model dude he looked.

"I'm sorry, I should have been wearing this badge, but I hurried here from a meeting," he said.

I glanced at the picture and the logo of the therapy company. Yep, he apparently worked there and he had initials after his name. He was a certified physical therapist.

"Maybe we should reschedule this appointment anyway." With another therapist. Mama wasn't about to let some white man with salon-scissored hair and a thousand-dollar suit lay a hand on her.

"That's not possible. I'm here to provide the therapy Mrs. Silvers's rehabilitation doctor ordered." He cleared his throat. "Are you going to let me in?"

All righty, then. I tried to save him. I stood aside.

"Let me introduce you to my mother." Lord help the man.

I led him inside. All of a sudden I was acutely aware of my nakedness under the bathrobe, the rough terry cloth rubbing against my skin.

"Who is this?" Mama demanded as soon as we entered the den. "My therapist is supposed to be here now."

"This is the therapist, Mama. Nick Cohen, this is my mother, Betty Silvers."

Mother didn't say a word but studied him from the top of his light brown, sun-streaked hair and blue eyes, down his expensive-as-hell Savile Row suit, to the tips of his Barker blacks.

"What the hell is this white man doing in our house, Sharyn?" Mama finally said.

Nick Cohen flinched.

"He's here for your therapy, Mama," I repeated.

"The hell he is. What fool is going to come to bend and

sweat with some old lady wearing that getup? You thought you was going to a party, boy?"

I noticed Nick Cohen's cheeks pinkening up nicely.

"No, ma'am."

So Nick Cohen wasn't dumb. That was the only right answer, as far as Mama was concerned.

"Well, then what's wrong witcha, boy?"

"Nothing that I'm aware of, Mrs. Silvers."

"Humph. Well, it's your suit that's gonna get ruined, fool. I leak. Sometimes us old ladies do. Anytime, anywhere, any orifice might start leaking, just like that. Leak, leak, leak, all over the place. Can you deal with that, boy?"

His eyes widened. "If I must, ma'am."

I tried not to grin and scored him a point.

She chuckled. "He's not too bad. Take off that jacket. Do you want Sharyn to get you a pair of her sweatpants and a T-shirt? They'll stretch. He's a tall one, isn't he, Sharyn? Look at those muscles."

I'd been looking. He must work out. Tall, well built and fine was a nice combo anyway you wrapped it.

"No, I'll be all right," he said as he swept off his jacket and rolled up his sleeves. Yessiree, he was as fine as wine. I turned to leave.

"Where are you going?" Mama asked.

"I need to get dressed."

"You're not going to leave me alone with this strange man. He could be a rapist or something."

I tried not to giggle at the strangled noise that emanated from Nick Cohen's direction.

"A rapist? Mama, please."

"You get over here and help this man."

"Really, I don't—"

"Shh. Be quiet, girl. First rule of the Silvers household—never interrupt Mrs. Betty Silvers. You got that? Under no circumstances mess up my train of thought, because once it's lost, I might not be able to find it again. Now, as I was sayin', go and get me my gait belt hanging on the back of the bedroom door."

There was no point in arguing with Mama in this mood. I went.

Nick was perusing Mama's chart when I returned with the belt a moment later.

"Put down that chart, boy," Mama ordered. "I know my own routine. First we walk to the bedroom and then we take a little rest while you bring us hot, sweet tea and cinnamon toast. You have enough sense to make cinnamon toast?"

"I believe so," he said.

"Good. Next time you'll get a chance to make it. Now, where's that gait belt, Sharyn?"

Fifteen minutes later I decided Nick Cohen really knew what he was doing. He expertly supported Mama so she was safe and felt secure, but she still did a good deal of work.

He was much better than Melissa, who coddled Mama too much. By the time Mama reached the bed, she was breathing hard.

"Sharyn, come over here and help me lie down."

"I'd also like to observe your transfer technique," Nick said.

He must have no idea that I was an RN and that heaving heavy patients around by myself was my bread and butter. I was small, around a hundred and ten pounds and short, while my mother weighed at least two hundred pounds. I forgave him because at first everybody thought I was going to have trouble.

I locked the wheelchair brakes, braced my knees against Mama's and flexed my hips. With one easy motion I leaned over and pivoted Mama around to the bed.

He cleared his throat.

I almost dropped Mama when I realized my robe had fallen open and the entire curve of my breast was visible. Mortified, I tightened the belt to my robe before I moved around the bed adjusting my mother's position. Mama closed her eyes and finally fell blessedly silent.

"Nice…nice technique. The way you moved really saved your back muscles and spine," Nick said, his voice husky.

I darted a glance at him. He was leaning against the wall, his hands in his pockets.

"If I didn't know what I was doing, I'd probably be in a wheelchair myself. I work med-surg at St. Margaret's Hospital. Speaking of, I better get dressed for work."

"Show him where he needs to make the cinnamon toast and tea," Mama said without opening her eyes.

I met his gaze and a wave of sexual awareness passed between us. Our gazes lingered too long, filling me with a warm, wet needing.

Nick's eyes were narrowed, his cheeks flushed, his hands deep in his pockets, hiding the arousal I knew without a doubt was present. Oh, Lord. He must think I exposed myself to every man who came into this house. That I was stuck in here caring for my invalid mother, desperate for some...

"The kitchen is that way," I said. "I have to get dressed."

I turned and fled.

His Second

When she opened the door, I wanted to peel back that sweet little white robe she was wearing and do her up against the wall, no words said, no questions asked or answered.

I couldn't remember any woman ever affecting me as much.

I'd been with plenty of beautiful women and I had no fetishes for any certain type of women. But something about this woman moved me like no other.

The feeling only intensified when she wouldn't let me in. The impish smile that had crossed her face only made me want her more.

Was it her delicate beauty or the difference of her glorious milk-chocolate silky skin and wet shoulder-length hair curling in tight, inky, coiled springs? Or was it her outspoken charm, the quick intelligence stamped on her features or the impish grin that crossed her face? Or maybe it was the more traditional appeal of huge doe eyes fringed with incredible velvet lashes and her kissable red Christmas-bow lips.

I was there that morning because there wasn't one therapist who'd agree to visit "the Dragon," as they referred to Betty Silvers, other than Melissa. When the office had called me to inform me of that fact, I'd rushed to the Silvers home from a meeting.

Right now wasn't the time to lose my most lucrative case to one of my competing agencies. It wouldn't look good at all since I was trying to sell my business I'd built from scratch to one of them. It was essential that I appeared a threat. Otherwise they'd be more hesitant to shell out the bucks to buy me out.

So I'd needed to handle this one myself. Then I could decide how to best present the problem patient to one of my better therapists. Betty Silvers might be difficult, but a difficult patient was something a good therapist should be expected to handle, right?

Wrong.

I was ready to wring that old lady's chicken neck within the hour.

I'd resolved to give Melissa a raise and a bonus and was trying to figure out some way she could conduct a therapy session on crutches, because the woman must be a saint to put up with Betty Silvers. If she called me "boy" one more time—

"Help me to the bathroom again, boy."

"Yes, Mrs. Silvers." The woman must have a bladder the size of a pea.

I helped her and waited outside the door, thinking about Sharyn.

"Boy! Boy, do you hear me?"

"I can hear just fine."

"Don't you get smart-mouthed with me, boy. Go to my daughter's room and get me a book from her bookcase, second shelf from the top, *Love's Fevered Passion*. I'm gonna be a while in here. Hurry up now."

Dear Lord.

Sharyn's room was neat, decorated with bright, sunny colors. It had a Caribbean feel to it, as if she'd rather be at the beach than in chilly Atlanta. She liked techie toys as much as I did. Electronics were scattered all over the room. Her walls were lined with bookshelves, and they were all crammed full of books. She had very eclectic reading tastes.

Then my gaze was drawn to the flickering computer screen. In her rush to leave, she'd left it on. Her screen saver was a lazy fish that flowed over her desktop, not really obscuring it. She'd been in a chat room?

I had to force myself to look away from the computer.

Second shelf of which bookcase? I looked over all the second shelves from the top, but I could find no *Love's Fevered Passion*. I hoped *Sin's Blazing Fury* would do.

On the cover, a man clutched a woman who was bent backward over his arm at her waist. He seemed to be sniffing her navel, his face contorted as if he smelled something awful.

The woman seemed dreadfully uncomfortable, arched back in a bow, her unnaturally red hair brushing the heels of her feet. Maybe she was dead. There was a tiny horse in the background and a misty caped figure with a sword.

I guess it was horror novel instead of the porn opus Mrs. Silvers had wanted to read—I couldn't help an involuntary shudder at the thought—but it would have to do.

I hurried back before Mrs. Silvers had another stroke.

She snatched the book out of my hand. Thank the Lord that *Sin's Blazing Fury* seemed to work as well for her as *Love's Fevered Passion*.

"It took you long enough. Now get out of here. I'll call you when I'm done. It'll be a while."

"I need to leave, Mrs. Silvers. I have another appointment. Can I call your daughter—"

"You don't need to do a thing in this life but stay white, die and do what I tell you. You best be here when I need you to get me off this toilet if my daughter isn't back. You know I can't be left alone."

I could see why this case billed so high. Extended daily visits at special-care rates indeed. And we probably didn't charge enough.

Sharyn had dressed and taken off as though those misty sword-wielding demons on the cover of *Sin's Blazing Fury* were after her. She'd mumbled that she'd be back in an hour or so.

The Dragon had screeched after her, "It's your fault if he rapes me!" I wished that somehow Mrs. Silvers would disappear and I'd be left alone with Sharyn so I could do my best to tempt her to violate my person, but those kinds of miracles just don't happen.

Anyway, I knew why Sharyn had abandoned me to the not-so-tender mercies of the Dragon.

She was embarrassed about the little bit of heaven she'd shown me when her robe had fallen open. I shut my eyes at the memory of that luscious curve of brown breast topped off by that hardened berry of a nipple. I'd had to bury my hands in my pockets to hide my erection as if I were a teenage boy.

When I'd followed her to the kitchen, it had taken every ounce of willpower I had to play the gentleman I once believed myself to be. Because I was no gentleman now.

Gentlemen don't want to sweep the kitchen table bare and throw a woman they don't even know on it. They don't want to shove that woman's robe above her waist while their tongues play around and their lips pull at her succulent nipples.

Gentlemen don't want to bury their fingers in her warm, wet slickness between womanly legs and tease, tantalize and touch until she opens wide, begging and pleading me to slide inside and stroke…oh, God, I was losing my mind.

I certainly had, because I found myself standing in her room in front of her computer, my hand on her mouse.

Match4Luv.com.

CHICCHERIE, 25 years old, Atlanta area. Lonely lady seeks friend for chat, maybe more.

I might have lost my mind, but this was a mighty interesting find.

* * *

Sharyn's timing was uncanny. She walked in through the door just when I had finished the rather unpleasant and involved job of helping her mother out of the bathroom.

"So, Mama, I assume your virtue is intact?"

"I suppose so, but that boy has a special way with a hand and a bottom wipe."

I felt my face turn red and I wished again that the earth would open up and swallow Mrs. Silvers. As always, the ground stayed as solid as ever, and so did the Dragon, Mrs. Silvers.

"Could you see me to the door?" I asked Sharyn. I had to have a word with her in private. I simply had to know if—

"Have you taken ill, boy? Why do you need help to the door all of a sudden?" the Dragon demanded.

"Uh, I need to ask Sharyn something."

"Something about what?"

"Um, billing?" Please, Lord, let me strangle her, just a little bit.

"I handle my own bills around here, damn it! Spit it out, boy."

"Mama, let me see the man to the door," Sharyn said. "For heaven's sake, I'll be right back."

"I know Mama can be a handful," she said, as soon as we got out of earshot.

"A handful? More like a dump truck full of cement," I muttered. "Look, I wanted to ask you if you had any free time this week so I could stop by and take you out for a drink."

She crossed her arms and leaned back. "Are you asking me on a date, Nick Cohen?"

"I believe that's the official term if you're into labels."

"I don't date my mother's therapists."

"Not even a cup of coffee?" I had to take another shot.

"Is that all you asked me out here for? I'm freezing."

Since it was, I really didn't have a reply.

She gave me one of those looks and closed the door rather firmly between us.

I wished I hadn't left my coat in the car. I was freezing—in more ways than one. Sharyn cut me cold.

Why? I knew I wasn't ugly. And like most men, I could pick up the scent of female sexual interest from a mile away. She'd been nervous but interested. Very interested.

So why wouldn't she go out with me? Psychically bleeding from the pain of rejection, I skulked to my Jag and pulled out my cell phone. I'd received seven calls—three from the office, one from a buddy and three from fine babes more than willing to soothe my pain. But they weren't like Sharyn at all, and for some damn stupid reason, she was the only woman I wanted right now.

Was it only my hormones talking when I knew that I'd do almost anything for her? But why, oh, why did that have to include braving the Dragon?

Then I remembered Match4Luv.com and smiled.

Her Third

It was past midnight when I got home. Mama was sleeping, her snores audible as soon as I walked through the door. I peeled off my scrubs and jumped into the shower to rinse off residue of my work shift at the hospital.

I dried off and pulled a flannel nightgown over my head, warm bunny slippers on my feet and padded to the kitchen for a snack. It always took me time to wind down after work. I usually didn't get to sleep until two or three in the morning.

I hadn't been able to get Nick Cohen out of my head all day. It was worrying me to death. The man looked good, was professional, clean, polite, educated, more than well dressed—Barker blacks, for God's sake. So why the hell did I turn him down flat?

I sighed. I knew why, I just didn't want to name it. A part of me wanted to step up to Nick Cohen's plate and take what he had to offer. But, to be honest, I wasn't looking for a white guy. Especially a white guy I'd flashed all my goodies to on the first meet.

I knew Nick Cohen wanted to taste this dark chocolate real bad. It was written all over his face. How could I ever know where I stood with him? How'd I know for sure whether I was just an exotic new sexual flavor he wanted to try and discard or a woman he'd possibly consider for the long haul?

I never would know unless I was willing to take that leap, to risk my heart if the chemistry between us took its natural course. I knew I was still too bruised to be able to easily do that.

It had taken me a while to admit to myself how badly Patrick had hurt me, but once I did, I also had to deal with how sore I was, limping around from the aftereffects. I needed a break.

This was the first holiday season in five years I'd be without Patrick at my side. We were supposed to marry. The invitations had already gone out, the marriage plans in place.

I'd thought I was lucky. Patrick was a corporate lawyer, and most importantly, I'd thought he had class, a quality black man. He'd done those things important to a woman— little things like opening the car door, surprising me with an unexpected bunch of flowers and attending church with me on Sundays.

But I wasn't lucky at all. The way I'd found out was a cliché. I'd caught him in bed with my best friend, my would-be maid of honor. I swear the ugly, jealous bitch had set me up to see it.

Then I'd found out Patrick had screwed every female

with a pulse that had moved within a yard's radius of his manhood, all the few friends I had.

They'd turned on me and then they'd turned on each other. Somebody was pregnant. Somebody didn't know if Patrick was the daddy of her child. Somebody said she'd had an abortion. My life had turned into a freakin' Jerry Springer special overnight.

Patrick had sat back and enjoyed the spectacle of all these fool women fighting over his magnificent member. And, believe me, in hindsight I realized that the member in question wasn't all that in either quality *or* quantity.

In the end, I had no man. I had no friends. And Mama got sick.

Mama told me the whole mess was a blessing in disguise. She said if I married a mad dog like Patrick, his bite might have killed me. I guess Mama was right. But since I didn't have the sense to know a good dog from one who'd turn on its owner, I'd been wary about entering the dog pound since, you understand?

But don't get me wrong; I'm a woman who likes the company of a man. It's just that, after Patrick, I needed to take it slow and easy next time. And there was nothing slow or easy about the sexual chemistry between Nick Cohen and me.

I sat in front of my computer and clicked the messages link of the Match4Luv site. My mailbox was full, but one message caught my eye. For one thing, he actually knew how to construct a sentence, understood comma usage and how to spell the word *and*. Also, unlike most of the other guys, he didn't demand a photo immediately.

I clicked on the chat-room window, and lo and behold he was there! I opened the window for personal chat and clicked his handle GH0ST30

CHICCHERIE: Hi. I liked your note.

He answered immediately.

GH0ST30: Your profile seemed like someone I'd like to get to know. Especially the part about taking it slow.

I opened his profile, but it was sparser than mine, which was pretty sparse. He hadn't posted any photo of himself, either. He'd listed his profession as an "entrepreneur". That was broad. He'd listed his interests as wood working, cabinetry, camping, hiking, mountain climbing, skydiving and mountain biking. Yep, a white guy for sure.

CHICCHERIE: You sound intriguing. Why are you interested in taking it slow?

GH0ST30: I've been on the market for a while.

CHICCHERIE: That doesn't sound like a good thing. Are you like a too-small fish? Are the women throwing you back?

GH0ST30: I don't think so. I'm ready to get real, but all the fish I'm meeting are a tad tiny. My reasoning is that if I start fishing a little slower, maybe I'll start catching bigger fish.

CHICCHERIE: Touché. So what are you looking for?

There was a pause before he answered.

GH0ST30: I want to fall in love.

Oh, snap. Stop pounding, oh heart of mine.

CHICCHERIE: Why no photo on your profile?

Ghost30: Why none on yours?

CHICCHERIE: I'd like someone to get to know what I'm all about without getting all wrapped up in my appearance.

GH0ST30: Me, too.

CHICCHERIE: But that could tip either way in the looks department. It's a risk.

GH0ST30: You mean I could be either a three-hundred-pound wheelchair-bound dwarf or a Calvin Klein underwear model?

CHICCHERIE: Don't get me wrong, I'm not shallow, but I hope you resemble the underwear model more.

GH0ST30: So do I.

CHICCHERIE: I don't blame you for wanting to look more like a sexy underwear model more than a three-hundred-pound dwarf.

Okay, time to put him to the test. I laid it on him before he got the chance to tap out an answer to my teasing.

CHICCHERIE: Can I ask you a question?

GH0ST30: Are you going to ask me what I look like?

CHICCHERIE. Not quite. I was wondering what you're wearing right now.

I giggled. Okay, so I was a bad girl. But this brought out the guys who were only about cyberslutting right away.

GH0ST30: :-D . Would you be disappointed if I told you that my black negligee is in the wash?

He had a sense of humor! This could be promising.

CHICCHERIE: No, I can deal with it, since mine has been sitting in the dirty clothes for days. Seriously, what *do* you look like? Stats, I want stats!

GH0ST30: I'm six foot one, average weight, with brown hair. I'm pretty average looking overall. My great personality is my claim to fame.

CHICCHERIE: Ha! What if I said that? Would you assume I was a three-hundred-pound dwarf?

GH0ST30: Undoubtedly. Now it's your turn.

CHICCHERIE: I'm five two, a hundred and ten pounds, with black hair. I could almost be a dwarf compared to you.

GH0ST30: You left the lottery question blank.

CHICCHERIE: What?

GH0ST30: The question on your profile that asked what you would do with the money if you won the lottery.

CHICCHERIE: Oh. You left that question blank, too.

GH0ST30: You noticed. I'm flattered. So what would you do? I won't tell anybody, I promise.

CHICCHERIE: Okay, I guess I can tell you, then. First I'd buy a new house with a separate wing for my mother and I'd get my mother a live-in maid. Maybe two maids. Then I'd pay off my all my brother's debt, including his mortgage, and set up a trust to send my nieces and nephews to college. Finally, I'd quit work to write novels full-time. That's it.

GH0ST30: No Rolls, no private jets, no mansions, no bling?

CHICCHERIE: Nah. I'd have an ace investment firm on it, though. I hate taxes. Your turn.

GH0ST30: I'd buy an EarthRoamer—that's a very expensive, environmentally correct, self-contained RV—and I'd take off to the wilderness. I'd build a house with my own hands and be entirely self-sufficient somewhere naturally beautiful, off the grid. I'd do woodwork and cabinetry and give the rest of the money to charity.

It sounded rather romantic, albeit exhausting. The Adam-and-Eve angle was sort of appealing to me. I hated to admit it, but down deep—okay, *waaay* down deep—was a craving to get back to the basics. A good man, a simple home, hard work, babies. Was that enough? Was that all I really wanted? I stifled an urge to make the sign of the cross to ward off my sudden insanity.

CHICCHERIE: Everybody's got a dream. What does "off the grid" mean?

GHOST30: It means not connected to utilities.

No electricity? No air-conditioning or refrigerator? Now *that's* crazy.

CHICCHERIE: What about your computer?

GHOST30: There'd be one. There's solar energy for power. There's wood. There's biodiesel. We could have most of the amenities you have now.

CHICCHERIE: Thank goodness for alternative energy.

GHOST30: So basically you want to write, help your family out and get away from your mother. I can't blame you for wanting to get away from your mother.

What was his deal with mothers?

CHICCHERIE: Why? Do you think most people want to get away from their mothers? Do you want to get away from your mother?

GH0ST30: My mother passed away.

CHICCHERIE: I'm sorry.

He must have had Mama issues. Oh, well. Nobody's perfect.

GH0ST30: It was a long time ago. What do you want to write? Horror?

CHICCHERIE: Why do you think I want to write horror?

GH0ST30: My favorite horror novel is *Sin's Blazing Fury*, but it's been a long time since I read it.

CHICCHERIE: I'd hope so, since *Sin's Blazing Fury* is a historical romance.

GH0ST30: You're kidding. There's a dead woman on the cover!

What weirdness was this? Did this dude have a romance-novel fetish? He was sounding crazy, which was too bad, because I was kind of enjoying him so far.

CHICCHERIE: ?

GH0ST30: You mean she wasn't dead? She sure looked dead to me.

CHICCHERIE: Right. Ha-ha. You're pretty funny.

GH0ST30: A sense of humor is the name of the game. Are you going to be online tomorrow? Same time, same place?

CHICCHERIE: Sure. I'll be back. Same time, same place.

Okay, so GH0ST30 was a little strange, but so far I enjoyed passing the time with him. I might as well see where this went, if anywhere.

His Fourth

I'm a bonehead and I blew it. Why did I have to bring up *Sin's Blazing Fury*? Was I fixated on that book or what?

I wanted to show we had something in common; I wanted to impress her. Instead I came off as foolish. Crap. I drained my beer bottle and threw it in the trash, scoring a perfect two points. It made me feel a little better.

I bet she wouldn't show online tomorrow night. What would I do then? I'd actually considered taking over Betty Silvers's case personally, that's how much her daughter turned me on. But there was no way I could do it regularly with everything else I had to do.

So I kissed profit goodbye and paid the case out at such a high rate I had therapists clamoring for the opportunity to put up with the Dragon. Cash helps anybody get along.

We needed to keep that case. Just a few weeks more and

the ink would be dry on the papers to sell and I'd be free, heading out West in my newly delivered EarthRoamer RV.

I wasn't lying about what I'd told Sharyn. What I didn't tell her was my dream was almost coming true. All that was missing was the woman I imagined accompanying me. I'd been looking for her the past couple of years, but I hadn't met her yet.

I knew I'd recognize her when I saw her. Don't ask me how I knew, I just knew.

I'd never believed in love at first sight. I still didn't, but I felt as if I had a chance with Sharyn—we'd work everything out, you know? It wasn't that I expected that everything would be smooth between us—in fact, I was sure it wouldn't. I just knew somehow we'd get through whatever. And I knew if we ever got together, we'd probably stay together.

But that's stupid. There's no such thing as soul mates. My overwhelming attraction to Sharyn had to be nothing more complicated than intense sexual attraction.

I shouldn't overthink things. The woman simply revved me up. Once we got to know one another better, things would follow their natural course and that would be that.

If Sharyn wasn't online when I signed on tomorrow, I'd create a new persona. Sooner or later, I'd find a persona that clicked.

Then what?

I'd cross that bridge later. My plan was to charm her first and then it would work itself out. Somehow we'd end up in bed and then I could stop thinking about her all the time.

Because there's no such thing as soul mates.

CHICCHERIE: I was waiting for you.

She was waiting for me and admitted it? Hot damn!

GH0ST30: I'm glad you're here. How was your day?

CHICCHERIE: It was all right. Yours?

GH0ST30: The same.

CHICCHERIE: I want to say something to you. Do you mind?

My stomach knotted up. That wasn't reassuring.

GH0ST30: Of course not. Go ahead and say it.

CHICCHERIE: Let's get real here. I'm not about wasting time.

I shifted in my chair, uneasy. What was she about, then?

CHICCHERIE: What do you expect out of this online thing, seriously? Are you really unattached? Or are you mainly looking for sex? Are you truly lonely? Or are you bored with your squeeze and just passing time? Do you date other women or are you strictly cyber? What *are* you all about?

She was direct. Then I would be, too.

GH0ST30: You really want honesty? Or do you want to hear what you want to hear?

CHICCHERIE: You know my answer to that. Otherwise why would I have asked?

GHOST30: That's what a lot of women say right before they get pissed off when you tell them the real deal.

CHICCHERIE: I'm not a lot of women. If you can't be real with me, don't bother to be with me at all.

GHOST30: All right. Fair enough. Okay, I date. I see women all the time. I don't have a committed relationship, though. I'm seldom online and I never cyber. This is a new thing for me.

CHICCHERIE: Then why are you doing it?

GHOST30: I'm looking to hook up with the right one. What I've been doing isn't working.

CHICCHERIE: What's wrong with the woman you've been seeing?

GHOST30: Women, plural. Nothing's wrong with them. But nobody has moved me to want to commit. Nobody's come close.

Except you, I thought.

CHICCHERIE: Have any wanted to commit to you?

GHOST30: Hell, yeah.

CHICCHERIE: A bit cocky, aren't you?

GHOST30: More than a bit, the ladies say.

CHICCHERIE: Bad boy.

GHOST30: I can be very bad, if that's what you want.

Her pause was way too long. Damn it! I'd scared her. But my replies had been automatic, hormone-generated. I'd have to be more careful.

CHICCHERIE: I'm an RN. What do you really do? Entrepreneur sounds a little shady. You're not in the mob, are you?

She'd changed the subject. I'd started treading on ground too dangerous for her. How much or how little should I tell her about what I did?

GHOST30: I own a heath-care-supply company. Not nearly as glamorous as Tony Soprano, I'm afraid. I only get to fantasize about shooting people.

CHICCHERIE: What about your family? Have you ever married? Are you widowed? Divorced? You know, if you wrote this in your profile like you were supposed to, I wouldn't have to ask.

GHOST30: I'm divorced. It was a brief interlude.

CHICCHERIE: I'm sorry. How long?

GH0ST30: Don't be. I've been divorced for about three years now. I was married two years.

CHICCHERIE: Do you want to exchange sad stories?

My story wasn't all that sad. But I really wanted to know her story. I'd have to show mine to see hers.

GH0ST30: Sure. You first. Are you divorced?

I'd never thought about her past. But she was twenty-five; she had a past.

CHICCHERIE: I'm more of an abandoned-at-the-altar girl.

GH0ST30: Really?

CHICCHERIE: Sort of. I called off my engagement less than a month before my wedding. We were supposed to get married last week. We thought a winter wedding would be nice, with the holiday season and all.

GH0ST30: Last week! You're a recent veteran of a broken heart.

She was on the rebound. Damn.

CHICCHERIE: I'm more mad than brokenhearted. Mad enough to wonder if I ever loved him in the first place and why I was insane enough to agree to marry him. I should be hurt, but where is the pain?

GHOST30: You have cause to feel hurt?

CHICCHERIE: More than enough cause. He cheated on me with not only my best friend but four other women I knew. There might have been more.

The man must have been stone crazy to cheat on a woman like that.

GHOST30: How could he do that to you?

CHICCHERIE: That's what I wondered. Can you imagine if I'd married him? It would have been awful. He would have tomcatted through the entire neighborhood—no, make that the entire city. I've been tested for every sexually transmitted malady under the sun and I'm clean, thank goodness. That's my sad story. What's yours?

GHOST30: My marriage collapsed because we were young and I was stupid. It's not a very sad story. We'd been dating for about a year. I went along for the ride. She had a strong personality and made things easy for me. Then all of a sudden she decided she wanted to be married. I think that's exactly what it was—she wanted to be married, not necessarily that she wanted to be married to me.

CHICCHERIE: That's tough.

GHOST30: I'm not guiltless. I added up the pros and cons and decided she'd be suitable. I settled for suitable and I don't want to make that mistake again. We had a big wedding, went to Hawaii on the honeymoon, moved into a big house. Then we discovered we didn't like each other very much. By the end of a couple of years, we couldn't stand each other's guts. We decided to split before we got any deeper. I think our divorce was more fun than our wedding. We threw a nice party.

CHICCHERIE: But isn't the breakup of any marriage a disappointment?

GH0ST30: Not really. We both decided that the best was yet to come.

The pause between us lengthened and I felt compelled to end it.

GH0ST30: So what are you doing for the holidays?

CHICCHERIE: Not much. My brother's flying into Atlanta with his family this year because of Mama's stroke—we usually fly out to California, mainly because we like the weather. We prefer palm trees to a cold Atlanta Christmas.

GH0ST30: It's just you and your brother? No extended family?

CHICCHERIE: Nope. My mother's an only child.

When they made her mother, they broke the mold, thank God. I've never chatted with anybody before. I didn't know what to do. Was this what chats were supposed to be like? I'd heard about cybersex, but revealing things about ourselves and innocuous banter would get old soon. This was going nowhere fast. I wanted to come out from behind the computer. I needed Sharyn to know the real me.

GH0ST30: My office throws a big Christmas party every year. Ours is coming up next weekend.

CHICCHERIE: Oh?

GH0ST30: I have to show, but I'm not really the party type.

CHICCHERIE: I know what you mean.

GH0ST30: Our party is at the Palace downtown.

CHICCHERIE: The Palace? Your company shells out big dough for this party, huh?

GH0ST30: It's expected for the making of friends and influencing of people. Actually, a lot of agencies get together and throw it. Anyway, I'd love it if you'd show. It's in the Grande Ballroom, formal dress. Hundreds of people will be there. It's a safe place for a first meet, and you can protect me from the hordes of partygoers.

CHICCHERIE: I'll think about it. We can discuss it later.

GH0ST30: All right. Same time and same place tomorrow?

CHICCHERIE: Same time, same place.

* * *

The next day all I could think about was Sharyn. I moved a few meetings around and took the Dragon lady's session myself, lovesick fool that I was.

I knocked on the door at the stroke of ten. Sharyn's big brown eyes widened at the sight of me. "No fancy suit today?" she asked.

"No sexy bathrobe?" I regretted my words when a slight look of irritation crossed her lovely face.

"No sexy bathrobe," she said. "Mother's waiting for you. She was excited to hear you'd be her physical therapist today."

"Me, too."

She let that one go with a raised brow.

"Hurry up, boy, I don't have all day!"

"Do you have something to do, Mrs. Silvers? Maybe an appointment?"

"Get smart with me and what I'll have to do is whup your butt."

"Butt whupping is a bit on the kinky side," I said, rubbing my upper lip. "But I suppose it's good for range of motion and an excellent upper-body exercise."

Mrs. Silvers's eyes narrowed as she stared at me. I steeled myself for the dragon blast to come but was surprised at the roar of laughter that emanated from her throat instead.

"Good one, boy, good one," she said, wiping her eyes with the backs of her hands.

Sharyn caught my gaze and winked. I caught my breath.

If I could tame the Dragon, would she grant me her daughter as a boon?

As I worked through the therapy session with Mrs. Silvers, I could hear Sharyn moving around in the kitchen. I was surprised at how pleasant the Dragon was today. She only called me "boy" a few times.

I got her settled into bed. "Okay, boy, get yourself to the kitchen and make me some cinnamon toast and sweet, hot tea."

"Sure." Cinnamon sprinkled on toast. How hard could that be? I headed for the kitchen.

"I have the cinnamon toast ready," Sharyn said. "If Mama is on schedule—and she always is—she sent you in here to get it." Sharyn smiled at me, and all was right with the world.

She pulled a cookie sheet out of the oven. Two fat slices of Texas toast lay there, with a rich sugar and cinnamon glaze.

My mouth watered. "Baking is involved in making cinnamon toast? I was going to sprinkle some cinnamon on some bread I put into the toaster."

"Mama would have a fit. It's not hard. You mix real butter, sugar and cinnamon together, spread it on the bread, set the oven on broil and brown the toast in the oven for a few minutes."

It sounded pretty damn hard to me. Putting a Pop-Tart in the toaster was about the level of my cooking skill. But I nodded as if I understood exactly what she was telling me.

"Take one of these to her. Here's the tray. I've already set up the teapot, too. Then come on back to the kitchen. The other one is for you."

That sounded better. "Thanks a lot." I infused the words with as much meaning as I could, because I meant them.

Really. If Mrs. Silvers wanted cinnamon toast as a part of her PT session, from now on I'd simply have to stop at the bakery on the way.

I set the tray on Mrs. Silvers's table in front of her and adjusted her electric bed, feeling more like a nursing assistant than a physical therapist.

"Pull up a chair. I like company while I eat," the Dragon ordered.

"Uh, I have to go the bathroom." I grabbed my lower belly and did a little dance. "I have to go right now."

The Dragon frowned, obviously not wanting her repast disturbed by any intestinal unpleasantness. "Well, get to going, then."

I got.

Her Fifth

Nick Cohen was adorable sitting across the table from me, trying to restrain himself from cleaning up every last crumb of cinnamon toast from his plate. I could tell by the longing in his eyes.

"Do you want another slice?" I asked.

"Please," he said.

I grinned. I like an honest man. I'd made a batch of cinnamon-butter, and it only took a second to slather it on the toast and slide a piece in the oven. Sure enough, as soon as I returned to the table, Nick's plate was as clean as if somebody had washed it.

"Can I ask you a question?"

"One moment. The toast is done already. It only takes a second." I slid the toast on his plate with a spatula and topped off his glass of milk.

I sat down across from him. "Ask away."

"I don't want to offend you, but I want to know. Is the reason you turned me down for a date because I'm white?"

My eyebrows shot up. I didn't know what I was expecting, but it wasn't this.

"You can be honest," he said.

"I usually am." I slid back into my chair, adjacent to his. "Maybe a little, but it wasn't most of the reason."

I looked away, not wanting to meet his eyes. "White men are basically men like any other, no big deal. If I'm ever hesitant, it's because I don't want to deal with this society's race baggage. But usually I don't care about society much. I figure the most important society is the one you make for yourself, you know?"

He nodded. "So what was it then?"

"It's you. I'm coming off a bad relationship and I sense it would be heavy between us. Our vibes are very strong."

"You think that's a bad thing?"

I shrugged. "It's a scary thing."

"I think if you know beforehand something is going to matter, it's going to matter. And you shouldn't let it pass you by."

His voice had lowered to a whisper and his face was close to mine, his ice-blue gaze intense. I couldn't breathe in for the sudden sexual tension that descended, but I could smell him, sharp, musky, clean and very masculine.

I wanted him to touch me, to kiss me. And he wanted to kiss me. I was certain of it.

We breathed each other's air, and our hearts beat a fast, staccato rhythm as the space between us grew smaller.

He stood, pushing the chair back in a sudden motion and grasping my shoulders, pulling me to him. I was boneless, more than willing to be crushed against his hard body.

Yes. I looked up into his eyes, surrounded by his arms, sinking into him, every nerve vibrating. It was as if I'd been waiting forever for this moment.

The feeling was strong, so that I had no hope of controlling it. Nick Cohen could hurt me for real, not merely bruise my pride.

I didn't care. The moment between uncertainty and surrender was only an instant. His head lowered and his lips neared mine. My eyes closed. My body quivered like a string waiting to be played.

"Boy, come here!"

Nick growled out a low, savage curse.

"Boy! What are you doing? You better get your behind in here before I call the po-lice."

He grazed my lips with his, like a thirsty man denied water. Then he strode away toward my mother, his steps wide and angry.

Mama, my bane and my salvation. I fled to my bedroom and started a bath.

I planned to retreat behind locked doors until Nick left. I shook with desire from a mere almost kiss.

This man could kill me. He could. I admit it, I'm a wuss, but the power Nick Cohen had over me terrified me.

GH0ST30: I was afraid you weren't going to come.

CHICCHERIE: Why is that?

GH0ST30: Maybe that I said the wrong thing or scared you off.

CHICCHERIE: I'm not that easily scared.

GH0ST30: That's a good thing to know. So have you thought about attending the party?

I hadn't, but why not? Another man might be just the ticket to dilute the frightening power of Nick Cohen.

GH0ST seemed pleasant enough. Meeting in a public place was safe enough. I'd been to a party or two at the Palace before, and the Grande Ballroom was very grand indeed. It was right off the main hotel lobby, as public a meeting place as any restaurant.

CHICCHERIE: Sure. Since we haven't done pictures, shall we exchange them now so we can recognize each other?

GH0ST30: Let's surprise one another. How about flowers? A red-green-and-white carnation on the lapel or shoulder would be Chrismassy. We can meet at the bar next Saturday at seven sharp.

CHICCHERIE: Is it a pay or an open bar?

GH0ST30: Would I invite you to a party with a pay bar? It's an open bar. The best thing about an office party is the opportunity for your coworkers and colleagues to embarrass themselves.

CHICCHERIE: But it works both ways.

GH0ST30: True. So we're on?

CHICCHERIE: Guess so. Oh, did I mention I'm a black chic?

GH0ST30: Your profile did. Did I mention that I weigh four hundred pounds?

CHICCHERIE. No.

GH0ST30: I'm kidding! But I am white. Do you have any problem with that?

CHICCHERIE: Whiteness was the default choice on Match4Luv, surprisingly enough, with only other races having to specify their race. So I assumed you were white. It's okay.

GH0ST30: Good. I want to let you know that you're going to be surprised. I don't want to say any more for now. But you're going to be surprised. I only hope you find it a pleasant one.

CHICCHERIE: What? No hints?

GH0ST30: Maybe you've heard of me before.

CHICCHERIE: Are you telling me you're famous? A celebrity?

GH0ST30: You haven't told me much about your family other than your mother is an only child. My mother passed away about five years ago. My father sold the house and went to live in a retirement apartment. He likes it there.

CHICCHERIE: Right. So you're just going to change the subject and leave me hanging. No fair.

GH0ST30: Saturday will be here soon enough for you to find out. The reason I was telling you about my father is what you said about your mother and maid service. I think she'd like a place like where my father lives. It comes with maid service, activities and people to order around 24-7.

CHICCHERIE: Really? But we could probably never afford it.

GH0ST30: I don't know. I just thought I'd mention it. Maybe you can bring it up with your other relatives when they get here for the holidays.

CHICCHERIE: You mean my brother.

GH0ST30: Is he married?

CHICCHERIE: Yes, and he has five children. They're biracial. He married a white woman.

   Given the amount of time GH0ST30 paused, I gathered he was surprised.

GH0ST30: Your mother was fine with this?

CHICCHERIE: Not like she had much say. And she's crazy about her grandchildren. I think her daughter-in-law gets on her nerves less than my brother. He's a minister.

GHOST30: Really? And that gets on her nerves?

CHICCHERIE: He's a minister of the Church of the Glorious Inner Light of Free Earth Beings in Space. That's the GILFEBS Church for short. Yes, that gets on her nerves a bit.

GHOST30: Wow. That almost has my brother beat, but not quite.

CHICCHERIE: How can that not quite have your brother beat?

GHOST30: My brother is a Mormon, an elder in the church. I suppose you could say he's also a minister. He lives in the Utah desert, a very rural area. He has four wives so far and probably twenty-odd kids. Dad thinks he's nothing but a no-good swinger who took on that religion to get away with getting a lot of young nooky on the side. He gets on Dad's nerves a bit, too.

CHICCHERIE: My goodness. It appears we have more in common than we thought. Is that your only sibling?

GHOST30: I have another. She's more like me. She's in Africa now. She's a World Health Organization doctor.

CHICCHERIE: You're sounding more interesting by the moment.

GH0ST30: I'm very interesting, as I'm hoping you'll discover Saturday.

CHICCHERIE: Is that a promise?

GH0ST30: If you want it to be.

His Sixth

It was a few minutes before seven. I hurried through the party crowd to the entrance, but it seemed as if I ran into human obstacles every few feet.

"Nick! It's been such a long time," some woman said in my ear.

"Later," I replied without slowing.

I grinded to a halt in front of a gilded figure who'd planted herself in front of me. Oh, Lord, it was Maureen.

"I will forgive you for not returning my calls if you bring me a martini, two olives. I love olives."

I looked at my watch. Damn, it was straight-up seven. Was that Sharyn in the red dress?

"What an ugly thing," Maureen said and plucked the multicolor carnation boutonniere out of my lapel.

"Give that back."

"I will when you bring me my martini."

Sharyn was looking around with the slight frown of a stranger at a party. I had to get to her. What if she left? I turned away from Maureen with an exasperated sound and made my way through the crowd.

"Nick! I'm surprised to see you here," Sharyn said. "I was supposed to meet someone…" she looked around.

I glanced down at my missing boutonniere that was supposed to explain that I was GH0ST30 to her in one glance. "About that…um…"

She looked up at me with her brows raised. The words to explain I was really GH0ST30 died on my tongue, an ignominious coward's death.

"Can I get you a drink?" I asked.

"Sure, a rum and Coke."

She had uncomplicated alcoholic preferences. No psuedosophistication or girlie, frooty-tooty drinks for her. I liked it. The band started up, playing an upbeat jazz tune.

Sharyn was at my side, and I knew the night was going to be good.

The night was as fabulous as the band turned out to be. We danced nonstop. Was it an excuse to hold each other tight? I hoped she thought so. Because for me, I knew it was so.

Her hair had been pulled back into a knot at the back of her neck, and my fingers itched to release it. Sexy wayward tendrils had escaped their confinement, and her red dress clung to every delicious curve she had.

The band was playing R & B slow-dance tunes. Sharyn had

called it "old school." Her scent of raspberries and roses intoxicated me more than any strong liquor. As her body moved against mine, at first I had to stick my butt out, way too stiff in more ways than one.

But the music moved us together like sticky honey. I'd long since given up trying to be circumspect as her soft curves melded against me. Burying my face in her hair, I longed to finish what I had started in the kitchen the other day.

She lifted her head and looked into my eyes. Our gazes met and something moved between us, something hot and so compelling, I couldn't look away. Neither could she. I didn't think as my mouth met hers, couldn't think for the feeling. Her lips were as soft as I had imagined.

The kiss deepened, grew more intimate. Urgency pulsed through me like the roar of blood through the arteries in my ears. She pulled away, breathing hard. "Your colleagues…?"

I glanced around. There were some stares, a few hostile glares from women I'd dated. I'd not made any polite rounds, not left Sharyn's side or sweet arms from the moment I'd arrived. I supposed people noticed.

"I couldn't care less."

"It's awkward," she said, her voice faint. I loosened my embrace and we continued to dance, our hearts thundering against each other's.

"Would you like to go—"

"I'd love to," she answered before I got my sentence finished.

I held out my arm and we went to retrieve our coats from the coatroom. I abandoned my own party without a moment's hesitation.

I felt shy with her in my car. It wasn't something I was used to feeling with a woman. "Do you want to go to a restaurant? A jazz club? Or if you want to dance, we can do that."

"I don't think I'm in much of a party mood tonight after all." She gave me a smile that almost took my breath away. "I'd like a quiet evening, a chance to get to know you better. A restaurant would be great. Simple food is fine." I could feel her gaze on me. "Or we could go to your place. I'm curious about how you live. It's only fair, since you've been to my house so often."

I caught my breath. A man's dream come true.

But I knew if I took her to my place I wouldn't be able to keep my hands off her. She had to know it, too. She thought she was in control, didn't she? Coming off a bad relationship, she needed to be in control of this. I'd bet money that was the case. She wanted to see if she could handle us, just me and her alone together, without it raging out of control.

She thought she could. But I knew we couldn't. And too soon for us would be disastrous.

"I know a great little restaurant I want you to try. Italian," I said.

"Merry Christmas, Mr. Cohen. Good to see you again."

"Merry Christmas, Tony."

He led us to a great table, his eyes gleaming with appreciation as he glanced at Sharyn. So Tony liked her better than some of the other women I brought here? I appreciated his taste. It was excellent in both women and wine.

"How about you serve us, Tony? House specials in everything."

"It'll be my pleasure, Nick."

"I hope you like surprises," I said to Sharyn.

"I love them when they're good."

"I trust Tony. I think he'll hook us up fine."

Tony appeared on cue with two wineglasses and a bottle of rosé. He proffered it to me to taste, and I shook my head, trusting him. He poured our wine with a flourish and then retired.

"It will be good," I said.

She sipped. "Excellent." Her finger traveled around the rim of the glass after she replaced it on the table. "You know, I'm glad I ran into you. I was wrong to turn down a date. I did want to go out with you."

"So why didn't you?"

She shrugged. "I was afraid to take a chance. I recently came out of a bad breakup. I'm still a little bruised, you know?"

I knew too well. I should tell her right now I was GH0ST30. I'd tell her about Maureen and the boutonniere. Everything would be all right.

"Trust is the most important thing to me in a relationship," Sharyn said. "After being lied to for so long, I want to get it right next time."

I was a squirrel in the middle of the road and an eighteen-wheeler was bearing down on me.

"I understand," I choked out, my throat dry. I emptied my wineglass. A waiter appeared as if by magic to refill it.

I understood too well. I'd broken her number one rule right out of the gate. How could I tell her now?

The waiter put our salads in front of us—the fresh vegetables, cheese and olives cut and arranged like a work of art.

"This looks too pretty to eat," Sharyn said.

"I've had it before. It's delicious. You'll be surprised how easy it is to eat once you get started."

I picked up my salad fork even though I was no longer hungry.

"Have you got your Christmas shopping done yet?" Trite, but I needed to fill the silence.

"You're right, this salad is yummy. Yes, it's done. My brother and his family will be here day after tomorrow. I'm getting in gear with the baking. I've got the holiday off from work this year. What are your plans?"

"It's just my father and I. We don't do much. And besides, we're Jewish."

"Really? Then why don't you come over? I warn you—it'll be wild. My brother has a passel of bad kids, but I think kids are what make Christmas fun."

"They are. You know what? I'd love to. I think I can drag Dad along for the ride, too."

She laughed, delighted. "Mama likes you."

"You could have fooled me. I think what she likes is to call me 'boy.'"

"She's trying to get a rise out of you. She'll grumble for the effect, but she'll be thrilled."

Sharyn had invited Dad and me to her home for the holidays? A grin spread across my face. Like that, my mood lightened, my trepidation was forgotten. Wine and laughter flowed.

The waiter served veal piccata. By the time Tony came to ask how we were enjoying the meal, I had relaxed again, enjoying Sharyn's company, enjoying the food, enjoying everything.

I'd worry about that trust thing tomorrow.

Sharyn looked at her watch. "It's almost eleven-thirty! Nick, I have to get home. May has to leave soon."

Everything comes to an end. We drove to her house in companionable silence. It probably was particularly companionable because we were both stuffed to the eyeballs. Tony had outdone himself and I'd rewarded him well.

I opened the car door for her and helped her out like the queen she was. At the door, I pulled her to me, hungry for a different meal. She met my lips with the same fervor, her arms twining around my neck.

"I want to ask you in for coffee, but…"

I thought about the Dragon guarding her lair. "That's all right. I'll pick you up for brunch tomorrow. Noon?"

"Perfect."

She gave me another kiss, before turning to unlock the door and disappearing inside.

Yes! I know it was undignified but I couldn't help a few air punches as I danced back to the car. I was the man! I was her man to be. We'd dated and we were going to date some more. Our families were going to spend Christmas together. Touchdown! Well, almost.

Her Seventh

I took my hair down, threw my red dress on my chair and studied my kiss-bruised lips in the mirror. Nick Cohen was hot. Tonight I'd been willing to get burned. There was something about that guy that turned me on all the way. He made what Patrick and I had had together seem like practice for the real thing.

Nick was the real deal all right. Thank goodness GH0ST hadn't shown up. But what if he had? Once Nick and I got together, we didn't take our eyes off each other all night.

If GH0ST had arrived, he would have seen me grinning up in another man's face, glued to another man's side. Would I have spoken to somebody if I were in a similar situation? Probably not.

Maybe GH0ST had shown, but what would be, would be. Given how I was feeling about Nick, it wasn't fair not to tell

GH0ST about it. I didn't want to string him along, and an online connection had no comparison to the flesh-and-blood immediacy of Nick.

Resolved to tell him, I signed on my computer and logged in to the chat room, but GH0ST wasn't there.

"You confused, boy? Somebody else already did my session," Mama said to Nick.

"We're going out," I said.

"Going out! Why are you going out with that boy, chile?"

"The usual reasons, Mama."

"Humph." She turned her baleful gaze on Nick, and I swear he flinched. "You take care of my child. And spend some money on her. We Silvers women don't suffer cheap-ass sorry fools, you hear?"

"Yes, Mrs. Silvers."

Trust Mother to put the icing on the cake of my mortification. That was why I never brought boys home in high school. I never met a man yet that Mama couldn't scare, but Nick was holding his own with Mother. This was one white boy she wasn't cowing. I smiled.

"What you grinning at, girl?"

"You, Mother, I'm grinning at you."

"You better get your hind end outta here."

I winked at Mama, grabbed Nick's hand and raced to the door.

"Are you sure you want to play with the Dragon like that?" he asked as the door shut behind us.

"Who?"

"Your mother."

"Don't you know by now that Mama's bark is the worst thing about her? So y'all call her the Dragon at your physical therapy place?"

He looked embarrassed, a slight pink spreading across his cheeks. "Yeah."

"Mama would be flattered."

"She would?"

"A dragon is a mighty formidable mythical creature, beautiful and strong. Who wouldn't want to be a dragon?"

"I guess that's a point." He opened the car door for me and then slid into his seat. "What do you want to eat?" he asked, starting the motor.

"I want to eat something I cook at your place."

I don't feel as if I really know somebody until I see how he chooses to live—and I wanted to know Nick Cohen.

"All right." His fingers tightened on the steering wheel. Just that tiny movement turned me on. I twined my fingers together to keep from touching him.

I frowned a little, wondering why something like that affected me so much. I bit my lip as I realized that Nick wanted to know me as much as I wanted to know him.

Nick lived in one of those luxurious high-rise condos downtown with a parking garage underneath.

"I left a mess," he said as we stood in the elevator.

"I always wonder about OCD or the down-low if a guy is too neat."

"Isn't that gender discrimination?"

"Nope. I'm suspicious of overly neat women, too."

"That type gets on my nerves, too. They're always following around, picking up something. Thank the Lord for cleaning services."

I nodded. Nick Cohen was a man after my own heart. He believed in cleaning services! He was damn near perfect so far.

We got off on a floor high enough to make me dizzy, and he turned the key in his lock. I drew in a sharp breath as he opened the door.

His place was stunning, both masculine and beautiful, decorated with bold slashes of color, reds, browns and black against white, and set off with silver.

"I love your place. It's very modern but not cold."

"I like it, too. I got a bargain. I would never have paid the prices that decorators charge firsthand."

I noticed he didn't say he couldn't afford it.

"Who decorated?" I asked.

"A friend. Want to take a look around?"

When we got to his bedroom, with a stunning platform bed, the tension between us gathered, thick and palpable as steam. I wanted him to kiss me. I craved his touch.

"Maybe we should go look at the kitchen and see what there is to cook," he said, his voice husky.

"Maybe we should do that."

"Yeah. I think I have some eggs."

"I like eggs."

"They're especially good with cheese," he said right before his lips covered mine.

It was as if the room filled with music. We moved against each other in our own special slow dance. Nick had a fluid grace, and I matched him move for move.

His sex rose and thickened, musk-hot, pounding and throbbing, out of control as he kissed me, his mouth demanding, our tongues hungry, wanting needing more.

He cupped his hands around my buttocks and pulled me close against him. I buried my face into his neck, inhaling his scent, musk and fire. Arousal hardened my nipples as I moved against his body.

Butter-silk smooth, I ground my pelvis against him, I didn't want control anymore. I wanted him. As I abandoned care and fear, all there was left was Nick and this feeling. Our mouths met again, our tongues dancing in time to an inner beat.

Overwhelming and urgent need for this man overcame me, and I gasped against his lips with the desire to have him buried inside me, his hands on my naked body.

"I can't get enough of you," he whispered, his mouth reclaiming and exploring my own.

I stepped away, my desire clear in my mind. Once I decided to do something, I liked to do it right. My mood was playful and happy, abandoned and free. *No control, no regrets.*

A small smile crossed my face. I wanted him to see me.

He tried to follow but I held up a finger. *No, no.* I pulled off my shirt, one motion over my head. My bra was red, my favorite, lacy and almost see-through.

He drew in a breath, his eyes narrowed.

I kicked off one shoe, then the other. I held out a foot for him to take off the sock, teasing him. "Now the other foot." His hands trembled.

"Slow down. Take your time," I said.

He looked up then, a sardonic smile on his face. "I always do," he said.

Oh, my.

I wasn't myself, but I didn't care. I'd decided to cross the line and I was going to go all the way. I dropped my belt to the floor, and my jeans followed right after. He made a convulsive movement toward me.

"No, not yet. I'm not done."

"Oh, God," he said.

I took off my bra. His tongue moistened his lips, his pupils huge in his light eyes. I stepped out of my panties.

"Merry Christmas, baby," I said.

He grabbed me, lifted me in the air and swung me around and gave a whoop. "I have died and gone to heaven. You're as crazy as I am! I knew it!"

I laughed with him. For a second, at least. He soon silenced me.

He trailed tiny kisses down my throat, circled his warm tongue around my nipple and sucked, pulling deep desire up from between my legs. Then the other nipple.

My hips churned, needing more, needing him.

He parted the curls between my legs and slid clever fingers around my most sensitive part. Then his tongue followed. He slid two fingers within me, in and out, at the same time.

Was it me making all that noise as I spun into freefall, spiraling out of control, clutching his hair, crashing and splintering to a million pieces?

I came back together slowly, gasping hard. Dang. For that alone, he was a keeper.

He moved up me and looked into my eyes. His light eyes were dark, stormy. "You want me?"

"You know I do."

He quickly put a condom on and slid inside me, moving slowly. He filled me up, so big. I loved it, every inch. He worked it hard and slow, stoking that fire within me again while he whispered words of adoration in my ear.

Wildfire. I burned. Wrapping my legs around his waist, I felt his deep thrusts filling up every inch of me, working and rotating round my slickness.

"Again. I want to feel you quake against me again." He burned me slow and easy, his fire moving inch by inch, unstoppable.

Then, like the thrust of a knife, sharp and hard, I cried out in surprise and ecstasy as I convulsed against him. He shouted as he met me in that place where we seemed to belong together.

I had to pull myself out of Nick's arms before midnight as if I were a fairy-tale figure. We'd had a magical day, making love, talking, laughing and being silly. Nick simply felt right, a real good fit.

I'd jumped into bed with him too soon, and the striptease was silly, but I didn't care because I'd made the decision to trust Nick Cohen.

Did he know the leap of faith it took me to hand him my heart along with my body? I'd whispered it in his ear, and he'd kissed me, reassuring me he was worthy.

It's not that I'm such a poor judge of men. I never trusted Patrick to this extent, not really. Patrick was never as transparent as Nick, though. His eyes had always been veiled, never showing outright longing for me. Lust, maybe, but never longing.

I'd never again trust a man who wasn't transparent, who was too quick with the easy put-down and too careful about his ego and persona to be fun. Nick was fun. He didn't give a damn about being cool.

I eyed the flickering screen of the computer on my desk. I wondered if GH0ST was on, for me to let him know about Nick. GH0ST was a decent guy. I should be trustworthy, too.

I sat down at the laptop and signed on. I'd almost decided to click off when he appeared.

CHICCHERIE: Hi GH0ST.

GH0ST30: Hi.

CHICCHERIE: I'm sorry I missed you at the party, but it's cool. I was preoccupied. I met this guy.

GH0ST30: Okay.

CHICCHERIE: I want to tell you about him. We said we'd be honest with each other. He's the guy I'm going to be seeing from now on.

GH0ST30: That's all right.

If I was a lesser woman, my ego would be a little crumpled at G's cool reaction, but it was all good.

CHICCHERIE: I'm happy you're fine with it. Sometimes you meet someone and you just know.

GH0ST30: Yes.

I was bubbling over to talk about my new squeeze, but GHOST was a guy!

CHICCHERIE: I can tell you, but you have to take it like a girlfriend.

GH0ST30: How's that?

CHICCHERIE: The job of a girlfriend is to listen and make appropriate sounds at intervals. You can handle the gig?

GH0ST30: I can't resist being a fly on the wall for this one.

CHICCHERIE: He's fantastic. I met him at your party. We danced. He's not the greatest dancer, but—

GH0ST30: Not the greatest dancer! What do you mean by that?

CHICCHERIE: It's not important. It's how he made me feel.

We shot live sparks off each other. It was almost spooky how he turned me on. Then, after the party, we went out to eat.

GHOST30: Live sparks, huh?

CHICCHERIE: Yep. I think you have the girlfriend thing down pat. And today…today he, uh, kissed me. Squeeee!

GHOST30: Squeeee? Dare I ask, is that good or bad?

CHICCHERIE: I haven't actually said squeeee since the eighth grade. But that's how it felt. I shouldn't be telling you this.

GHOST30: Please do go on. You were referring to the way he made you feel. Feel free to use all the descriptive adjectives you like.

CHICCHERIE: Have you ever gone off the deep end like this?

GHOST30: More than you know.

CHICCHERIE: I invited him and his father to our house for the holidays. He's coming over for Christmas Eve dinner.

GHOST30: It sounds like you want this guy in your life.

CHICCHERIE: I think so. I hope you find what you've been looking for, too.

GHOST30: You know what? I think I've gotten lucky, too.

CHICCHERIE: GH0ST! Really?

GH0ST30: Really.

The pause was so long I wondered if he'd left.

CHICCHERIE: You still there?

GH0ST30: Yeah. But I better sign off. I'm tired.

CHICCHERIE: Good luck with your somebody. Take care.

He had to know I was saying goodbye.

GH0ST30: You, too.

Guys aren't that sentimental, I guess. I signed off and went to the kitchen to make myself a cup of chamomile tea. I'd better get some sleep. I needed to be at the airport early tomorrow morning to pick up my brother and his family.

His Eighth

"I was going to go over to Maury's on Christmas Eve," Dad said. "We were going to double date and play some cards. You know how he always gets depressed this time of year."

"I really want you to come and meet her family," I said. "Her mother's about your age. You'd be crazy about her."

I was glad that Dad had long since lost the capacity to beat my ass, because he'd certainly deem the whopper I'd just told him as deserving a beating after he met Mrs. Silvers.

"Usually you go out with one of your women on Christmas Eve, and so do I. Why the sudden change of plan? I got things to do and people to see, Nick."

"How many times have I asked you to meet one of my girlfriends' parents, Dad?"

"It's serious?"

"It could be."

"I guess it's about time you settled down…again."

"Yeah, but we just started dating. Don't embarrass me by bringing that topic up."

"Is this one of those fancy, rich, goyish affairs where I'm going to have to wear an uncomfortable suit?"

"No. Very down-home, small family probably wearing jeans. They'll have good food, too."

"Good food, huh? Your girlfriend's got a good-looking mother, too? It might not be too bad."

"Thanks, Dad. I'll pick you up Tuesday around five-thirty."

He was going to kill me once he laid eyes on Betty Silvers, since *fetching* wasn't a word I'd used to describe her. But she wasn't ugly, and I'd bet she was a looker in her day, so it wasn't a complete lie.

But, man, was Dad going to be surprised! But I didn't feel like telling him all about the Silverses up front. I didn't want him to back out and I had to go buy Christmas presents.

The next day I was at Neiman Marcus enduring the hell of frenzied-eyed women stampeding down the sale aisles. I decided to get everybody a sweater. A one-size-fits-all unisex sweater. They had a good selection of outrageously expensive cashmere sweaters—kids, women's and men's, so that's what everybody was going to get. I'd given the salesperson a list and he began fetching and wrapping. I'd hidden from the hordes of shoppers in the men's department and was playing games on my cell phone when it rang.

"Hey, Nick," Sharyn's sweet voice said.

"Hey, darlin'. What's up?"

"I'm still cooking. What are you doing?"

"Finishing up my Christmas shopping."

"I'm finishing up the Christmas feast, but I've retreated to the bathroom so I won't choke my sister-in-law."

That sounded interesting.

"Tell me the tale," I said.

"They're strict vegans. They want tofu instead of meat for Christmas!"

"That sounds rather grim."

"I told her I was cooking duck and turkey. She tells me that I'm not and goes out and buys a tofurkey!"

"A what?"

"A tofurkey, a tofu turkey. It doesn't look like food, Nick."

"Don't you always spend the holidays together? What do you folks usually eat?"

"We do spend the holidays together, but we usually go to her place, so I deal with whatever she serves. I respect other people's kitchens. If they want to pass off soy by-products as food in their own damn house that's fine, but—"

"You cooked the duck, didn't you?"

"Three ducks, a turkey and a ham." Sharyn sniffed. "I dealt with all the other culinary weirdness she was laying on me. I thought, live and let live and she'd do the same, right?"

"But, no, she didn't," I said. I was getting the hang of this girlfriend thing. It was rather fun.

"That's right. She said her kids' Christmas would be ruined if they had to look at dead animals sitting on the table. She said it wasn't sanitary to have dead animals where people intended to eat."

"Dead animals?"

"She looked at my glazed ducks, ham and turkey breast and said they looked like rotting, maggot-infested roadkill, Nick. She insisted on serving the horrid Tommy Tofu tofurkey instead. I lost it. I can't believe I cussed my sister-in-law out the day before Christmas Eve."

"It's going to be all right. Tell her you won't put the meat on the table. But it's going to smell so good people will be sneaking into the kitchen to get it. Your food will disappear and her tofurkey will sit there abandoned."

"For real. That thing doesn't look edible. What if I sneak some real stock into the dressing to get her back?"

"C'mon, be nice. Use vegetarian broth and let them sneak their meat-laced foods knowingly."

"I know you're right, but I'd still like to hold that heifer down and ram a hamburger down her throat."

I grinned at the vision. "Any chance of you getting away today?"

"Nope, not until dinner tomorrow. It's the usual before-Christmas preparation. We're simply overflowing with holiday cheer. Want to come by?"

"Uh, I can wait till tomorrow."

"Coward. But it's probably for the best. This place is a madhouse. I hope your father has a good sense of humor. I don't know what I was thinking, inviting you over to experience the full force of my family this early in our relationship."

"I'm thinking you're wonderful. Dad has a great sense of humor. He'll be entertained way before he's offended. And I met your mother, remember? If that's not full force, what is?"

She laughed. "Five bad kids, a militant vegan sister-in-law and a space-alien minister."

I wanted to tell her about my crazy family, but I think I'd revealed it as GH0ST, and now wasn't the time to break the uncomfortable revelation. "Dad and I can handle it," I said.

"I feel better, thanks. I'm ready to go back to the kitchen."

"Tell your sister-in-law if she doesn't zip it, the blood in the kitchen will be hers."

Sharyn gave a delighted peal of laughter.

I have a sense of humor, too, and I knew Dad's reaction to the Silvers family was going to be priceless. I couldn't wait.

At six o'clock sharp on Christmas Eve my father and I stood on the Silverses' porch and rang the doorbell. A pleasant-looking plump blonde dressed in silky flowing blue robes answered the door. "Welcome, and sweet winter solstice," she said.

"Merry Christmas to you, too," Dad said, handing her his coat. "Is she the one?"

"No, Dad." To the blonde I said, "I'm Nick, Sharyn's friend. And this is my father, Saul Cohen."

"Pleased to meet you," she said. "I'm Sharyn's sister-in-law, Carole Silvers. Let me take your coat, too."

Shrieks of children greeted us. A bunch of kids raced toward us, circled, and one ran straight into Dad's stomach.

"Oof," he said, doubling over. He straightened and adjusted his clothes. "What's with these little brats? Don't they know how to behave?"

"Those are my children," Carole said, looking none too pleased.

"Hello, Nick." Sharyn exited the kitchen, wiping her hands on a dish towel. Dad's brows shot up. Yep, he was surprised.

"Is she the one?" he asked me.

"Yes, she's the one."

"Dad, this is Sharyn Silvers. Sharyn, my father, Saul Cohen."

"Pleased to meet you, Mr. Cohen." Sharyn had a glint in her eye and she shook hands with my father. "You remind me a bit of my mother."

"I agree," Carole said, her voice faint. "I better go and see what's going on with my children." We followed her to the living room.

"Mama, we don't handle them that way," a tall, slim black man said to Mrs. Silvers, who brandished her gait belt over her head. "We put them in time-out. Jared, Jeremy, go to those two corners right now."

"No!" the two boys shouted.

The little boys took off in different directions. I looked around. Sharyn's usually neat house looked as if a giant had picked it up and shaken it.

Mrs. Silvers gave the belt a decisive shake. "Time-out? What's wrong with you, boy? No wonder you got such badass kids."

"Kids, get over here this instant," I heard Carole's voice scream from the backyard.

"Mama, you know that we don't believe in striking our kids or letting anybody else do so."

"That's why their little bad asses are so damn bad."

"They are not bad," the man said, exasperated.

"You need some glasses and hearing aids, then. You've been spending too much time reading all those ignorant books written by psychobabblers who raised a bunch of crazy badass kids themselves."

"Calm yourself, Mama," Sharyn said.

"I am calm. It's your brother and his wife those badass kids are driving crazy." She sucked her teeth. "Time-out. I can't believe I raised a son without a lick of horse sense."

The man started to say something.

"I know you're not going to open your mouth and talk back to me," the Dragon snapped.

The man's mouth closed.

"Butt-whipping is quick, effective and efficient when used properly. Other discipline is a lot harder to carry through. You gotta show a lot more resolve and backbone than I see you two showing."

Her son fidgeted and the Dragon lifted her hand. "Let me finish. Those kids don't do anything you say because you don't back it up. Your word doesn't mean a damn thing to them. If you tell that boy he's gotta go to the corner, you make him go there, even if you have to put a foot on his neck to keep him there. Do you understand? All that screaming and yelling of empty words has to stop."

"Yes, ma'am," he said.

"You and your wife need to stop chasing after those kids like they're the boss of y'all. Just let them know what's going to happen if they run—and follow up. Boy, are you paying attention to me?"

"Yes, ma'am."

"What would I do to you if you ran from me?"

"You'd whip my butt until I couldn't sit down, ma'am."

"Was that a promise?"

"Yes, ma'am."

"Did you ever run from me?"

"No, Mama, I didn't."

"Go get your wife. Those kids will get tired and want something soon. When they drop, tell them they ain't getting nary a present tomorrow morning unless they calm their little bad asses down and fly right. Tell them Grandma said it so they know it *will* happen."

The man turned and fled.

Dad had settled on the sofa near Mrs. Silvers and was watching her, fascinated.

"Now who is this old white man in my house and when is somebody going to introduce me to him?"

"Mama, please. You know Nick. This is his father, Saul Cohen. And this is my mother, Betty Silvers."

"Delighted," my father said. He took Mrs. Silvers's hand and held it too long, looking deep in her eyes.

"Is somebody going to offer this gentleman something to drink?" the Dragon demanded. "We have some good eggnog. I made it myself."

"Then I must try some," Dad said.

"Get us two glasses, Sharyn."

"Please call me Saul," Dad said to her.

"You call me Betty." Was the Dragon batting her eyes? Lord.

I was relieved when Sharyn returned with the eggnog.

Watching the old man put the move on the Dragon was somewhat disgusting, if I can be frank.

I guess they hit it off. I supposed they were both equally obnoxious in their own ways. The Dragon wore her age well. Besides, Dad liked them plump.

"C'mon, Nick. You can help me put out the food," Sharyn said. I was more than willing to trot after her to the kitchen.

Dad and the Dragon had three glasses of eggnog apiece and were getting rather loud and raucous by the time the food was set out and everybody was settled around the table.

I'd finally been introduced to Sharyn's brother, Robert. He was a quiet man with no immediate eccentric appearance other than the multicolored robes he wore.

Dad rolled the Dragon's wheelchair to the table. "Son," she said to Robert, "you being the eldest male in the family, I'd ask you to say the grace," the Dragon said. "But I still haven't recovered from last year. Saul, will you do the honors?"

"I afraid I'm going to have to pass on the Christmas blessing," Dad answered.

The children tittered.

"Robert prayed to somebody named Metatron last year. I wouldn't be surprised if that wasn't what brought on Mama's stroke," Sharyn whispered in my ear.

"I'll say the prayer, Mama. After all, I am an ordained minister."

"Not in my house you won't unless you make it clear you're praying to the Lord God Almighty Heavenly Father Jehovah in the blessed name of our Savior Jesus Christ."

"All right, Mother, but—"

"Ump, ump, nope. Don't want to hear it. Say the prayer right or don't say it at all," the Dragon ordered.

Dad was pretending to cough in his napkin. I was surprised he wasn't choking with gales of laughter by now.

Robert cleared his throat and delivered a heartfelt and respectful prayer to the appropriate deity.

Sharyn squeezed my hand. I looked into her gorgeous brown eyes and decided this was the most entertaining Christmas Eve I'd had in years. I hoped that this was only the first of many family Christmases together.

Dinner was delicious. Sure enough, just as I'd foreseen, the animal carcasses disappeared like magic from behind the closed kitchen door.

My head snapped toward my dad and the Dragon. *Had he just asked her to bingo?* That qualified as a date!

Sharyn's gaze followed mine. "They're hitting it off," she said. "Surprised?"

"Very."

"Mama was something of a player back in the day."

"So was the old man."

"They make quite a match."

"We should lay a bet on who does the other in first."

"No fair. Your dad can run."

"Nick," the object of our conversation said. I swung my head toward Dad, feeling guilty.

"Gina Reavis is moving down to Florida to be closer to her daughter," he said. "Her apartment would be perfect for Betty."

"I can't afford that place," the Dragon said.

"What are you talking about?" Robert asked.

"Saul lives in a retirement center. It sounds great. Lots of activity, enough support so I could be independent. You know I never wanted to be dependent on my children," the Dragon said. Then she shrugged. "I can't afford it anyway."

"I love having you here, Mama," Sharyn said. "You sacrificed and gave a lot to us, now it's time for us to give back a little."

"I did no more than what a mother is supposed to do. I could have done better, could have done worse. That doesn't mean that I gotta live up under my kids until I'm dead and buried."

"You can live the way you want to live," Robert said. "It's not as if you don't have options."

"What are you talking about, boy?" the Dragon snapped. I had a guilty sense of satisfaction hearing that term directed at someone other than me.

"I don't have the option to get the hell up out of this chair and dance," the Dragon said with a snort.

"You have financial options," Robert said. "Ballpark, how much are we talking?" he asked Dad.

Dad told him. It wasn't a small amount.

The Dragon snorted louder. "What lottery you won, boy?" she asked.

"All right," Robert said.

"All right, what? I know you don't have that kind of money and I know Sharyn doesn't, either."

"We have that kind of money," Robert said.

His wife nodded in agreement. "It's doable," she added.

"Ya'll done won the lottery?" the Dragon asked.

I noticed Sharyn leaning towards her brother, her brow raised. She was wondering what was up, too.

"The church of the Glorious Inner Light of Free Earth Beings in Space is financially very well supported," Robert said.

I thought the Dragon was going to fall over, she snorted so hard. "What? The space aliens got funds?"

Robert looked a little offended. "We're popular with the celebrities and the affluent. The light beings have a wonderful effect of the inner and outer bodies, freeing the way for emotional and financial success."

"He got a scam running," the Dragon said. "Saul, you hear that?"

Dad nodded. "I know of similar cults that are very financially well-supported by certain segments."

The Dragon surveyed Robert, disbelief written on her face. But it was that tinge of admiration in her gaze? "Sharyn, you hear that? My boy's getting paid."

"I heard him." Sharyn's voice was dry.

"Investigate this apartment, Mama, and if that's what you want to do, let me know," Robert said, picking up his fork.

The Dragon sniffed. "If the boy has fool's money to spend, I'll let him spend it."

"Are you talking about me?" Robert asked. "I'm right here, Mama. And I'm a grown man, too," he reminded her.

"Yep. I'm talking about you. As far as I'm concerned, you're always going to be my boy," the Dragon replied. "But I gotta say, you're chock full of surprises this evening." She took a bite of her food. "This dressing is wonderful, Sharyn. You didn't sneak any meat-based broth in it, perchance?"

Sharyn had the grace to look a little guilty.

The Dragon beamed at her. "This is turning out to be a dandy Christmas, isn't it?"

The kids were in the bedroom watching Christmas DVDs and the grown-ups were sitting around stuffed; sipping rum-spiked eggnog, listening to mellow Christmas soul music and watching the lights blink on the tree.

Sharyn leaned back in my arms. It felt great, a wonderful Christmas Eve. Just one more thing would make it perfect. "Coming home with me?" I whispered in her ear.

"Let's go," she whispered back.

I yawned. "Dad, we better get going. It's past ten."

"So soon?" Mrs. Silvers asked.

"Yeah, Nick, we can stay a little longer."

"I think Sharyn and I better turn in. Tomorrow is a big day," I said.

Silence.

"I'll go get my bag," Sharyn said in her perkiest voice. I braced myself for the Dragon's roar.

But the Dragon was too busy giving her digits to my Dad to bother.

Her Last

"I got you a Christmas present," Nick told me as soon as we'd reached the privacy of his condo. "I just didn't want to give it to you in front of all those people."

"I got you one too, baby." I reached for him.

"I'm talking tangible goods," he said.

"And what makes you think I wasn't?"

He walked toward a shelf and took a small package off it and handed it to me. "Merry Christmas."

I love gifts, and it's true—the best things come in small packages. I opened the box, eager. My eyes grew moist as I stared. "It's too much."

"It's not enough," he said. He took the gold chain with the perfect square-cut ruby dangling on it out of the box and fastened it around my neck.

"How did you know this was my birthstone?"

"I asked your mother. She said it was your favorite and that you seldom spend money on yourself or the pretty things you love."

I threw my arms around his neck. "Thank you. I love it."

It didn't feel as if we had just met, as if we didn't really know each other that well. Nick seemed like my soul mate, trusted and loving enough to feel like an old friend, edgy and enticing enough to be flaming-hot.

I sank into his kiss, my body molding to his, ready and yielding. But then I remembered and pulled away. "I have something for you." I moved to my purse. "It's not nearly as grand as your gift, but I liked this."

I held a delicate Christmas tree in my hand, carved and exquisite, gleaming with tiny lights. It was a beautiful object. "I noticed you didn't have a tree. I thought a small one that you could keep with you would be right."

He took it from me and studied it. "This is great."

"But it's not all." I handed him another package. I'd bought him a compilation of comedy CDs and DVDs, the best of the best, from old classics to the newest emerging talents. "I thought this would be right up your alley."

"How did you know I love stand-up comedy?"

"Guessed."

He kissed me again. "God, I adore you."

"We don't know each other yet."

"It feels like we do."

I couldn't answer that because it did. His tenderness soon ignited a passion within me, and our kisses grew hungry and wild.

We fell on his bed together. I was as greedy as I always was for him and pulled him free from his slacks.

He gasped as I held his heaviness in my hand, my thumb rotating around the bead of moisture at the tip. What a beautiful man. I wanted him, all of him.

"You're going to make me explode." His voice was husky, and he pulled away my clothes, dropping them over the side of the bed to the floor. My blouse, my bra.

His tongue swirled around one nipple, then the other, teasing them to erect, taut peaks, breathing hot breath over them.

It felt so good. He pulled heat from deep within my core as he sucked. But, greedy, I wanted more.

I couldn't wait, wouldn't wait another moment. I rolled over on top of him and kissed him, our tongues as frantic as our bodies as I rid us of the rest of the cloth barriers between our skin.

He was rock-hard, so big and beautiful. I straddled him, expertly slid a condom on him, and took him inside me in one motion.

He grabbed my hips and sucked in his breath harshly. The large ridged head of his penis slid slow and easy into my velvety wetness.

"So good," I said, barely able to whisper through the intense feeling as my hips churned against him.

He groaned and thrust up against me sharp and hard. His clever, expert fingers reached and spread my juices over me.

It seemed as if I felt every vein of him as he moved inside

my buttered wetness, plunging, filling every inch. The storm inside me was building, rising, inexorable.

Then a crack of thunder, unexpected and violent, ripped through me. Everything went black for a moment as it rocked me, making me convulse on his hardness, clutching him tight inside me.

His body tightened and he rolled me over, plunging deep, his penis working in and out. I met him stroke for stroke, and a moment later he buried himself deep within me, shuddering.

We subsided against each other. I felt as if I'd come home, wrapped within his arms.

I woke up and looked at the clock next to the bed. Six in the morning. I was far too alert and clearheaded for the hour.

I got up, careful not to disturb Nick's slumbering form. I took a quick shower and dressed in one of Nick's robes, padded into his kitchen to see if he had any green tea.

He didn't. I made some instant coffee in the microwave instead, too lazy to figure out how to unset the preset coffeemaker. I went into his office and booted up his computer for a quick game of solitaire.

To my surprise, I saw an icon for Match4Luv.com on his desktop. I frowned as I clicked it. He'd saved all his passwords in his browser and on the site. My frown deepened when I saw his handle.

Nick was GH0ST30.

I swallowed as I turned off the computer. I made sure I left his office as I'd found it. I poured the coffee down the drain, then washed and rinsed the cup, feeling as if somebody had punched me in the stomach.

I went back to the bed and lay next to Nick, stiff, staring at the ceiling. I'd trusted him. We'd promised not to lie to each other, but he'd been dishonest with me from the beginning.

I'd gambled my heart and taken a chance on this relationship. What was wrong with my judgment with men? What was wrong with me? I wiped at my eyes. I waited.

About an hour later Nick rolled out of bed and went to the bathroom. When he returned, he saw I was awake and slipped back into bed, pulling me to him. "Merry Christmas, baby," he said.

I stiffened and started to speak.

"Shush," he said. "I have something that I've been trying to tell you for a long time. I want to get it out now, so I need you to listen for a moment."

I looked away, unable to meet his eyes.

"The first time I came to your house and saw you, I knew you were the one for me. You left, remember? But you left your computer on."

He cleared his throat.

"I'm GH0ST30. I know I was wrong and I apologize. I should have told you, like I said, but I haven't been able to get it out."

I didn't move, didn't look at him. The pain of betrayal still felt too raw.

"Are you going to say something?"

"Did the things you said to me as GH0ST…were you lying, too?" I asked.

"No, I was telling the truth."

The hardest question of all. "Were you only trying to get me into bed?" I asked.

"No, no. I adore you. I've been crazy about you from the beginning. You have to believe that. That's the only reason I pretended—I thought it was the only way to get next to you."

I didn't know what to believe. An hour ago, I believed everything he said. Now, after one lie, I had trouble believing anything.

"Without trust, there isn't anything left," I murmured.

He looked as if I'd punched him.

I looked away. "The kids are probably up by now. I'm going to get dressed, then I'll be ready for you to take me home."

I'd just picked up my purse in preparation of following Nick outside the door when he grabbed my hands.

"You have to talk to me. We need to work this through."

"Please take your hands off me."

He stepped back. "Sharyn."

"Nick, I'm hurt. I'm in shock. I'm deeply disappointed. I don't want to talk right now. I need to process this."

"You have to talk to me."

"I don't have to do anything but stay black and die," I snapped. When stressed, I admit a bit of Mama comes out in me.

"When people have a difficulty in a relationship, they work it through. That's what I expect."

"And I expect not to be lied to. I made that abundantly clear from the get-go." I sighed. "Take me home. Now is not the time to talk. Things might get said that don't need saying. You need to leave me alone."

Nick got out his keys and opened the door. He waited for me to exit, tight-lipped. Christmas was no longer merry, not one little bit.

There was a strange car in front of our house, an older Mercedes.

"Dad's here?" Nick said.

Loud traditional Christmas music was playing and the kids were yelling and laughing. Nick followed me into the living room. Sure enough, his father was there, next to Mama, both beaming at the kids, who were surrounded by so many presents it looked as if Santa's workshop had exploded.

We were definitely going to have to ship all this back to California.

"The kids were up at the crack of dawn opening presents," Mama said.

"Santa was good to us," my nephew Jeremy crowed.

"It sure looks like it. Where's Robert and Carole?"

"They went back to bed."

"Did you eat, Mama?"

"Saul brought us breakfast. It's in the kitchen. Are you going to open your presents?"

"Later, Mama," I said and escaped to the sanctuary of my bedroom. I carefully locked the door before I threw myself on the bed and let my tears escape.

* * *

I emerged from my room an hour later.

"My son says you're upset with him. He went on home."

Nick's dad looked a little pissed off, but it was Mother who verbalized it, as usual. "It's Christmas, for heaven's sake, chile! Haven't you ever heard of Christian forgiveness?"

"I need to take a run. I'll be back in a while."

"Carole brought a tofu ham for Christmas dinner." Mama gave me a meaningful look and Saul shuddered.

I laughed. "Yes, Mama, I'll be back in time to help Carole with dinner."

I got in my car and drove to Piedmont Park. I ran a couple of miles, wind in my face, sweat in my eyes. Then I got back in my car and drove to Nick's place.

"Who is it?" Nick asked when I pressed the button on the intercom.

"It's me."

He hesitated an instant before he buzzed me in.

When I got off the elevator, he was leaning against his door frame, unshaven with bare feet, ripped jeans and a scruffy T-shirt. He looked sexy.

"You've decided you're ready to talk?" he asked.

"I need a little time and space when my emotions are high, Nick. Believe me, it's better. Do you have anything to drink?"

I followed him to the kitchen and sat down at the table. He put a bottle of mineral water out for me, took out a Heineken for himself.

"I thought about things," I said. "I know that if I hadn't

had the experience I did with Patrick, it wouldn't have been that big a deal to me."

"I knew it was a big deal to you. I have no excuses. I was a coward. I was afraid to screw up the possible relationship."

I took a swig of water. "When I was running, I thought about the things that are important to me, the questions that I need answered in an important relationship."

"Anything," he said.

"Can I trust you when it matters? Can I trust you not to hurt me? To love me and keep loving me even when it's hard?"

Nick started to answer, but I held up my hand. "Wait. You can only answer these questions with words. That's all any man can do. These are questions that I have to answer myself, right here." I put my hand over my heart.

Nick was silent, staring at the bottle of beer. "Anytime you trust in a relationship with another human being, it's a leap of faith," he said.

"That's right. Love equals having faith. And if you don't have any, you don't love. It's all about taking chances. But I gotta ask you one thing."

He tipped his bottle, swallowed and nodded.

"Is it true about your brother having four wives? That's just too freaky."

The dimple in his cheek creased. "It's true."

He reached out and took my hand.

It looked as if we were just sitting there to anybody else. But we were really jumping, almost flying—taking that huge leap of faith together.

* * *

Christmas dinner was more modest than Christmas Eve. We had lots of leftovers. I think Mama and Saul were hungover, too; they were much more subdued. They talked in the corner.

The kids were quiet, tired out from excitement, playing hard and too much food.

"We'd better get up and straighten this mess," Carole said, making a halfhearted effort to struggle off the couch.

"Chill. I pre-booked an after-Christmas housecleaning with Cheerful Cleaners tomorrow."

Nick listened to his comedy CD through earphones. He laughed at intervals.

I lay on a floor pillow, watching my family, watching him. Nick and I were brand-new and shiny. I didn't know if we'd work out or not, but so far it felt good. The gambles were that we'd keep being real and keep it right.

I glimpsed this beautiful place in my mind, full of flowers and trees. Birds sang and a waterfall cascaded into an idyllic pond. Nick was at my side. Was it a premonition or a fantasy? I had to take the chance.

Nick was at my side. We were hand in hand, still leaping, flying into that wide-open unknown wilderness of the future. Together.